Life and Liberty

Aidan Parr

Set in Stone: Book One

Life and Liberty: Set in Stone, Book 1

ISBN-13: 9781092761376

"Freedom, high-day, high-day, freedom,
freedom,high-day, freedom!"

The Tempest, Act 2, Scene 2

Contents

Chapter 1 – Santa is a Son of a Bitch 7

Chapter 2 – Growing Up Troubled 13

Chapter 3 - The Crisis Point 48

Chapter 4 - Sean of Hope? 56

Chapter 5 – Woosterville Nightlife............................65

Chapter 6 – A Death in the Family 91

Chapter 7 - On the Run 113

Chapter 8 – On the Run Part 2 119

Chapter 9 – So Near and Yet… 127

Chapter 10 – Medical Marvels................................137

Chapter 11 – Alvin Unleashed...............................169

Chapter 12 – Floyd, Grilled 180

Chapter 13 – Floyd Catches His Breath...................193

Chapter 14 – Boredom Strikes...............................202

Chapter 15 – Alvin and Sean Scheme 210

Chapter 16 – Master and Slave 217

Chapter 17 - Gwen...230

Chapter 18 – A Near Miss 243

Chapter 19 - Brains and Beauty.............................251

Chapter 20 – Girls, Dates and Being Primitive 283

Chapter 21 – Revelations.....................................295

Chapter 22 – Rehabilitation and Resolve 313

Chapter 23 - Testimony 333

Chapter 24 – Arrested Developments 346

Chapter 25 – Trials and Tribulations 370

Chapter 26 – A Night on the Town..........................403

Chapter 27 - Trial and Error...426

Chapter 28 – Moving On 437

Chapter 29 – Burying the Past? 480

Afterward 484

Chapter 1 – Santa is a Son of a Bitch

"Santa is a son of a bitch," muttered Floyd as he trudged on into the darkness. He was a young man, around seventeen years of age, nondescript, but his stance curiously like a boxer, hands balled into fists by his side and his face set in a scowl. There was aggression dancing in his piercing grey eyes, showing a too-familiar acquaintance with casual violence.

The rain continued to fall. It was what his Mom called 'wet rain', the kind that would soak you in a minute. Floyd had been out in it for hours. He's tried to dodge the potholes as cars go by, but the drivers seem to want to deliberately soak him.

"Bit late for that, assholes..." he grumbled.

The supervisors at the store had made him move all of the Christmas trees from one part of the yard to the other. As a punishment, on top of spending all day long filling sacks for 'Santa'.

'Santa', as everyone knows really is a son of a bitch...

Mayor Theodore Sanchez. 'Santa'. Always the centre of attention at Christmas. Sanchez had to be 'Santa'. Sanchez had to switch on the Christmas lights and Sanchez always had to be the one Christmas revolved around. Sanchez's face was on the picture of the Three Wise Men. All three of them. Floyd sometimes thought that Sanchez wanted to be the baby in the crib too.

Floyd eventually got home, past midnight, soaked to the bone. His Mom was still up, waiting.

"Where have you been, son?"

Floyd's mother worried about every move Floyd made and with good reason.

"The supervisor kept me back. Then Sanchez turned up and yelled at me."

"Oh Jesus, Floyd! What for?"

Floyd was silent. Everyone hated Sanchez, but no-one dared cross the guy who could take a job away as easy as clicking his fingers. Or make someone just disappear.

"Oh Floyd, what sort of idiot are you working for this time?"

Floyd sighed. Although he was called 'stupid' by everyone in the town, he usually picked up things quickly, an earnest learner who annoyed those who tried to force him to be just like them. Every job it was the same:

"Floyd, you ain't clever enough to get that so quickly. Do it again properly."

"Young man, when you have been here less than two days, don't you think it's bold to want to change things already?"

So Floyd inevitably got bored. And a bored Floyd was a mischievous Floyd...

People knew he could work hard and he was focused if left alone. But leaving him alone to do a job was beyond the people of Medusa. 'Marlene's Bastard' was never to be trusted.

Floyd's Mom continued, "Floyd, I know something else is wrong. You can't fool me, boy, I know you too well."

"Nothin'…"

"Come on, boy, out with it."

Floyd gave a sigh. "The manager fired me. Then Sanchez arrived and shouted at me for another ten minutes"

"Oh Floyd, what did you do this time?"

"Well, I… I pasted a picture of Sanchez on the baby Jesus' face."

Floyd's mother looked at him in astonishment, her face growing red. Then she gave a huge snort. In between laughing she struggled to speak: "Floyd... you... you didn't?"

"Sorry Mom, but I did!"

She started to giggle again, her normally tired and worn face lit up with delight. "F... Floyd, what... am I going to do with you?"

Floyd, relieved at his mother's reaction, began to chuckle too. This set his Mom off again. Soon they were both breathless with laughter.

"What... what did Sanchez say to you?"

"I lack respect."

"Who respects Sanchez?" said Mom, letting out another contemptuous snort of laughter, which set them both off again.

"What else did he say, Floyd?"

"Mom I need to go and dry off."

"Oh no you don't. What else did he say?"

"He was pretty pissed with me. Grabbed me. He said that just because I was your son didn't mean I could hide behind you anymore. That I should think about being somewhere else if I couldn't behave like everyone else 'in this fine town of Medusa'."

"Oh, Lord, Floyd... 'This fine town.' I warned you to keep your head down. You should have remembered what happened to Zeke."

"I just didn't think. I'm sorry, Mom."

Mom's face became more serious. "God knows how Sanchez will make you sorry, boy. You know how he's done that to me and to everyone I've loved. All except you."

Floyd burned with curiosity. "In what way, Mom?"

Floyd's Mom paused, as if collecting her thoughts. "I had a boyfriend here. Once. A long time ago. Before you were born. I was real sweet on him. And he loved me too. We had plans. He fell out with Sanchez's father. And he disappeared too. I know what happened. You can probably guess too?"

Floyd's eyes filled with tears. "Was... was he my Dad?"

Floyd's Mom seemed faraway for a moment. "No, he wasn't. But... but he would have been a good father to... to you and you would have loved him too. Of that I'm certain."

"So... so who is my Dad? Mom, you never said. And you got so upset when I asked as a kid I never dared? Who was he?"

Mom's face hardened. She wiped her own tears away. "OK son, get yourself a hot shower, I don't need you getting all sick on me with the cold."

Floyd protested. "But Mom..."

"Floyd! Shower. Now. Get a good night' sleep." She kissed him on the cheek and hugged him. "My Floyd... what am I going to do with you?"

Floyd was embarrassed. He knew his Mom loved him. But she was not usually this affectionate.

Floyd kissed her on the cheek too. As he walked up the stairs he shouted:

"Goodnight, Mom."

"Goodnight Floyd" she called back. And softer to herself, "What will you do, Floyd, when I'm gone?"

Floyd's Mom sat late into the night, worrying. Maybe it was time for Floyd to leave Medusa. Before it was too late.

Chapter 2 – Growing Up Troubled

The first thing Floyd remembers is being with his Mom: her unique scent, the crooning she makes as she rocks him. The smell of her starched clothes. The smell that is her. The odour of the kitchen, the sweet scent of the perfume she sometimes wears.

She is Floyd's Mom and to Floyd she is gorgeous, beautiful and everything to him. His early years are usually full of contentment, but even then he senses something...

Floyd sees few other people. There are no visitors except for one in particular who comes now and then.

'The Man', as Floyd begins to think of him, is so big! He frightens Floyd with his angry face and his roughness and what he does to Mom. Floyd knows that she is frightened and he hears her cries when the visitor drags her into the bedroom.

When he leaves, 'The Man' always looks happy and whistles a jaunty little tune as he walks out the door.

Floyd waits for a long time, huddled in the corner next to the couch. Mom comes out of the bedroom eventually and makes straight for the bathroom. She never looks at him. She stays in the shower for a long time and when she comes out, he can see the bruises on her face and the one's on her arms, in the shape of fingerprints.

She who is everything clasps Floyd tightly, so tightly that he fusses and complains. That's when she cries, the tears running down her face. It isn't the Mom he knows and adores, this is the Mom who weeps. Always caused by 'The Man'. Floyd learns to hate and dread these visits.

Later Floyd gets to know the Mom who is harsh. This Mom shouts at him over nothing. This Mom looks worried and angry and even as a small child he senses her fear and her rage. This Mom is a stranger who frightens Floyd, disturbs his contentment and makes him unsure.

Floyd asks who 'The Man' is and why he hurts Mom, but she flies into a ferocious temper and screams at him for what seems like forever. Her words mean nothing, but the terror in her eyes speaks volumes.

When he is two, Floyd is left on his own while his Mom goes to work. She checks on him several times a day. She feeds him, plays with him, but then she is gone again. The lonely hours are filled with books and the scraps of paper and coloured pencils she leaves him. The books and his scrawling are his true mother and father: the colours and the pictures, but later, words contained in the books. Books are his family.

Floyd's Mom does her best, but she has to work to earn a living and there is no-one else she can leave the small boy with. For Floyd, being on his own is natural.

Floyd at four years old is a quiet boy who thinks before he opens his mouth. He never knows which Mom he might be speaking to. He watches her to see which Mom she is that or day or in that moment.

It's only when she takes him to the local kindergarten for the first time that he begins to understand her fear and anger. It is not just about 'The Man'. Floyd notices something about people who he meets. Their reaction to his Mom and to him. Over and over.

The women greet his Mom and are full of sympathetic smiles. They happily turn to Floyd in welcome, but then their smiles fade. There is something in him that they don't like. Something about the way he is. They are polite to him, but they make no effort to involve him with the other children. Floyd happily plays on his own, but when he sees the other children together, he sometimes feels sad.

When he asks why no-one likes him, harsh Mom shouts at him. "Don't be so stupid! There's nothing wrong with you or them. Just try to fit in and be nice. Is that too much to ask?"

The first day of school aged five is a nightmare full of more strangers who seem actively angry with him. All the time. They silence his halting words, they insult him and his Mom, and they isolate him from the other children in his class. He is a child that works on his own. A pariah. The bookshelf and his imagination are his only friends here too. Floyd learns to watch people and the other kids in his class. They fascinate him, but he knows he is not allowed to be friends with any of them.

Floyd learns more from the books than from any teacher and that makes them extra angry and contemptuous. They mock the formality of his words. He talks like the things he reads: a little formal, a little precise. He does not talk like any of the other kids. He hates them in turn.

"Mom, they're all hayseeds. Dumb hicks. They don't like anything but bein' stupid!"

At home there is fear and anger and at school there is rejection and contempt. Floyd, like any small child who is isolated, turns in on himself. He is his own world and he has little contact with other children or adults. Books and drawing remain his only reliable friends. Until Zeke arrives...

Zeke. A new boy in Floyd's class. Black skin. Mouth in a big smile. Laughter in his eyes and in his voice. Zeke is chatty and full of mischief and he wants to talk all the time. To everyone. Even to Floyd, who is shy and reluctant to speak, is amazed at this boy who speaks enough for the two of them. For the whole class sometimes. Zeke wants to know about everything and everyone.

The teachers and Floyd's classmates soon show Zeke how unwanted he is, because of the colour of his skin and his happiness. No-one speaks to him and his joy begins to dim. But when Floyd giggles at Zeke's antics, Zeke is delighted and laughs back. Floyd, after being so shy, begins to respond to Zeke's endless chatter, starting with a shy 'Hello'.

Zeke's brilliant grin gets even wider and they soon begin to talk endlessly about the things that only five year old's care about: their toys, favourite cars, their Mom's and food. Floyd tells Zeke about the book he is reading: 'The Cat in the Hat'.

16

"It's about a cat who wears a hat and a bow tie and he goes to visit Sally..."

Zeke laughs and they both share the book, reading a page alternately. Floyd corrects Zeke when he says a word wrong and Zeke encourages Floyd to speak out loud. They begin do everything together.

The genie is out of the bottle: they find joy and laughter and mischief in each other: the isolated Floyd comes out of his shell and the outgoing Zeke learns a little caution when dealing with others. Sometimes.

Their friendship is a match made in heaven for them and a match made in hell for their teachers. Neither boy pay much attention to what anyone else is doing. They aren't particular naughty, but they are a little class of two, on their own. And they like it that way.

Floyd never feels completely alone again. Each has the others back and there is nothing that one does without the other there to defend against bullies. And there are many bullies in the school. Over the years both the boys learn to be quick to violence in defending the other. The quieter Floyd is strangely easier to temper and uses his fists quicker whenever anyone crosses him or Zeke.

Anyone who crosses Floyd can expect a swift punch in the face and a good kicking if you've really made him pissed.

But it's not just at school: neither boy really understand what is yelled at them in their early years, but the 'nigger boy' and 'Marlene's Bastard' soon understand that no-one in Medusa is fond of either of them.

Floyd and Zeke learn that they live in the town of 'Medusa'. That it is a beautiful place. That the Mayor, Mr Sanchez, will look after them. That it's best to behave and do as they are told, or Mr Sanchez will be angry.

Mr Sanchez owns most of the stores on Main Street. Mr Sanchez has farms all around Medusa. Mr Sanchez provides work for nearly everyone in the town. There would be nothing at all in Medusa without Mr Sanchez helping them all.

It's only after seeing a picture of the Mayor, that Floyd realises that Mr Sanchez is 'The Man'. The one that visits now and then and always hurts his Mom, then whistles his little tune as he goes away.

Floyd notices the grubbiness of Medusa when he walks home from school with Zeke. There's just one road through, called 'Main Street' that has smaller lanes off which contain even smaller houses. He sees the boarded-up store windows with their peeling paint, the sidewalk with its poorly fixed potholes run-down roads with their poorly fixed potholes and the people with their heads always down. There's no music and little movement. People drive in, get their groceries and then get out. Everyone looks tired and wary.

He is foolish enough to say this in class.

The teacher, Ms. Lombard is annoyed "You are an ungrateful brat, Floyd Jensen. Medusa is a beautiful town and we are a happy community. Mayor Sanchez runs a fine town. If you or your mother don't like it, why, you should find another place to live. Frankly, we'd be better off without you."

Floyd is cowed by the teacher's anger and cries.

"Crocodile tears, is it? Perhaps you'd be better learning how to behave?"

Zeke sits very still next to Floyd and waits until Ms. Lombard is busy with another student in the class.

"I don't like her, Floyd. She's mean. She shouldn't say those things to you."

Floyd remains silent but takes comfort in Zeke's words.

When he goes home, he repeats what Ms. Lombard has said to him. Mom is furious.

"You idiot! Complaining about Medusa will do you no good. Keep that yap of yours shut. And don't ever say anything bad about the Mayor. Do you understand, Floyd?"

"But... But Mom? If Mr Sanchez is so good, why does everyone look so unhappy? Why is everything closed down?"

Mom's anger reaches fever pitch. "You must learn, Floyd. Never, ever mention Sanchez to anyone else. Not in school or to anyone you know. It won't do you, or me any good."

His Mom's words made Floyd even more fearful and he becomes quiet again at school, except when he is with Zeke. As more years go by, Zeke and Floyd's friendship grows. It wasn't as if they had anyone else.

Floyd occasionally meets Zeke's Mom and Dad. They are hushed and withdrawn too. Zeke's Mom is kind to Floyd and welcoming, but Zeke's Dad is distant and grim when he sees the boys together. Here is another adult who disapproves of him, although Floyd still does not understand why.

Zeke's Mom cautions the two boys to behave. "Us folks don't want to attract too much attention, understand, Floyd? Understand Zeke?" But it is hard for the boys to restrain their energy and any fun is immediately halted as 'bad behaviour' by the townsfolk.

Floyd's Mom also pressed him. "Zeke is a good enough boy, Floyd. But he's a magnet for trouble. His folks are decent too, but they worry about his antics. Don't get dragged into something you'll both regret, son."

When the two boys explore the edge of town, they see fields of wheat and barley, as far as the eye can see. It's flat. "Flat, flat and more friggin' flat" is a local staying, but there are hills and mountains far away in the distance. No-one in the town mentions them.

In Floyd's imagination, the mountains contain castles and monsters and wizards and adventure. One day he and Zeke will go there and they will never come back. When he says this to Zeke, they both relish the idea. One day they will never come back. At eight years old, the boys already long to get away from Medusa.

'The Man' who is the Mayor still visits Floyd's Mom. When Floyd goes home there's now three or four men outside Floyd's house. They take turns going in the house and they come out looking pleased with themselves.

These are the group of men who seemed to be able to do whatever they like in the town. Sanchez's men are employed to keep the law officially and unofficially in the town. Floyd and Zeke dodge them whenever possible, but they notice the anxiety in the locals whenever Sanchez's gang are around.

Floyd hates them too. With a passion.

"The Mayor is talkin' to your Mom. Go and play until they're finished," says one of them.

Floyd is embarrassed and runs away as the men laugh. He runs because he is frightened and he runs because he knows no-one will help him or his Mom.

Floyd avoids contact with the Mayor whenever possible, but it is inevitable that their paths sometimes cross. Although Sanchez is normally reclusive, he sometimes visits the school or organises some compulsory event in the town.

When Floyd is nine, the school is 'honoured' by a visit from the Mayor. Floyd and Zeke and his class are assembled with the rest of the school. Up on the stage is the Principal and the schoolteachers and sitting in the middle is a very large man. 'The Man'.

Big, broad shouldered and strong looking, but going to fat. Dark brown hair and dark complexion, tanned from the sun. He looks hard and strong and frightening. There's a ferociousness and something like an animal, like the aggressive dogs the neighbours have. Like a Rottweiler. Floyd notices Sanchez's piercing eyes that miss nothing as he looks over the children.

Floyd squirms as Sanchez's eyes fall up him. The man looks at him for a long time in a mixture of fascination and then irritation. Floyd keeps looking back, puzzled at the attention, until his ingrained shyness takes over.

Sanchez ignores Floyd for the rest of the day, but the boy occasionally catches the Mayor looking at him. When Sanchez visits the boy's class, he even speaks to Zeke.

The Mayor is charming to everyone and the kids seem to love him, but Floyd is ignored. Floyd sees the charm Sanchez has with the female teachers and the way they respond: the coy smiles, the blushes and the simpering. The boy can't fail to see the way the male teachers at his school are quiet and respectful. They never look Sanchez in the eye.

When Floyd gets home, he mentions the Mayor to his Mom. Later he realises how much he should know better. Mom yells at him in anger and in tears.

22

"You don't let that man see you. Hide away, boy!"

Mom holds Floyd tightly and weeps. "It's not safe for you to have anything to do with him. Floyd, you must understand. Whenever the Mayor comes to your school, I will keep you home. You must tell me, Floyd."

After that, Floyd has 'a fever' or 'a stomach bug' when Sanchez visits school.

School continues to be a problem for Floyd. The teachers repeat over and over: "You're just plain useless."

The other kids in his class often chant at him: "Doesn't listen, doesn't do, doesn't remember, doesn't have a clue!"

Floyd believes what they all say, despite Zeke telling him they are being spiteful, and it makes him resentful, so he retaliates with his fists, as usual. He doesn't realise that he is a bright child, but his early years have been spent doing and learning and reading whatever he likes, when he likes. No-one has shown him any other way. He resents the kids, the teachers, the school and the whole education system.

Lessons seem designed to take him away from this thoughts and his writing, reading and his drawing. What is all this rote learning? Multiplication tables, history and religious studies?

"What use is all this to me?" he often thinks.

Floyd excels in creativity. He is quick to learn and apply ideas when he see things that attract his attention. It infuriates his teachers that he asks so many questions that seem to come from nowhere.

"You never wrote this. Who helped you? You must have got it out a book?"

"You never drew this. Where did you take it from? Be honest, boy. This is stealing."

"Where do you get these damned-fool questions from? Who puts you up to this?"

His protests are ignored and often his work is torn up or thrown in the trash bin. In the beginning, he cries when the teachers destroy his work. But he sees how much that pleases them and that their later words of comfort are intended to make him compliant and obedient, just like all the other kids in his class.

"Hayseeds and dummies, all of them," complains Floyd repeatedly to his Mom.

Sometimes he manages to retrieve the scraps of paper and take them home. He fixes them together with tape and puts them on the wall of his bedroom. As he gets older, he also makes copies of what he's written or drawn, in case they are ruined too.

As they grow into their teens, Zeke and Floyd's rebellion grows. Although he remains quiet, Floyd's anger targets everyone and anything in Medusa. Floyd's temper even worries Zeke.

"Dude, just let it go. No-one at school messes with you or me anymore. They learnt the hard way. Just chill out."

"I hate 'em all, Zeke. The whole place is a dump. Nothin' to do. Always bein' bothered by the adults. We can't even sit on a bench without bein' hassled."

Zeke sighs. "I know. They won't let us be. I'm just sittin' and you scribblin' away in that book of yours. What are you writin' about anyways, Floyd?"

Floyd is embarrassed. "Just what I see. The people. The way they look. The way they look ground down. The town. The peelin' paint. The way nothin' happens. Why everyone looks so unhappy. "

Zeke chuckles. "I don't know why you do it."

Floyd smiles back. "I dunno, Zeke. I just want to do it. This place is weird and I don't get it. So I write what I see, even if I don't understand. I don't get why everyone in Medusa is so frightened."

"Sanchez," replied Zeke.

"The Mayor?"

"Yeah, Floyd. I heard my folks talkin' a few nights ago. They're plain scared of Sanchez and his guys. You know the ones?"

"I know them. Mom gets crazy when I mentioned them."

Floyd doesn't dare tell Zeke about Sanchez and his visits.

"No offence, Floyd, but your Mom gets crazy about everything."

"I know, Zeke. I daren't ask. She gets in a panic: Sanchez, the town, the people, school, even you. She keeps tellin' me to stay away from you and your folks too."

"Why?"

"I don't know. Remember when I told her that Sanchez was visitin' the school?"

"Yeah, she shit herself."

"She screamed at me about him. 'Hide away, boy!' It's like she's a crazy witch sometimes."

"Maybe she is, Floyd?"

"Maybe. But do people get crazy for no reason? Everyone in Medusa seems crazy in one way or another."

Zeke thinks for a moment. "Let's stay outta town for a while. I've had enough of this place. We could get away on a Saturday. No need to be here."

"Let's do it, Zeke. Pack some snacks for the day and get away."

"Will your Mom go for it?"

Floyd looks annoyed. "Nah. She'll go apeshit again. But she'll go apeshit for somethin' else. She's always on my back, wanting to know where I am or what I do. Let's go for it."

Saturday they meet early, just after seven am. Medusa is quiet as they walk out towards the town limits.

"Where are we goin', Zeke?"

"I don't know, Floyd. But that's part of the fun."

They turn once they've left the town, just past the worn welcome sign:

Welcome to Medusa

Your Kind of Town

27

"Fuck Medusa," grumbles Floyd, as he picks up a rock and throws it at the sign, luckily hitting the 'Y' dead on.

The two boys laugh as they see the results:

'our Kind of Town'

Floyd and Zeke spend the next ten minutes throwing rocks at the letter 'Y' on the sign until it is completely obliterated. They only stop when they see a car coming and they dive behind a bush until it has gone.

"We better make ourselves scarce, Floyd."

"Yeah, sure. Let's go."

They spend the whole day discovering the area around Medusa. It is a beautiful time of year with every flower in bloom, heavy with scent and the smells of growth. The countryside gently rolls into the distance, full of massive fields full of wheat almost ready to harvest. Getting out of Medusa was the best thing they have ever done. But even here they have no peace from adults.

A battered Jeep suddenly stops near them on the road and an older man gets out. He looked mean and angry, like all the adults the boys have ever met.

"Who are you boys and what are you doing here? What's your names?" he demands.

Zeke begins to speak but Floyd interrupts. "What's it got to do with you? We ain't botherin' no-one."

Zeke tries to quieten Floyd down but that just makes Floyd's temper go up another notch. "We ain't hurtin' anyone, we're minding out own business."

The man is annoyed. "I'll call the sheriff…"

"You can call the friggin' President for all I care, mister. It's our business what we're doin', not yours."

Zeke drags Floyd away and they turn to walk back to Medusa.

"You shouldn't sass people like that, Floyd. He was just some old guy."

"Fuck him, Zeke. I ain't been bullied by some nosey old guy. We get this all the time at home. I ain't been bullied out here too."

"That doesn't mean you have to want to fight everyone, Floyd."

"Screw them and screw you, Zeke if you don't like it!"

Zeke tries to reason with Floyd but in the end they walk home in sullen silence. They are both worried about the man and their dispute and they part company without a word.

As expected, Mom shrieks at Floyd when he gets home.

"Where've you been? I looked everywhere for you? I was worried sick? You ain't causin' trouble again are you?"

Fourteen years of having abuse from his Mom, the school, everyone in Medusa and now the argument with Zeke causes Floyd to flip. He yells back at her for the first time.

"What if I did go out? What if I spent the day with Zeke havin' fun? What makes you think I was in trouble? Why don't you quit whinin' at me all the time? Why can't you be a normal Mom like everyone else?"

With that, Floyd runs up the stairs to his bedroom and slams the door with all his might, not seeing his white-faced Mom slump into her armchair, shocked by Floyd's response. She sits there silently and hopelessly weeping.

Ten minutes later, she hears impatient banging on the door. It's the Sheriff and one of his deputy's. Her heart sinks. The Sherriff is yet another crony of Theodore Sanchez.

"What do you want?" she snaps.

"Where's that kid of yours, Marlene?"

"I don't know."

The Sherriff grins at her. "You always know where your bastard is. Do I need to come in and get him myself?"

"What's he done?"

"There's vandalism of the town sign, abusing one of the farmers outside Medusa. Him and the knuckledragger he hangs around with. Will that do for starters?"

Mom's shoulders slump. "You'd better come in. Go sit in the parlour. I'll fetch him."

Slowly she ascended the stairs, dreading facing her son. Tapping gently on the door, she speaks quietly.

"Floyd. Floyd! The Sheriff's hear. Wants to speak to you. What have you done?"

There is no answer. Opening the door, she sees the window, curtains flapping in the breeze. Floyd has made his escape.

Floyd's Mom shouts down the stairs. "He's not here. I thought he was upstairs."

The Sherriff pushes her out the way as he too walks up the stairs and sees the wide open window.

"He's skipped out on you, Marlene."

Mom shakes her head. "He would never do anything like that to me. He's a decent boy."

The cops laugh at her.

"Decent boy? He's trouble at school, he hangs around the town with that knuckle-dragger and he's destroyed the town sign. 'Decent boy' my ass!

"Tell Floyd we want to see him and that black friend of his. If I have to keep searching for him, he'll be sorry."

It takes them a week to find Floyd and they only finally catch up with him at school in a room with no escape route.

The teacher, Mrs Bennett, comes into the room with one of the Sherriff's deputies. "Jensen, the Sheriff wants to see you. Up to no good again?"

"I ain't done nothin'," protests Floyd.

"If the Sheriff wants to see you, you must have done. Get to the Principal's office. Now."

Floyd sullenly makes his way to the office, all the while looking for a way out, but the deputy stays close.

"Don't even think about trying to get away, boy," the man mutters.

Floyd's face gets harder and meaner as they walk into the office.

The Principal speaks first, to the Deputy. "Grayson, have a seat. No, not you, Jensen, you can stand."

"Why am I here?" asks Floyd.

"We want you to tell us why you destroyed the town sign," replies the Sherriff.

"I didn't do nothin'."

"We know it was you, Jensen."

Floyd grins at them. Insolence is a useful weapon and a distraction. "Where's your proof?"

"Your little pal Zeke told us."

Floyd's grin gets even wider. "I don't think so. Zeke knows nothin'. You know nothin'. I've done nothin'. Prove it."

"Don't you talk to us like that, you little prick!" snarls the Deputy.

Floyd glares back and then settles for more impudence. "Oh I'm so sorry, Principal Morton. And to our wonderful police. Please do forgive me."

His sarcasm is biting.

"You're a nasty piece of work, aren't you Jensen?"

"If you say so, Sheriff. You and the Principal and everyone in Medusa seem to know what I've done even more than I do."

Floyd observes with satisfaction how the three seated men have got angrier. He knows they've got nothing on him and that Zeke would never squeal.

"Why did you damage the town sign, Jensen?"

"Who said I did?"

"We know you did it, boy."

Floyd smiles again. "You know nothin', Sherriff. You ain't got a clue who did it, so you try to pin it on me."

The men pause for a moment, glaring at Floyd.

"Get out!" shouts the Principal.

Floyd grins back. "With pleasure. Nice to meet you, Sherriff."

He enjoys shutting the office door with just a little bit too much˙ force.

Floyd walks straight out of the school gate and down to the town library. He spends all afternoon reading the worn and faded books. He has enjoyed riling the Sherriff and the school Principal, but reading these grubby and well-used books is even better.

Miss Montague, the librarian, is the only adult who tolerates him. She's in a conspiracy: he comes in and reads quietly, she denies he was ever there. She knows Floyd is harmless and she enjoys having at least one regular customer. The books are worn and old and there is no money for anything new. She survives on donations and books she has begged, stolen or borrowed.

A handful of library members come and go but they keep themselves to themselves. Floyd and Zeke often sit quietly and read and sometimes they talk in whispers about what they've learnt.

Miss Montague smiles as she sees these young men fill their heads with learning, knowledge, fiction, poetry, history and anything they can get their hands on. She's pleased that she's able to do something for them.

Back at the Principal's office, the conversation continues.

"We can't touch the little bastard without a reason," said the Sherriff.

The Principal agrees. "Same as at school. He's an impertinent little fucker, but he never gets caught."

"Maybe we could get someone to teach him some manners, Chief?"

"Good idea, Grayson. I'll get the Mayor's guys to explain it to Jensen that he needs to behave."

The Principal smiles. "I wish I could join in too. See the smirk wiped off his face."

"You'll see that in a few days, my friend," grins the Sherriff in turn.

Zeke meets Floyd the next day. "You've upset everyone, Floyd. Why?"

"They all blame me for everythin', Zeke. So why not have some fun with it?"

"Dude, don't push everyone too far."

"What can they do to me? I ain't been caught, no-one knows anythin'. Fuck 'em, Zeke."

"I hope you won't be sorry, Floyd."

Over the next few days Floyd notices the four goons around the school and his route home. He gives the impression of being calm, but wonders what they might do to him. He knows they wouldn't kill him, or so he hopes, but he understands they could hurt him bad if they wanted to do.

Floyd and Sanchez's men play cat and mouse for a few days. Floyd sees them and makes a detour. He can see they are getting more and more annoyed with him. But there was no way he was going to let them get him that easy.

They eventually catch him running down the alleyway next to the library. One minute he is heading full pelt for home, the next he's jerked off his feet and slammed against the wall.

"Well, well. Lookee here. If it ain't Marlene's Bastard. We've been looking for you for a while now, boy."

"I ain't done nothin'," repeats Floyd again, for what seems the millionth time. He is frightened but he can't, he simply won't let it show, even if it's Tony Moscarra who has grabbed him, one of the worst of Sanchez's gang.

"Maybe that's what you say, kid. But we don't like you much. Time for you to learn some manners."

Moscarra slaps Floyd across the face, so hard he almost falls to his knees, his head reeling from the blow.

"Now. Tell us how sorry you are for upsettin' the Sherriff and the Principal for your damned cheek…"

Floyd mumbles under his breath.

"What was that, boy?"

Floyd speaks loud and clear. "I said 'Fuck you, asshole'."

The man slaps Floyd harder. "I see we've got a bunch of manners to reach you, Jensen."

"Good luck with that, dickhead."

The man rains slaps and blows on Floyd to break him, but Floyd will not apologise. He will never give in.

Another of the gang intervenes. "Any more and you'll hurt him too bad, Tony. The Boss told us to be careful."

"I can't let this little shit go without getting him to say 'Sorry', Jake."

"Look at him, Tony. You've tried to knock some respect into him and he won't. We have to let him go. For now. I'll talk to the Boss later."

Moscarra strikes Floyd one last time. "Get outta here, you little faggot!"

Floyd staggers away, not making a sound. He mutters curses against the gang and everyone in Medusa as he stumbles his way home.

When he gets there, his Mom is still out. Floyd goes straight to the bathroom and sees himself in the mirror.

He Is a mess, with bruises forming all over his face. He winces as he removes his shirt. His torso has more bruises which merge into a dull throb all over his upper body.

He grabs some Tylenol and heads for bed.

A few hours later his Mom comes into Floyd's bedroom.

"What are you doing in bed? I thought you we're supposed to be doing homework? Something? Anything?"

Then she sees his face.

"What in God's name have you been doing, boy? Fighting?"

"I was..."

His Mom interrupts. "I didn't bring you up to fight like a low-life. Who was it with?"

"Will you let me get a word in edgeways?" Floyd yells and then falls back on the bed, the throbbing in his body and head increasing.

"Our wonderful Mayor's guys beat me up."

His Mom looked frightened now. "Oh my God! Floyd! They coulda killed you. I warned you."

Floyd snarls back at her in contempt. "As if they'd kill me. They'd never get away with it."

His Mom stares at him for a moment before she speaks.

"You stupid, fucking moron. You dumbass! How could I have brought a child up to be so stupid? So completely stupid?"

For a change, her voice is soft. Almost despairing.

"How many times have I warned you, over and over? How many times have I said to you about being careful in Medusa? Be careful what you say, who you say it to and whatever you do, you don't in any way tangle with Theodore Sanchez?"

Floyd is still dismissive. "He ain't nothin'. He's the big guy around here, that's all. No-one's got the balls to take him on."

"And you have, Floyd? Barely fourteen and you can take on the Mayor and those brutes of his? And the Sherriff who's in his pocket?"

"I ain't scared 'a no-one."

"Then you're a fool. Remember Gunter Roland?"

"Yea, I liked Gunter. Didn't he go off and join the army? Lucky guy, he got outta this shithole."

"Yes. He came back last year. Do you remember?"

"Yeah. He looked so different. Confident and he didn't take no bullshit from no-one."

"Do you know what happened to him, Floyd?"

Floyd looked unsure. "He musta gone back to the army."

"It was very sudden, don't you think, Floyd? One moment he's here and the next he's gone?"

"He musta gone back. Where else would he go?"

Mom smiled sadly at him. "He's where most of the people who upset Sanchez are."

Floyd scowls in puzzlement. "Like where?"

"Somewhere outside the town limits. About six feet down. That's where Gunter is."

Floyd looked shocked. "I don't believe you."

"Then don't believe me. But you'll find out why everyone is so terrified in this town. And you'll end up somewhere alongside Gunter. "

"But... but how can they get away with it?"

"Who is going to stop them, Floyd? You?"

"I can't believe they could do that."

"Believe it, boy. Over my life there's been many."

"How many?"

"I'm not sure, Floyd. Maybe fifteen people. One's I've known. Sometimes friends. And then there was..."

She pauses, as if in thought, her eyes full of regret.

"Was who?" asks Floyd.

"I've said enough. Let's get you fixed up. Come on downstairs."

"Who?"

Mom becomes angry again. "Floyd! I have no time to answer your questions. I need to make sure you're OK. Get your ass out of that bed and downstairs."

With a grunt, Floyd gets out of bed and follows her down the stairs and into the parlour. She cleans his bruises and small cuts.

"It isn't too bad. Take it as a warning. Please don't antagonise them, Floyd."

She hugs him close and ignores his hiss of pain.

"I don't want to lose you too. There's too many lost and there's too much to bear already."

Floyd burns with curiosity, but he knows he'll get no more from his Mom when she's like this. He's seen it far too many times and been yelled at more than enough.

After that, he tries to behave. Zeke and Floyd keep their mouths shut, but from the ages of fourteen to sixteen the Sherriff and Sanchez's gang bother them, wherever they go. The goading, especially of Zeke, infuriates the boys, but they know they need to clam up.

The stress of Medusa life is written though Floyd: the fists permanently clenched by his side when he leaves the safety of home, the fierce scowl and the body language that says, 'leave me alone or you'll regret it'. It hides a vulnerable boy who has only aggression as an outlet and for a measure of protection.

Zeke is the only other outlet: someone to talk to and to share books and ideas. Floyd has no idea what he would do without Zeke.

When he can't be silent, or when he takes them on when they bother Zeke, Sanchez's gang rough him up, but he soon learns an important lesson: get your retaliation in first. When they grab him, he reacts with a punch. His bravado is met by laughter and they return his blows.

Floyd's fury now has an outlet. With these guys he can really cut loose. They seem to enjoy his defiance and his violence too. He always ended up beaten, but he manages to land some blows in turn. His natural aggression grows and grows with each meeting. It starts with fists but it often ends up as kicks and bites and scratches as Floyd gets more desperate. At this point Floyd is like an animal: a red haze of violence.

When he gets out of line, the beatings escalate until his is down on the ground, panting, still wanting to fight back, but with nothing left physically. He's just a fifteen year old boy trying to take on three or four older men. But he will never tell himself that.

There's one thing puzzles the boy: they could easily make cat-meat of him, but something stops them. Floyd doesn't know why. Why did these mother-fuckers not do to him what they had done to so many others? Can he use this to his advantage to protect Zeke, his only friend?

"Zeke, I told you what Mom said. You can't let them get to you."

"I know, Floyd. But it gets worse by the day. What I wouldn't give..."

"Me too, but you know how that works in Medusa. We have to wait it out, then get gone. We have a deal? We'll get out of here together."

"Sure, Floyd. I just hope we can last it out."

Floyd is now in a permanent temper that occasionally strains their friendship. There's nothing normal and nothing to look forward to but a hopeful escape.

At sixteen, Zeke is good at debating, but he's ignored at school. He's big for his age, but no-one wants him on the football team, the wrestling team or any team. He tries to hide his disappointment but Floyd can see it: Zeke, his only friend, has no place in Medusa either. Because Zeke is black. They both know this and the yearning to be free of the town grows ever stronger.

Floyd is still hurt by his own rejection, but he hides behind sneers and feigns indifference.

Girls are a torment too. Zeke and Floyd can't fail to notice them, but they despise the young men just like everyone else. Just a look from them invites accusations of harassment.

Girls do look at Floyd. They don't like him, but they are fascinated by him.

"It's not as if you're that pretty, Floyd. It's them eyes 'a yours, that's what they like."

Floyd laughs and flutters his eyes at Zeke. "Do you like them too?" he teases back.

Zeke pretends to stick his fingers down his throat and makes puking noises while trying not to laugh too. They still enjoy each other's company: both of them versus the world, which at the moment is this disturbed shithole of a town.

Zeke and Floyd eventually take to meeting out of town, spending the summers exploring the countryside. They swim in the cold water lakes around Medusa: anything to cool down in those red hot, dry summers. It's the only peace they'll ever get.

In the winter they hide in the library, reading and whispering about what they've read or learnt, away from the endless cold and rain of Medusa, away from Mom's desperate anger and away from Sanchez's men.

They still help each other. Zeke is still chatty and likes to debate ideas. He talks better than he writes, but there's a brain in there with more ideas and things he wants to know about than there's hours in the day. Floyd helps him with the written work, but Floyd learns how to communicate from Zeke: how to charm, how to stay sane. Or at least try.

They survive, but it's not a great life. Two more years and then they hope to leave Medusa behind.

Chapter 3 - The Crisis Point

The first of the two years went by. Slowly.

Floyd's Mom constantly reminded him. "Don't get caught with Zeke or anyone the people of Medusa disapprove of, boy. They don't forget in a hurry and if Sanchez notices, were all in trouble. You already tangle too much with those men of his. You understand, Floyd?"

Floyd stubbornly retained his friendship with Zeke. If Floyd's Mom knew what he was up to, she never let on.

Floyd and Zeke were nearly seventeen and approaching manhood, as far as they were concerned. Floyd began to shoot up in height, but remained skinny and slight. Zeke, in contrast, seemed to explode in size. He got a foot taller over the summer and began to bulk up. His voice got deeper although sometimes it cracked, which made both the boys laugh. Their adolescent surliness at the poor treatment they still received made them all the more angry and resentful.

Medusa had taken a turn for the worst: one of the three stores left in Main Street closed for good: now there was only two left. One owned by Sanchez and one owned by a local family. Choice went down, prices went up, but there was nowhere else to go to buy food, clothes or hardware.

The slow death of Medusa disturbed the boys.

"We gotta get outta here, Floyd. This place is dyin' and we're stuck here."

"But where, Zeke? I ain't got money and neither have you. I'm as tired seeing you treated like dirt by Sanchez's men, those losers at school and those ass-kissers in the street."

Zeke had started to be targeted even more by Sanchez's men, particular as he had become taller and bigger than most of them.

"I dunno, Floyd, but if we don't, there's gonna be trouble. Ma and Pa are gettin' hassled by Sanchez too."

"For what reason?"

"Does Sanchez ever need a reason? Maybe he just feels like it. Who knows what that son of a bitch thinks? I only know my folks are a target and you is too because we're friends."

"What are we gonna do about this, Zeke?"

"I don't know dude, but a black kid like me can't stay in this place. May as well paint a target on my back. You seen my folks. They're scared. Just plain scared. I don't wanna end up livin' like that."

Two days later Zeke was deliberately jostled by one of Sanchez's men in the street. It wasn't the first time. But this time, Zeke angrily rounded on them. "Can't a guy walk on the street without the likes of you retards botherin'?"

"Screw you, nigger! You ain't got no rights here. Keep your Goddamned yap shut."

"Fuck you!" snarled Zeke in return. "You walk around like you're kings, but you're just white trash."

Floyd pulled Zeke away before the confrontation could get worse and they quickly got out of the centre of town.

Zeke was still enraged. "I can't stand this much longer, Floyd."

"I know, Zeke. So have you got some ideas?"

"Mom and Dad have some money together and they say I ought to make for Woosterville or farther parts. They are tempted too. It's gettin' worse for them. Maybe we should all get gone?"

Floyd felt confused. He was going to lose his only ally in Medusa? Seeing his face, Zeke continued.

"I want you to come too, Floyd. But I ain't got enough money for the two of us. If I can make it you can come later?"

"Thanks, man. But I have to pay my own way. Just as soon as we get out of school I can get a job and save some money too."

"Do that Floyd. You'll never prosper in a place like this. I have to get back to my folks... see you tomorrow, here?"

"Yeah, sure. Give your Mom and Dad my best?"

"Will do. See ya Floyd."

Floyd never saw Zeke ever again.

No-one in Medusa mentioned the missing young man. Floyd asked around quietly a few times but the whispered scolding he got from people made him fearful too. The tension in the town was almost tangible.

Floyd's Mom told him off, "I hear you been asking questions. Don't mention Zeke to anyone again. Understand? It might happen to you too and I couldn't bear it. Promise me you'll not ask anyone else?"

"But Mom, a guy can't just disappear. Zeke's my friend. He's the only one who ever stuck up for me and I watch his back in turn."

Floyd recoiled from the slap. His Mom had hit him! She had sometimes punished him physically as a child, but she had just slapped him across the face with all her might.

51

"You stupid idiot child... Don't you see how things are? Haven't I already told you what happens in this Godforsaken town? You're seventeen years old. Open those God damned child's eyes! Zeke is more than likely buried out there past the city limits. Zeke's parents haven' been seen in two days either. If they've got sense, they're long-gone. "

Floyd was horrified. "Zeke is dead?"

"Floyd, you fool! If he ain't dead he's a sorry man and he soon will be a dead one. You don't know the half of it with Sanchez and the men he surrounds himself with. Time to grow up, Floyd. I can't protect you now. I always managed when you were a child but I can't now that you're gettin' towards being a man.

"I... I never realised. Mom..." Floyd stuttered.

"You should know. I've warned you enough. You should know what every other man and woman in this town knows: cross Sanchez or Sanchez's men and you're dead. Promise me you'll keep that in your mind. I couldn't bear to lose you too to that bastard, Sanchez. I've lost enough already..."

When Floyd remind quiet, she spoke again: "Promise me, Floyd. Please, son?"

Floyd made the promise, but he remained troubled. Floyd kept his eyes open for Sanchez's gang and avoided their attention. As much as he could. Even their squabbles became rare in the next few months. He became more isolated in school and avoided the town as much as he could.

At school, Floyd spent his time writing in a battered notebook and ignoring the lessons around him. The teachers tried to take it off him, but his rage and resistance soon made them back off. He sometimes got into fights with classmates as they tried to find out what he was writing, too, but Floyd's savagery soon taught them to leave him alone.

He was often sent to study alone, but it was no punishment. He spent all that time obsessively writing and writing and writing. He wrote down his thoughts, feelings and what he'd seen and heard. Notebook, reading, reading, writing, drawing. It wasn't as if he now had anything else in his life.

Floyd's writing had no particular depth, but the daily writing made him an acute observer of people and their activities, but never as a participant. His involvement in school was always severely curtailed, as it was in town society.

Floyd stopped going to school shortly after. It was clear from the teachers' attitudes that they didn't want him there. They made him feel 'stupid' and they continued to delight in telling him so. But the truth was that they didn't know what to do with him. Floyd excelled in what he liked doing, but he was unable by his nature to ever sit, learn and regurgitate academic learning at the command of someone else.

The boy had no ambitions to be a 'team player' and subsume his personality and interests to that of others.

The Principal, finally had enough and told Floyd to "Not waste any more of our time". There was no thought of the things that Floyd excelled at, because the school did not at all understand 'Marlene's awkward bastard'. They had no ambitions or ability to try and understand. The next week he was employed part-time evenings at a local store by an 'associate' of his Mom's.

Floyd continued to write in this notebook, slouched on a bench in the street, out in the countryside or when he had breaks from working in the store. "Always scribblin' that boy. What's he writin'? Does he think it makes him clever?"

Floyd's workmates bothered him about his writing as well. "Come on boy, it can't be a secret. You better not be writin' about us. We want to see." Floyd's fury and aggression made them all back off, as it had at school.

His behaviour caused problems with the manager at the store, but because he was otherwise amiable, they let it go. He remained withdrawn. The isolation bothered him still, but it was a relief to not to be noticed by the locals with their spiteful words.

Work, for Floyd, seemed to be the same as school, just a lot nastier.

He thought he was settled at the store when he was summoned by his manager and fired. The manager looked upset and embarrassed but refused to explain why Floyd was losing his job. A few days later, he learnt that Sanchez now owned the place.

The new job lasted an even shorter time, before he incurred Sanchez's wrath.

Chapter 4 - Sean of Hope?

Floyd was soon busy looking for a new job, but got nowhere in the town. The word had got out about Sanchez's face pasted on the baby Jesus in the crib. No-one would employ 'that boy who made Sanchez look like a fool', although they probably laughed about it in private. Sometimes Floyd saw Sanchez's men in the distance and made himself scarce. Money became tight as Floyd was not earning and his Mom began to have occasional days off feeling 'under the weather'.

Floyd noticed how his Mom had become a little tireder and her brown hair a little greyer. Her already slender frame was much thinner. Her shoulders became a little more rounded as if she was carrying a heavy weight. She never asked for help and refused any offers of help from Floyd, taking it as an insult.

"The day I can't run a household is the day I should be dead," she replied.

Most of the time Floyd was a typical teenager, too self-absorbed in his own problems, but sometimes he did jobs around the house when his Mom was at work: cleaning, laundry, sweeping up. Mom never commented and Floyd never let on.

His one attempt at cooking her a meal was a disaster and she shrieked at him for half an hour about his 'uselessness'. "Can't you even make scrambled eggs without burning the damned house down?"

The weeks turned to months. Still no job. Floyd began to think that he would never work again. So early one morning he walked the two hours to Farnsfield and then took the bus thirty miles to the nearest city: Woosterville.

Woosterville was huge and seemed to go on forever. It took just as long from the outskirts of the city for the bus to travel from Farnsfield. He was in near terror at the lanes of cars and how the bus driver negotiated his way to the city centre. Then he was out of the bus terminus and out the door and into the city, swarming with people.

For a boy brought up in tiny, isolated Medusa, Woosterville was an intoxicating mix of cultures, ethnicity, sights, smells and sounds. Floyd soon became distracted from his original task: finding himself a job.

He explored the city: its skyscrapers, squares, stores, museums and galleries. There were so many things he never seen before or even knew existed. He scolded himself as he nearly got run over in the busy traffic – there were cars everywhere here too.

Floyd watched the people playing music in the street. He smelt spicy food in the air and looked around seeing people of every race under the sun: Asians, Chinese, Russians, Africans and people from South America. He heard more different languages in one hour than he had before in his whole life. For a boy raised in a white, racist and intolerant fiefdom, it was overwhelming.

People were dressed in suits and in other fine clothes. He gawked until they glared back at him. But as soon as one peacock passed by, there was another. Beautiful women wearing daring dresses, with vibrant colours swayed as they walked by. The teenage Floyd was mesmerised.

He was slightly shocked to see 'pictures of naked-ass wimmin' in the Woosterville's City Gallery, but he found it hard to drag himself away. There was little art of any kind in Medusa and it wasn't of women dressed literally in nothing.

One picture particularity attracted his attention: "Venus of You-are-beeno? How the hell do I say that? By 'Titty-ann'?" He giggled to himself.

Floyd took his notepad out and began to scribble down ideas. He knew that he'd forget most of what he'd seen that day and wanted to capture his feelings and thoughts about the picture. He wrote about the nude form on the canvas before him. After what seemed like minutes he noticed an older man looking at him with a faint smile on his face.

"You like the picture, son?" said the man.

Floyd flushed in embarrassment. "It's OK I suppose", he replied, trying, but failing to curb his enthusiasm.

"'OK' enough to be here for an hour then?" The man smiled more. He was chubby, red-faced and balding, with a huge ginger moustache almost covering his cheerful smile and wore a worn tweed jacket and a badly-knotted tie.

"An hour? I thought it was a few minutes?"

"That's the nature of art. It captivates you. What's your name, son?"

"Floyd."

"Pleased to meet you Floyd, I'm Sean. Sean Lynch. I'm the curator here. This place captured me a long time ago and it still inspires me. I don't think it will ever let me go, but I'm fine with that."

"I've never been here before, but I want to come back here again and again," said Floyd, his words tumbling out.

"What do you like about the picture, Floyd? Apart from the obvious?" Sean smiled again.

"Obvious?" Floyd blushed again. "You mean she ain't got a stitch on? Well maybe it's that."

He paused. "Yeah... it's a lot of that" Floyd smirked.

"Is it just that?" pressed Sean.

Floyd paused. "It is and it ain't." He stopped to think. "It sorta makes me..." and he blushed again.

"But it ain't just that. She ain't got a stitch on but she's so... so bold. She ain't ashamed. I ain't ever seen a woman like that. Even the whores in Medusa, they don't look a nothin' like her?"

"So you're from Medusa, Floyd. 'The Place Set in Stone?'" smirked Sean

Floyd grimaced. "That's what they call it."

"So what else about the picture do you like?"

"I was wonderin' what she had in her hand? I can't tell. And what's the dog doin' there asleep on her bed? And what's the women in the back doing? One looks like she's prayin' and the other looks like she's rollin' her sleeves up to give the other one a good tannin'?"

Sean paused. "Floyd you're an unusual young man. You've noticed many things others just don't see. "

"'Unusual' ain't what they call me at home. 'Stupid', 'lazy' is more like it. 'In a dream'. I can't help the way I am and they all think it's deliberate!"

Sean looked annoyed. "Floyd! Don't let anyone ever tell you you're stupid. If I had more students than you I'd be a happier man. Many of them are 'stupid' and 'lazy', but don't ever think that applies to you."

Floyd began to get annoyed. "Yeah... sure." He had no experience of praise and he thought the older man was making fun of him. "No-one ever said that to me before so why would you? What do you want from me?"

"I was curious what you liked the picture, Floyd..."

Floyd interrupted. "I might have known there'd be something. I've heard 'a guys like you. I ain't that sort of guy. Find a pretty boy to say nice things to."

Floyd stood up from the bench angrily stuffing his possessions into his pack.

"I'm sorry son. I meant nothing by it. I teach art and most my students don't think like you. And I wish more did."

"Enough already, dude." And with that, Floyd stormed off.

"Shit..." muttered Sean to himself as he sat on the bench. "That went well. What did I say? Such a bright boy and he sees things. What made him so angry?"

Then he noticed the battered notebook on the floor. "It must be Floyd's?" he thought. "Maybe I could catch him up?"

Sean rushed back to the gallery reception. "Hi, James" he said to the man on the desk. "Did you see a young man walk out of here in a hurry?"

"Hi Sean. Yeah, looked in a mood. Didn't see anything on CCTV so I just let him go. Has he done anything to you?"

"No not at all. Just a bright kid and I said the wrong thing…"

"Teenagers? What can you do with 'em? I've got two aged thirteen and fifteen and I wonder who they take after. Me and Monica like a quiet life but the two boys are hell at times."

"But did you like the quiet life when you were thirteen? Or fifteen?" smiled Sean.

James laughed in reply. "As a matter of fact I did, but it never seemed to quite work out like that. Sometimes I just wanted to be left alone but older folks just didn't seem to get that."

"That's true", sighed Sean. "I think I shouldn't have pushed too much with that kid."

"Looked like a nasty piece of work to me."

"Nasty? Sure. But it's his mind I liked. A strange way of thinking. There's something there… but he doesn't know it or doesn't believe it. And he dropped his notebook."

"Do you want me to keep a look out for him, Sean?"

"Yes. Give him one my business cards if he comes back. I feel such an idiot. I might have frightened him off. But he loved this place, I could see it. Keep an eye out. Try not to spook him like I did?"

"Do you want me to keep the notebook?" asked James.

"No. I'll keep it. It might give me a chance to talk to him again. He's certainly worth talking to."

"OK Sean. You heading home?"

"Yes, I think so. See you tomorrow. Don't forget to print out the invites for the competition next week?"

"Will do. Take care of yourself, Sean. Give my best to Gabriel."

James watched Sean stride away. Sean was a good guy and so was his partner Gabriel. He'd never seen Sean be so concerned over some kid before, though. Couldn't be that special, surely?

Floyd hurried down the street, as quickly as he could, away from the gallery. He was angry and upset. He'd enjoyed talking to Sean but he'd let his temper get the best of him. "Damned fool... he talks to you and you get all angry. Maybe he was after your ass but maybe he just wanted to talk. Now you'll never, ever know. Dipshit!"

The experience had disturbed him. He simply wasn't used to people asking his opinion or suggesting he was clever or capable of anything. Floyd couldn't make sense of what Sean had said. "Yeah, he was just after my ass. Screw him!"

Lost in thought, Floyd wandered the streets of Woosterville. He had no direction or purpose and no sense of time. He was too upset to think straight. It was when it began to go dark that he realised he had missed the bus back home to Medusa.

Chapter 5 – Woosterville Nightlife

Floyd was completely lost. It took him an hour to get his bearings and then another half an hour to get back to the bus terminus. It was now seven pm and the rush hour was ending. The bus station was nearly empty and gradually grew quieter and colder. Floyd started to walk up and down to keep warm.

"How am I going to stand it when it's really cold?" he thought.

Floyd continued to pace back and forth. He looked at his watch again, ten more minutes had passed.

After a while he noticed others arrive. They kept to themselves, which Floyd appreciated. "Unsavoury lookin'," he thought.

Then the women arrived. He knew what they were straight-away. Short skirts, "Tits hangin' out" he muttered to himself. He sat down in a corner to try and avoid attention, but it didn't work. One of the prostitutes slowly sauntered up to him.

She was pretty but looked hard-nosed. She wore a short skirt and a grubby yellow halter top. She was pale skinned, with bruises around her eyes. She had a sore in the corner of her mouth. And looked tired looking and drawn. "Drugs?" thought Floyd.

"Hey honey. You cold? I betcha I could help? Or lonely? I can help with that too," she cooed, as she pushed her chest out at him.

Floyd was mortified. "I'm... I'm fine as I am, thanks, ma'am" as he tried to stop staring.

"You're a polite one, aintcha? No-one calls me 'ma'am'. But you like what you see, don't you sweetie? I can tell. What can I do for you...?"

Floyd flushed beet red. "I ain't got no money. I ain't gonna want anything off of you."

"OK, sugar... But I got what you need. And when you got money, we can have a little fun, won't we? Take one of these..." She handed him a card.

And with that she slowly walked away. Floyd was transfixed by her walk. That sensual strut. The wiggle. Even though he knew exactly what she was, he still couldn't help but look.

"Jesus..." he mumbled. "What I wouldn't give..." as he continued to watch her. She turned and gave a smile again. Her smirk turned to a frown as she spotted a big black guy, who quickly walked up to her.

"Sleaze-bag..." was Floyd's immediate reaction.

"What's the deal, bitch? I give you what you need, you get me some money! Where's your customers?"

"It's early, Zaden. There's no-one here yet, It's too early."

Floyd was shocked as the black man slapped her hard across the face. She doubled over in pain but he dragged her up by the hair. "Listen here, ho. I gets you what you want and need and you get money with that body of yours. Get me? Now if you want to go without or wants to be in the river, you keep up doin' nothin'!"

And with that he slapped her again. She fell to the floor and lay there, sobbing.

Floyd was shocked, and then very angry, How could that guy treat a woman that way? Before he knew it, he was walking quickly towards them.

Zaden turned to him. "What d'you want, kid? A piece of this...?" as he pointed to the women, still weeping as she tried to get to her feet.

Floyd was enraged further. "You son of a bitch! You leave her alone or I'll stop you..."

The black man scowled at him in annoyance. "And how do you propose to do that, kid?"

Floyd immediately lunged at the pimp trying to aim a fist. Zaden stepped back quickly and reached into his pocket to produce a knife. A very big knife with an evil looking hook on the end.

"Come on kid, let me introduce you to my best friend." Zaden stabbed back at Floyd, waving he knife wildly.

Floyd knew he was in big trouble. An older and stronger man with that knife was more trouble than he needed. He quickly decided to make a run for it.

Zaden called after him. "Run you little pussy! I see you here again, you is dead! Come back here and you'll see..."

Floyd ran for about ten minutes. Anywhere to get away from the guy with the knife at the terminus. There was nothing he could do for the prostitute with her bruises and drugs and her abusive pimp.

Floyd scolded himself as he ran, out into the night-time streets of Woosterville. "Jerk! Why get involved? You'll end up dead!"

The next few hours were a nightmare. Solicited by more whores, offered drugs, threatened by a crazy man and two attempts at being mugged later he was hiding in an alleyway, nursing his bruises and exhausted by the experience. He felt his fat lip with his fingers and came away with blood on his fingers.

"Sore, but OK" he thought. His tongue explored the front of his mouth.

"Damn it, I think one of my teeth is loose?"

He felt his right eye. One of those bastards had managed to stick one on him but in the jumble of fists and bodies he hadn't noticed. He'd have a shiner tomorrow...

Floyd didn't know what to do. The bus terminus was dangerous, but the streets were just as bad. No-one seemed to want to leave him alone. They wanted his money or they wanted his life. This was too much for a small town boy. He was upset enough to remember his Mom. "Shit, she'll be worryin'. As if she ain't got enough on her plate."

A police car went by and then stopped. A cop got out. Floyd immediately tensed.

"Hey! You..." shouted the cop. Floyd just ran for it. He'd never liked the cops in Medusa and he didn't want to get acquainted with the Woosterville variety, neither.

The boy charged down the nearest alley, out onto to the next street and dodged down the opposite alleyway again until he thought he had lost the cop. He dropped to a nearby doorway, breathing heavily. "What's gonna happen next?" he gasped.

He didn't know how long he sat on the doorstep, unable to relax or think straight. But his grumbling stomach had gotten his attention. He was starving and shaking...

"I've gotta eat," he thought, as he looked at his watch. "Jesus, it must be seven hours since I had that sandwich?"

Floyd cautiously peered out into the street. No-one about. How about that way? He had no idea where to go, so any direction was as good as the other. After twenty minutes of aimless walking, he spotted the diner. He was so hungry. It was quiet, with one or two people coming in and out. He didn't want to be seen going in, so he waited until there had been no movement for a few minutes.

Floyd quickly got himself through the door and into a well-worn seat, pulling his cap over his face, sitting hunched in the chair. He didn't want anyone to see how beaten up he was. The waitress approached.

"What'll you have?" she asked. Then she saw the bruises. "What the hell's happened to you? Are you OK?"

"I'm fine. Don't worry about me, ma'am. Can I have coffee and a piece of the pumpkin pie?"

She looked at him again. She was a nice-looking lady, with light brown hair and a friendly smile.

"Are you sure? You look awful!"

"Lady! I'm OK. Pie and coffee would be good...?"

"OK! OK!" she said, hands up in defence. "Pie and coffee coming up..." and she briskly walked away.

As he waited for his coffee, Floyd looked around. It looked like the one's he'd seen in magazines: old-style and worn, but clean. He thought it might benefit from a lick of paint. The other customers sat on the own, singly to each table. They kept themselves to themselves, although they smiled at the waitress who just served him. She smiled and spoke to them with affection and familiarity.

"This," thought Floyd, "is a decent place."

A few minutes later the waitress came back, dropped the pie and the mug of coffee on the table and walked away again. She didn't bother him again and Floyd appreciated that.

He quickly demolished the pie but tried to sip the coffee to make It last. Hunched over the table and soothed by the warmth of the diner, he began to doze off...

The waitress watched him warily for a while. "Young" she thought. "Been beaten up? Not another street kid? He better have money to pay for this?"

She looked around the diner. No-one else had come in and no-one inside had ordered anything else. She walked into the back of the diner. "Alvin...? Alvin..." she called out. "I think we've gotten another one of those kids."

She was met by an older man in his late fifties with thinning black hair, powerful looking but kind of overweight. He scowled at her. "What is it, Janie?"

"It's another one of those kids. A boy. Looks around sixteen or seventeen. Someone's whaled into him, but he's trying to hide it under his baseball cap. Over on table seven."

"OK, baby, I see him. Trouble, d'you think?"

"Don't think so. But never can be sure. He seemed polite, but got surly when I asked if he was OK."

"hmmmm... I'll keep an eye out. You stay near the alarm, OK?"

"If you're sure, Alvin?"

"He doesn't look a bad kid, but let's be safe than sorry, baby?"

They stood, watching the boy as his head began to droop. "He's asleep..." whispered Janie.

"Yeah, I see. Let's leave him be, but he'll have to be out of here when we close."

An hour later, the diner was empty, apart from Floyd, who was fast asleep, with drool running out the corner of his mouth. Alvin walked up to the table, trying to be as loud as he could manage, but Floyd did not move. He looked back at Janie and shrugged his shoulders.

"Hey... hey you..." he said softly, but there was no response. He tried again.

"Hey... Hey, kid... You need to get movin'..."

There was still no response. So Alvin gave him a gentle push.

Floyd erupted out the seat, confused and completely disorientated but his fist ready. Alvin jumped back, taken by surprise.

"Alvin? You OK?" called Janie.

"Yeah, baby. He moves fast!" He turned back to Floyd. "You OK, kid?"

Floyd paused, wobbling with tiredness. "Yeah… yeah. I think so. Where am I?"

"You're in my diner kid. Alvin's diner. You've been in here for a couple hours. You aren't on drugs are you, kid?"

"No! No… just tired. I got attacked by these guys… didn't know where to go…"

Alvin tried to calm Floyd down. "Kid, just sit down. You're safe here."

Floyd dropped back into his seat, still confused. Alvin looked over his shoulder.

"Bring the kid some more coffee, Janie," he called out.

"OK, I'll be there in a second," replied Janie, as she went for the pot.

When the coffee arrived, Janie found Alvin sitting opposite Floyd. "Have this on us, kid... what's your name by the way?"

"Floyd."

"Well Floyd, I'm Alvin and I own this place and this is Janie who works here."

"He means I do all the work and he takes credit, Floyd."

Alvin smiled, but Floyd only grunted his understanding.

"So what's going on, Floyd?"

"I missed the bus back home and got into a spot at the terminal. Some pimp waving his knife at me when I tried to stop him beatin' up this lady. I mean, not a lady. Y'know what she was... And then some guys tried to rob me... it happened twice?"

"This is a bad place to be Floyd, at night. You look like a punch bag."

"I got my own shots in," said Floyd defensively.

Alvin smiled. "Sure you did. Where are you from, kid?"

"Medusa..."

"Medusa? Stone City? What the hell are you doing way over here? Woosterville is no place for a small town boy like you. You in trouble, Floyd?"

"No." But then Floyd paused. "Well, maybe a bit... but I can take of myself," protested Floyd.

"From what I can see, kid, you couldn't take care of a paper bag. Or fight yourself out one at least."

Floyd began to well up. Zeke, the last few weeks, no job, no prospects, the massive experience of Woosterville and meeting Sean in the gallery. Then being attacked and lost in a big city was too much.

Janie came back over with the coffee pot. "Honey don't cry. We'll see you're OK. Won't we Alvin?"

Alvin sighed. Janie and her collection of lost chicks. It looked like this Floyd was going to be the latest. "OK Janie, what do you want to do with this one?"

Janie sat down next to Floyd who had begun to calm down. "Honey, we'll make sure you're OK. Floyd, look at me. We've seen plenty of guys like you. We want to help."

"Th-thanks," spluttered Floyd, his voice thick with emotion. "It's been a weird day. It's just been too much..."

Floyd tried to pull himself together. "But... but there's no place in Medusa for me neither. Sanchez, that son of a bitch has me blacklisted. There's no work and no-one will bid me the time of day because of that mother..."

"Sanchez? I heard 'a him. Mean tyrant. There's a reason Medusa is so backward, kid and its name is 'Sanchez'".

"Is it really that bad, Alvin?" said Janie.

"Yes, it really is. I'm surprised Floyd here didn't end up with a few bones broken or worse if he upset Sanchez. No-one respectable ever goes to Medusa if they can help it. He's like the mafia and every worse kind of bastard I ever heard of."

"Can't anyone do anything about it? Surely the cops..."

"Decent cops stay away, baby. The local cops are crooked. Medusa's too small to be worth their while. I hear the Feds would like to snoop about, but unless Sanchez makes a mistake they have nothing to go on."

"So what about Floyd here? We can't send him back to that? "

"I have to go back", said Floyd. "My Mom's there and she needs me."

"And you need her too kid," said Alvin gently. "Look we've gotten a place here you can crash for the night. Tomorrow we'll get you a ticket home. Can we let your Mom know?"

"We ain't got no phone."

"No cell phone?"

"No, we can't afford anything like that."

"Any neighbour we can tell?"

"No they all snoop for Sanchez, everyone's too scared. I don't want them or him knowin' what's going on. "

"Kid, you've got to get out of that place... How old are you?"

"Seventeen."

"When are you eighteen?"

"About a year's time."

"Kid, when you get to eighteen, you come back and see us, OK?"

Floyd paused in thought. Why were these two people helping him? "Sure. Thanks, Mr Alvin."

"Just call me Alvin. If I'm not about, you talk to Janie here. I mean it Floyd. You're in a bad way living in Medusa and if someone like Sanchez has his eye on you, you better watch your back. Got me?"

"Yeah, thanks Alvin."

"By the way... what did you do to Sanchez that got him so riled, kid?"

Floyd smirked. "I stuck a picture of his face on the baby Jesus at the Nativity."

Alvin began to laugh. "You little shit! He must have been furious. You're a lucky man to be still in one piece, Floyd."

"I couldn't help it, I got sick and tired of him runnin' everythin' and everyone is frightened. Or dead, like Zeke."

"Who's Zeke, kid?"

"My best friend. My only friend in Medusa. Had an argument with Sanchez's men. We never saw him again, or his folks. Mom said he was probably somewhere out there buried."

Janie looked shocked. "Floyd! You can't mean that?"

The older man interrupted. "He can, baby. Sanchez has been doing this for years. And his father before him, rest his soul in the darkest pits of hell."

"How do you know so much of this stuff, Alvin?"

"That isn't important now, Janie. But helping out this young idiot is... come along kid let's get you sorted."

"Thanks, Alvin," said Floyd, quietly, still bewildered at the offer of help.

Alvin smiled as he got out of his seat. "Don't thank me until you've helped clean up, Floyd."

Janie looked outraged. "Alvin! He's exhausted. He's been attacked. Come back here!"

Alvin silently walked away in the direction of his office.

"Wait here Floyd" said Janie as she went in pursuit. "And finish your coffee."

Janie rushed into Alvin's office and she leaned over his desk. "That's boy's exhausted and been beaten up and half-way to being terrified. And you want him to help clean up?"

"Janie, you like to collect lost kids but some of them have stolen from us and caused us more trouble than they're worth. I have to stand the bill, otherwise no-one would insure us."

"But Alvin..."

"No-one gets help from us now until they prove they are at least trying to be decent. Remember those guys all in black? Jesus, even with black lipstick? They stole from the cash register and we saw it in the news two hours later. Trying to score and busted by the cops using my money."

"But Floyd looks like a good kid?"

"He does, but he gets nothing until he proves that."

"OK, you're the boss," conceded Janie.

"I am. So get to it, Janie?"

Janie stuck her tongue out at him, smiled again and then went back in to the dining area. She found Floyd putting his coat on.

"Floyd, honey, where are you going?"

"I don't want to be no trouble to you or Alvin. I ain't one for charity."

Janie frowned. "Honey you aren't any trouble to us. But Alvin wants you to help me clean up. You'll earn your keep, young man." she smiled even as she tried to sound like a voice of authority.

Floyd couldn't help but smile back. Janie was kind of pretty for an older lady and funny too. "OK, I work, what do I get?"

"You help clean up and wash up. You get a bed for the night. The door's got a lock on it. You help set up tomorrow. We'll feed you well and you get your bus ticket home."

Floyd looked puzzled. "Why are you helpin' me? No-one's ever done that before. Most people treat me like shit." He looked embarrassed. "Pardon my language."

Janie smiled again. "Polite too? We don't mind helping polite young gentlemen, Floyd. We don't care what the people of Medusa think about you. We'll help you tonight and send you on your way tomorrow. But first you need to start washing up..."

Floyd took his coat off. "Where am I going?"

"Kitchen's that way," she pointed. "Now move that skinny ass!"

Alvin was waiting for him in the kitchen. "OK, kid?"

"Yeah, sure. What do you want me to do?"

81

"See that stuff by the sink? It needs washing."

Floyd turned and looked. His heart sank. It was a mountain of plates, cups, saucepans, trays and cutlery.

"Holy shit, all that now?"

"If I was you, kid, I'd get to it?" Alvin grinned.

"OK! OK! I'm on it." Floyd set work rinsing pots and pans and filling a huge metal sink.

"Once you've cleaned 'em up, stack 'em in the dish washer," shouted Alvin from across the kitchen.

"Huh? If you've got a dish washer, why am I washing them by hand?"

Alvin smirked. "Because your lily-white hands do a better job that any machine. And it's character building, don't you think?"

Floyd gave him a dirty look and muttered to himself.

Two hours later he had done. Alvin made him clean all the work surfaces down and then mop the floor. Floyd really was beat. Janie came back into the kitchen.

"Hi baby," greeted Alvin. "Money all sorted?"

"Yeah. Takings OK. But it's down since last year. We aren't losing money, but we aren't making much profit, Alvin. I'm not worried now, but we need more customers."

"I don't get it Janie," scowled Alvin. "The foods good, we treat customers well, no complaints, but takings are down again?"

"They are. Can we talk tomorrow? I'm dog-tired. And Floyd here is nearly asleep on his feet."

Alvin turned to the boy and saw him, standing on unsteady feet and eyes glazed, but still working away. "I never noticed. He just got on with the job. No fuss, just steady work."

"So he was OK, Alvin?"

"More than OK, baby. I'd give the kid a job based on what I've seen."

"Let's think about that tomorrow, too? But let's get him to bed. And then let's get you into bed too...? She gave him a sultry look.

"Your place or mine, Janie?"

"Do you have to ask? Always yours. Always..."

"I feel a bit livelier now, Janie..."

She walked up to him. "I might feel livelier too… if you play your cards right?"

And with that, she walked over to the exhausted boy. "Come on Floyd. Time for you to get some sleep."

Floyd docilely followed her, out of the kitchen and up the stairs.

"There's the bathroom. Here's your room. Get some beauty sleep, Floyd. You really need it. Apart from those pretty eyes of yours?"

Floyd grinned, embarrassed yet again. He wasn't used to anyone flirting with him like that and he enjoyed being praised, even if it was in fun.

"Off you go. Up at seven am, so get going…"

Floyd closed the door and lay on the bed. He almost immediately fell asleep, but his dreams were strange: full of whores, pimps, Alvin, Janie and Mom all mixed in. Sanchez and his men pursued him through the streets of Medusa. A strangely lifeless Zeke called out from the alleyway "Don't end up where I am, Floyd…"

Sanchez kept staring at him curiously, then in anger. "Doesn't listen. Doesn't do. Doesn't have a clue" chanted thousands of children surrounding him while the teachers looked on disapprovingly.

He woke in the night, soaked in sweat, disturbed by the nightmares. He had to go home to Medusa, but planned to leave again, as soon as he could.

"But what do I do about Mom?" he whispered to himself. "Will she come away too?"

Despite his busy thoughts, he fell back into a heavy and thankfully dreamless sleep.

The boy woke again to knocking on the bedroom door. "Where am I?" he wondered groggily for a second. Then the previous day slowly came back to him.

"Floyd? Floyd? Time to get moving." He recognised Janie's voice. "You awake Floyd?"

"Yeah..." he groaned.

The door opened and Janie walked in. "We've got no clothes that fit you, but clean yourself up. Here's a towel, you need a .
shower." She pulled a face. "Floyd, you really need a shower. Breakfast in twenty."

And with that, she was gone.

Floyd struggled out the bed, still tired and struggling to think. "Shower..." And with that, he hauled himself out the bed and through the bedroom door.

The shower helped him to wake up and he was almost feeling human when there was another knock at the door. "Hey, kid! Breakfast is ready. Get it while it's hot?"

"OK, Alvin," he replied. Floyd realised how starving he was and quickly left the bedroom again and walked down the stairs.

"Out the front, Floyd," called Janie.

Alvin and Janie were sitting there tucking in to breakfast. Bacon, eggs, toast, hash browns and coffee. Floyd's stomach gurgled loudly at the food smells.

The couple turned and smiled at him. "You need feeding, kid" laughed Alvin. "Take a seat and tuck in."

Floyd didn't have to be told twice He was soon inhaling the breakfast and the hot coffee.

"Floyd, don't eat so fast!"

Janie laughed. "Growing boys, eh, Alvin?"

"I don't want him choking to death, Janie. Not exactly good for custom, is it?

Janie smiled again. "Probably not? Slow down, Floyd."

Floyd grinned through his latest mouthful and he struggled to chew and swallow before he could reply. "But it's so good. I wish I could eat like this every day."

"Not if you want to end up looking like Alvin, Floyd?" giggled Janie.

"Hey! I resent that. I'm not fat. Just a little middle-age spread. Most guys have it."

Floyd looked at the two of them. He was embarrassed, but fascinated by the couple. They flirted so much. And their innuendo... he wasn't sure people of their age should act like that? It was disgusting in a way, but he also liked what he saw.

Janie and Alvin clearly loved each other and Floyd realised it was something he'd never seen before. His Mom kept to herself and he had little contact with anyone else in the town, men especially, outside of the 'visitors' both he and his Mom detested and feared. Zeke's Mom and Dad had been very reserved and he never saw them as much as look at each other, let alone with open affection.

"OK, kid. Well fed?"

"Sure," replied Floyd. "I ain't never ate like that before. Thanks, Alvin" and he shyly turned to Janie. "And thank for looking after me too..."

"You're welcome, Floyd," she replied and patted his hand.

Alvin chuckled again. "You ain't competing for my baby's affections are you, kid?"

Floyd stuttered, "No sir. I... I ain't used to a pretty lady like Janie being nice to me." His face fell again. "I ain't used to anyone bein' nice to me, period."

"Well we want to help, Floyd," said Alvin, who handed him an envelope. "Here's a reference from me and a few dollars. Take it wherever you want to go, kid. But when you're eighteen, you come back and see us, OK?"

"Are you sure?" replied Floyd, hesitantly. He tried to hand the envelope back. "You don't really know me that well."

Alvin pushed it back. "Look, Floyd, you don't have any future in Medusa. You seem decent, so you're welcome here. If you ever want another reference, I'll be happy to do that too. Think about your future. I know you haven't had much of a good time here but there's always a place in Woosterville for an honest kid like you, OK?"

"Thanks, Alvin. And thanks, again Janie."

"Now, it's time for you to get. Go home, talk to your Mom and see if she will move with you. She sounds a decent lady too and she'd do better away from Medusa too."

"I will. Thanks guys..."

Alvin and Janie noticed that the boy had started to become upset again. They wondered why this kid had such a low opinion of himself and they were horrified by what he had told about his life in Medusa.

They all got up out of their chairs. Alvin shook his hand. Janie hugged him and gave him a kiss on the cheek. He blushed yet again. They both laugh at his reaction.

"Floyd," grinned Alvin. "We gotta get you used to being kissed by pretty women."

Floyd took his coat off Alvin and put it on. "Time to go..."

With a final handshake and another hug and kiss from Janie, he was gone. As Floyd walked away, he kept looking back, like he didn't want to leave. He laughed as they started making 'shooing' motions and then he turned and strode away.

"Hope he'll be OK, Alvin?"

"He's a good kid. Tougher than he thinks. There's a bit of temper and steel in there. I can see it. If he comes back, we'll help him. If that's OK with you?"

"You know me, Alvin, always another chick to mother."

They smiled at each other. "OK Janie, let's get back to work," and he went into his office.

When he was sure Janie was occupied, he shut the door and made a phone call.

"Hi it's Alvin? Yeah good, thanks. I may have a useful contact from Stone City. A kid from there. Yeah, he's got a lot to say about S. Needs protection. A parent too. Yeah... I know. I should keep my nose out. Yeah, yeah... I'm retired. Got it. But wouldn't you like to nail that son-of-a-bitch? OK. There's a missing kid. Black kid. Yeah. Called 'Zeke'. Parents missing too. Deceased? Yeah, probably the usual. If we can nail one of S' men we'd know where. Will let you know. Say 'Hi' to Elaine for me? 'Course... any time. For free? Not a chance, Hanser."

And with a smile, he put the phone down. There was something about that kid. And he mentioned this 'Sean' at the City Gallery. Maybe a predator looking for a young guy, maybe not. Sounded OK. Might be worth a snoop around.

"But first, time to get through the breakfast rush..."

Chapter 6 – A Death in the Family

The trip back home was uneventful. Floyd walked back to the bus terminal and caught his bus on time. He fell sleep and only woke to the driver shouting, "Farnsfield and final destination!"

It was late afternoon and the sun had set by the time Floyd got back to Medusa. His mood worsened as he quickly walked down the Main Street to get home and to his Mom. He heard a voice shout from behind him, "Hey kid!"

It was one of Sanchez's goons: Tony Moscarra. Floyd knew that he was in trouble if he'd attracted Moscarra's attention.

Floyd ran as quickly as he could to get away. He heard Moscarra's voice, "You can't run for ever, you little shit. We're coming to see you soon..."

Out of breath, Floyd got near to home. He was wary, looking for any other of Sanchez's men. Floyd snuck around the back of the house and through the kitchen door. There was no-one around.

"Mom? Mom...?" Floyd called out softly. But there was no response. He looked through the downstairs room but there was no sign of his mother. The room looked tidy and unused.

He climbed the stairs. His worry silenced him. Where was she? All the doors were open – his bedroom, the bathroom and the spare room. His Mom's room, however, was closed. He tapped gently at the door.

91

"Mom? Mom...? It's Floyd..." he called out gently. There was no response. He opened the door.

The scent of vomit and excrement met his nose. He couldn't help but recoil at the stench. "What the hell...?" There was a shape in the bed, covered in blankets, but there was no movement. He saw her head on the pillow.

He shook her gently. "Mom? It's Floyd. Are you OK? Mom...?" but there was no reply.

He shook her again. She was warm in the bed and that consoled him a little. Why would she not wake or speak?

He shook her more violently this time. "Mom? Mom! Are you OK?" and this time, with a little grunt, him Mom moved.

"Flddd..." she mumbled. "izzit yooou...? Her speech was slurred and confused.

Floyd pulled back the bedclothes and was met by the renewed smell of vomit. His Mom, lying in it, continued to mumble.

"Jesus, what's happened to you?" He was shocked at her. Pale and hot and skin and bone. She was clearly very ill.

He moved quickly to the bathroom to get a wash-cloth, wet it in the sink and grabbed a towel. As he entered the bedroom again he saw her moving, trying to sit up and still muttering incoherently.

He gently supported her to a seated position and cleaned the stale puke from around her mouth. The smell almost made him vomit too, but his fear for his Mom kept him on. He went back to the bathroom to get a glass of water. When he returned, Floyd sat on the side of the bed and tried to get her to drink.

"Here Mom, drink some water. It will make you feel better."

Floyd's Mom took a sip and then began to greedily gulp the water. Just as quickly it all came back up, bile and water running down her front.

"Jesus, what is wrong with you?" but she sat there, drained and distant. "I have to get the Doctor for you."

"Flddd... Flddd" she mumbled.

"What is it Mom?"

"Listennn... t'me..."

"I have to get some help."

"Nnno... listen..."

93

"What is it, Mom?"

She paused, getting her breath. "Sanchez's men came... said they kill you... then... then you weren't here. All night waitin'. Thought you were dead. That bastard Sanchez he killed you..." She began to drift away again.

"Mom, I'm here. I went to Woosterville. Missed the bus. Got back as soon as I could. Here, try some water, but sip it."

He placed the glass back to her mouth and she took a few mouthfuls.

"Flddd... Floy..ad..? Is it you?"

"Yes Mom, it's me. I'm here. Don't worry."

"You're a good boy Floyd..." She stopped again, as if gaining strength. "Sanchez is gonna... he's gonna kill you Floyd. His men said so."

"When was this?"

"Last night..." I waited and you didn't come. "I thought you were...were dead. You aren't dead though?" She was becoming confused again.

More sips of water and she gathered her strength once more.

"In the dresser… bottom shelf… bottom shelf, Floyd. Money… all my money… take it and go, boy…"

"I can't leave you like this, Mom. I have to get a Doctor for you."

She closed her eyes again. Her breathing became shallow and laboured. Floyd shook her again.

"Mom? Mom…? Mom…!" but she didn't reply.

Floyd eased her back down on the bed, on her side, with a towel under her head in case she was sick again. She needed a Doctor right now.

He raced down the stairs, two or three steps at a time and then out the front door, slamming it behind him. The Doctor? Where? He had no idea. "Where's the phone book?"

He went back into the house. Although they had no phone, the company still delivered a book every year. He knew there was one in the kitchen cupboard. Of course, it wasn't there.

Five minutes later, he was almost at screaming point. "Where the fuck has she put the phone book?" Then he paused. "The parlour?"

There it was, under the coffee table. He sat and flicked to the General Practitioners'. "Murphy… McMillan… where are you…? Masters…"

He found it. 'G.J Masters, GP'. And with that he was off, out the door and running towards Medusa.

He was too focused on getting to the Doctor's home to notice Tony Moscarra and the rest of Sanchez's gang sitting in a pickup parked on the side of the street. Four of them. Mean and cruel, looking for trouble, as ever.

"Hey! There's that little shit, Jensen. I thought we'd warned him off? The Boss don't want him in the town anymore."

One of the gang responded. Sam Dempsey, a dark-haired cold looking guy with dead eyes. "Anyone else, we'd have sorted them by now. Why's Sanchez so soft on this one?"

"Best not talk about it, Sam. But no-one says we can't beat the crud outta him, do they? Teach him some manners?"

Delight shone in Dempsey's eyes. It made the other gang members shudder. He frightened them a little too. They knew that once Dempsey started, he never wanted to stop…

Moscarra accelerated off, pursuing Floyd down Main Street. They soon caught him up and the four of them jumped out of the pickup.

"Well if it ain't Marlene's Bastard. Time for you pay for upsetting the Mayor and all the decent folks of this town..."

Dempsey grabbed Floyd and dragged him into the nearest alleyway.

"Please! My Mom's ill! I need to get to the Doctor for her."

"Do we look like we give a fuck?" snarled Moscarra.

Floyd never even saw the first blow coming, but he instinctively responded with one of his own. That goaded Sanchez's men even more as they began to rain down punches and then kicks as he fell to the floor. As usual, they all had to drag Sam Dempsey off the unconscious boy.

"That's enough, Sam. The Boss said to teach this little shit some manners, that's all. OK?"

It took a moment for Dempsey to pull himself together. The raging madman gradually got himself under control. And then he grinned, a cold frightening smile.

"Maybe another time?"

"Maybe, Sam. But not now."

They took turns to spit on Floyd and then one pissed on the unconscious boy.

"Might improve the odour 'round here?" laughed Moscarra.

The rest joined in. With a last kick or two at Floyd, they made off.

"If that don't encourage the little shit to stay out of our decent town, I don't know what will, guys? Let's get a brew? Maybe we'll get a girl or two?"

The other thugs readily agreed and the pickup took off in the direction of the nearest bar.

Floyd woke half an hour later. He was in agony and bruised all over. He was groggy and confused and it took him a few minutes to realise where he was, but he still didn't understand what had happened to him.

Why was he in this alleyway? "Somethin' important?" He groaned as he tried to sit up. He rubbed down his arms and over his torso, groaning again where he felt the results of his beating.

"What am I doin' here?" he grumbled to himself, as he struggled to his feet. "I must be in the town? What was I doin' here?" he repeated.

As he finally stood up, he began to think again. "Maybe I should just get home..."

And then it hit him. 'Home'. 'Mom'. 'The bed'. 'Her sickness'.

"Jesus, I need to get the Doctor." Off he stumbled, out the alleyway and into the main street of Medusa.

As Floyd struggled along the street, he was spotted by some of the townsfolk. They could see he was bloody and beaten. Some were shocked and horrified, but they'd seen this happen before and they knew very well who had done it. One by one they crossed over the street to avoid the beaten boy.

Floyd ignored them. His pain and determination to get help for his Mom drove him on, until he finally reached Dr Masters' house. He paused at the door and then began to ring the bell and bang on the door repeatedly.

The door was opened suddenly by a woman in her thirties. She was attractive, brunette and well-dressed. "What's the meaning of this, haven't you got any..."

Then she saw the condition Floyd was in.

"My Mom, ill..." Floyd mumbled.

The woman turned. "Gregory? Gregory! Come quickly!"

"What is it darling?" came the reply. "Who is it?" Then he noticed Floyd's injuries. "God's sake? Who did this to you?"

"Floyd Jensen. My Mom, sir. She's so ill!"

"You're the boy who upset Sanchez? Is this from his thugs?"

Floyd did not answer, unsteady on his feet. "My Mom..."

"I'm Doctor Masters. Get in here, son. Joyce, get my first aid kit?"

Dr Masters led him into a side-room. "Sit on the chair, Floyd." and he began to examine the battered boy. Floyd hissed with the pain.

"Floyd. This is going to hurt." The Doctor began to help Floyd off with the shirt. His body was covered in emerging bruises.

"OK. A cracked rib..." Floyd groaned again. "Make that two. Lots of bruising forming. It will look and feel much worse tomorrow. Who did this to you? They could have killed you?"

"My Mom... please, Doctor Masters, she's sick... they wouldn't listen and they beat me up."

"Lots of bruising round your eyes. Lucky they didn't blind you. Can you see my fingers? How many?"

"uhhh… three…"

"Good. There's some blood in your left eye but your vision seems to be OK. Follow my finger… I think you're concussed. I want to get you to a local hospital."

"No! Mom is ill. I need help with Mom. Me later."

"Floyd, you need proper medical attention. You're badly bruised with two broken ribs. I can't rule out internal injuries. You've also got a mild concussion."

"No! We need to see Mom. You need to help her."

"Floyd you need…"

Floyd grew more frustrated, his fingernails digging in his palms with frustration as he glared at Masters. "No!"

Masters stared at him for a moment. He knew he couldn't reason with the boy. "OK. I'll get you some painkillers. It's just codeine. It'll make you woozy but you'll feel a heck of a lot better. Once we've helped your Mom, you're back here with me."

He moved to the door. "Get your shirt on and I'll get the car. Take your time."

The Doctor was back a few minutes later, with his bag. Floyd was still seated and looked uncomfortable. "How are you, Floyd?" he asked.

"mmm...OK," came the muttered reply.

Masters folded his arms in impatience. "Yeah, sure you are... come on, let's get to your Mom."

The mention of his sick mother brought Floyd back to life. He was quickly on his feet and making for the door. Masters called to his wife, "Joyce! I'm going with the Jensen boy to see his mother. Not sure what's wrong?"

His wife came back into the hallway and kissed him on the cheek. "OK honey. But you be careful?"

"Always, Joyce. But I doubt Floyd is any threat to me," he smiled.

Joyce looked seriously at him. "It isn't Floyd or any of the ordinary folk I meant. You know who I worry about here. And not just you or me. Our daughters too."

"I know. It was a mistake coming here. I thought a place with no resident GP would be an opportunity. I'm looking for another practice. Anywhere far away from this place. I can't just leave overnight. You know that?" Masters hugged and kissed his wife back.

"Come on Floyd…"

As they travelled in the car, the Doctor questioned Floyd about his Mom. "So tell me what's wrong?"

"She was in the bed. She'd been sick and… and she messed herself. All confused. Kept repeatin' herself."

"OK, that sounds consistent with her condition. She hasn't seen me for a few months. I did write to her…"

"What condition?" asked Floyd, alarmed by Masters' comments. "What's wrong with her?"

"She didn't tell you, Floyd?"

"No. What didn't she tell me?"

The Doctor paused. "She has bowel cancer, Floyd. Untreatable. I thought she'd have told you?"

"She told me nothin'. Why didn't she tell me?"

"I don't know Floyd. Maybe she didn't want to worry you. Did you notice anything about her? Any difference in behaviour or appearance?"

"No? She was always the same. Maybe a little tireder lookin'? But she was always tired…"

They arrived at Floyd's house and quickly went through the front door and up the stairs. Floyd went first into the room. He called out, "Mom? Doctor Masters is here." But there was no reply.

Floyd's Mom did not responded to his gentle shake of her shoulder, either.

Doctor Masters intervened. "Floyd, let me take a look at your Mom?" and he moved around the bed to take a closer look. There was a pool of fresh vomit near her mouth. Immediately, Masters knew she was dead. "Choked on her own vomit?" he thought.

He checked for a pulse but there was none. She was cool to the touch. "Dead about an hour ago?" the Doctor thought.

"I'm sorry, Floyd, but your Mom has passed away."

"Passed away?' What do you mean?" said Floyd, standing by the bed, too battered and sore and upset to see what was lying there before him.

"She's dead. Floyd. I'm sorry, son."

Floyd hesitated. He couldn't take the Doctor's words in.

"Dead? But she can't be? She was ill but… she can't be…" Floyd slumped into the nearest chair.

"I'm sorry Floyd. She'd been ill for a long time. Like I said, she had cancer."

"She never said. And I didn't notice."

The Doctor went on, gently as he could. "There was nothing anyone could do about it. I kept her as comfortable as possible wIth palnkIllers but it was only a matter of time."

"She never said…" repeated Floyd dully. "She never told me she was ill…"

"She was a good woman, Floyd. She didn't want you to worry about her."

"But she shoulda said… why didn't she? I could have taken care of her?"

The Doctor replied, more firmly: "Floyd, there was nothing you could have done for your Mom. She didn't want you worrying about her. Look… I have to notify the police."

"The cops? No way, they answer to Sanchez, I don't want that son-of-a-bitch involved!"

"Floyd, it's the law. My hands are tied. The nearest clinic is in Farnsfield. The Sherriff is the first one I have to talk to in Medusa. There's no-one else who can help. We need to get your Mom looked after. Then we need get you to Farnsfield."

"No! I won't let them touch her." Floyd hauled himself out of the chair, grunting in pain. "She's my Mom. They'll treat her like dirt. Like they always did…"

"Now, son. I know you're upset. Look, you stay here with your Mom and I'll contact the police. Just try to relax. No-one is going to hurt her or you."

But Floyd was in too much of a rage to listen. "Just look at me! They beat me to shit and because of them, Mom is dead! I'll kill every last one of those bastards if I have to!"

Doctor Masters knew he was out of his depth. The boy was furious and would not listen to reason. To anyone. But it sounded like he had good reasons to be angry. Even though he had only been in Medusa for six months, Masters had seen how poorly some members of the community were treated, especially if they crossed Mayor Sanchez. And the Jensen's seemed to be treated worst of all. Tolerated barely. The things they said about Marlene Jensen. He'd never been able to find out what that was all about. The boy was supposedly illegitimate, but so what?

"Floyd, just wait here with your Mom. I won't let anyone hurt her or you, OK?"

Floyd still looked angry, but agreed. "OK, Doctor Masters." He sat back on the bed next to his Mom with his head in his hands.

Masters descended the stairs and out the front door and made a call with his cell phone. "Hi it's Greg Masters here. Yeah, that's right. I'm at the Jensen place. Yeah, that kid. No, not him, but someone's worked him over real good. No, he'll have to. Look I can't just ignore... but they beat him badly. No, I don't want trouble... How dare you talk to me like that...?"

Masters' face went red. "Look I don't want trouble. I just want to report the boy has been assaulted. What do you mean? Look I don't care about that. His Mom is dead. Yes...

His voice became more formal. "I have to report the death of Marlene Jensen. Yes... No! I didn't imply the boy was involved. She died of natural causes due to bowel cancer. She will need an ambulance from Farnsfield. No, there are no bruises. I can tell when it's an assault. It isn't. What do you mean? I won't do that. The boy was with me. I can't do that..."

Masters ended the call. He couldn't do that to Floyd. But his wife and daughter... he wanted to help. But what could he do? He turned and walked back into the house and up the stairs.

"Floyd? Floyd? I need to talk to you now."

Floyd, sat on the bed still, cradling the body of his mother. "Go away, leave us alone..."

"Floyd, for God's sake, listen! The police are coming soon. They are implying that you attacked your Mom. We both know that isn't true, but..."

Floyd angrily interrupted, "They said what? I would never hurt my Mom."

"Floyd. You were right. The police do have something against you. They are pushing me to say you hit your Mom. I've refused to say it, but they threatened me too. I have a wife and two daughters... you were right son. I can't help you, but you have to get out of here. Right now."

"You can't be serious?"

"I'm deadly serious, Floyd. You need to get away, right now."

"But where? How...?" Floyd had no idea what to do.

"Have you got money?" said Masters.

"No, nothin'. Not a cent to my name."

"Did your Mom have any money?"

"No... Wait... Yeah, she did. She said. Mom said she had money in the dresser?"

"Well get it now. I'll help you with any money I can. Get moving, Floyd."

Floyd moved to the dresser, unsteady on his feet and dropped to his knees with a hiss of pain. "The bottom drawer" Mom had said. But when he opened the drawer there was nothing. He pulled the drawer completely out. Taped to the underside of the drawer was a padded envelope.

Floyd got up off the floor and sat on the bed. Opening the envelope, he cursed with surprise. In it was hundreds of dollars. More money than he'd ever seen in his life.

Masters came back to the bedroom. "Find it?"

"Yeah. All this money. What was she doing with all this money?"

"Floyd, it's just money. You need to get out of here. Here, this is my wallet. Take it. My credit card is in there. The pin number is..."

"I can't take your wallet, Doctor Masters? I ain't no thief?"

"Floyd. I think the police are going to set you up for the ssault and murder of your Mom. This is nothing. Take the wallet and remember the pin number. You can get cash, at least for the next few hours. OK?"

Floyd took the wallet. A thief? A murderer? Of his own Mom? "This is like a nightmare!" he said.

"The pin number is 7884. Can you remember that? Say it back to me."

"7884... are you sure about this, Doctor Masters?"

"As sure as I'll ever be. Now get going Floyd. God bless you kid. Don't think too badly of me in the days and weeks to come. I need to protect my wife and kids."

"I won't, Doc. You have to protect your own."

"Now kid. Time to threaten me. Get a kitchen knife from downstairs"

"Say what?" replied Floyd incredulously.

"You're robbing me, Floyd. With violence. It protects me, son, if they think you forced me to give you my wallet."

"I can't believe this?"

"Neither can I, son. Now do it."

Floyd quickly came back with the biggest and sharpest knife he could find and squared up to Masters, but he couldn't do it as if he meant it.

Masters saw the boy struggle. "Too nice and too decent," he thought. "Nothing like the way the people in this godforsaken town speak about him." Then the idea came to Masters.

He used all the things he'd heard about the boy to make Floyd angry.

"Floyd, can't you do it? I thought you had more about you. 'Doesn't listen, doesn't do, doesn't have a clue?' Marlene's stupid bastard?"

Floyd was too upset to know he was deliberately being goaded. His temper was heightened by the last few days and with hearing those old taunts, it erupted white hot. Before he knew it, he'd dropped the knife and punched Doctor Masters square in the jaw. Masters went down like the proverbial sack of potatoes.

He stood over the GP, face full of his fury, his fists ready to strike again.

Masters gasped on the floor, rubbing his face. "Floyd, don't get angry at me again. I think you almost broke my jaw. Boy, that hurts! Now go, Floyd. Run! Don't let them catch you or we're both for it."

111

The Doctor reached up to hand Floyd his wallet. Floyd briefly paused to look at his Mom and then rushed out of the bedroom without a further word. He was gone, into the night and into an uncertain future.

Chapter 7 - On the Run

"Where the hell am I going to go?" muttered Floyd as he limped down the road. "I can't be seen by anyone. Who will give me a ride looking like this?"

He climbed over the neighbour's boundary fence, groaning with the pain. If he doubled back to the other end of town, he could head for Farnsfiled where there was an ATM. Get the money using the Doctor's card. Then where? He knew no-one outside of Medusa. Or did he?

Sean? "Nah, too prissy. He'd have a fit seeing me like this. And anyhow I still think he might be too sweet on my ass. Janie? She'd freak. But Alvin might help or know people who could help. Who the hell else have I got?"

He had decided. Make for the south, stop at the K-Mart near Farnsfield to the east and get a new set of clothes. Wade through the river just in case. Maybe a towel?

Over the fields he went, stumbling into ditches in the dark. He heard the sound of sirens in the distance. He couldn't stop to rest. A few hours later he saw the K-Mart in the distance.

He spotted the ATM near the store entrance. "What was the Pin code?" After three tries, he was able to withdraw $2000 in cash which he shoved in his pack. Then into the store with his baseball cap covering his face and the noticeable bruises. He quickly went to the men's section. A new pair of jeans, heavy shirt. A tshirt. Underwear and thick socks. It was gonna be cold out of town this time of year. Big coat. Don't forget a hat? Thermal longjohns?

He took his purchases to the self-checkout section. Packed his bags and headed of the door. Nearly there...

"Excuse me sir?" asked one of the security guards at the store exit. Floyd panicked and ran. Out the door and across the parking lot.

The guard quickly spoke into his walkie-talkie. "Got a young guy run out of here when I tried to speak to him. No, paid for everything. Alarm never went off. Check the CCTV? OK, let me know?"

Ten minutes later his walkie-talkie squawked. "Yeah? Nothing? Bought everything? No theft? Why did he run for it? This job, more frigging nuts than in pistachio ice cream... OK, thanks Ron. No, all quiet apart from that."

Floyd was off down the road heading for the river. He hissed as he waded in up to his waist in the freezing water, bags held up to stop them getting wet. Ten minutes later, cold and exhausted, he got to the other side.

He dropped to the floor. It would so easy to sleep, but he couldn't give them satisfaction. Floyd stripped out of his clothes. He had forgotten to buy a towel. "Idiot!" he grumbled to himself.

He was quick because of the cold, using his old sweatshirt and tshirt to dry himself off. Then into the new clothes. He deliberately went downstream for a mile and dumped his old stuff in the rapidly moving water.

Floyd walked upstream, cutting away from the river and to the south of Medusa. He could travel south for about five miles, then make for the west towards Woosterville. Although worn out, his stubborn anger kept him walking throughout the night until he saw the beginning of the dawn.

"Where am I going to lay up?" he asked himself. The road and fields were empty. He was tired beyond belief and in pain from his beating. He really needed some time to rest. He remembered the codeine that the Doctor had given him. He spotted a bunch of bushes in the distance, well away from the road.

Ten minutes later, he was fast asleep in the bushes, wrapped in his new coat, hood up and pain-free.

Back in Medusa, Greg Masters was being questioned.

"So the boy called at your door looking like he'd been fighting with someone?"

"No! I said, someone beat him badly and he said his Mom was ill..."

The sheriff interrupted. "Now, Dr Masters, we know this boy. A no good little shit. We know that he hurt his Mom."

"I never said that."

"But of course you did, Dr Masters. In this statement here." The sheriff pulled a document out of his desk drawer. "The boy came to see you. He admitted he'd been fighting. He went home and argued with his Mom and then struck her. She fell and hit her head. That's what happened, Dr Masters, didn't it?"

"There's no way I'll fake..." but the Sheriff interrupted him.

"Then he came to you, asked you for help and you drove him to the house. You found the body of his Mom and you asked Floyd if he had hit her. He then flew into a rage and attacked you. Didn't he, Greg?"

"But that's not how it happened."

"Greg. You found a disturbed teen, likely high on drugs, who killed his mother and then attacked you. He stole your wallet and that was the last you saw of him. You feel lucky he didn't use the knife we found, don't you? You can testify to his agitation and his dilated pupils which made you suspect intoxication or drug use? Yes?"

"Floyd was not on drugs."

116

"Greg. You have a decent reputation in this town. People trust you. You don't want that trust broken. Your career would be at an end. And think of your beautiful wife and lovely daughters. What could happened to them?"

"You fucking son of a bitch…"

"Now, Doctor! Sign the statement. Go home. Comfort your family these upsetting times. Have a think about who your friends are in Medusa. And who could be an enemy and try to hurt you or your family. Then get your story straight. Understand?"

Greg was silent for a moment. "Give me a pen," he said tonelessly. And he signed the statement.

"Thank you Dr Masters. Always a pleasure to have the support a pillar of the community like yourself. Let him out, boys. See you around, Doc?"

Masters stood and as he went to leave, the Sheriff grinned again. "And don't leave town, Doc. We value your services far too much. Understand?" The smile faded.

"Yes, I perfectly understand," mumbled Masters as he was led out the door.

The Sheriff reached for the phone. "Hi Ted. All done. That poor Marlene, murdered by that little shit. Yeah… yeah… we're on the lookout. Resisting arrest? I know... yeah sometimes we have to be rough. Take care yourself, Ted."

The Sheriff put the phone down and chuckled to himself. "Now to find you and bring you to justice, Medusa-style, Floyd Jensen."

Chapter 8 – On the Run Part 2

Floyd woke to the sound of birds singing. He was disoriented and confused. "Where the hell am I?" he thought. "Middle of a friggin' bush?"

The first attempt at moving made him cry out. Everything hurt. He was in agony from head to toe. Any movement made things worse. "Th… those painkillers? Where are they?" but he couldn't remember.

It took him a while, with every movement making him curse with the pain. Of course, the codeine was in the last pocket he searched. He quickly took two guzzled down with some water. As the discomfort slowly receded he began to think of the events of the previous two days.

He scrambled from out of the bushes and looked around. He reckoned he was about eight miles from Medusa and a few miles from the main highway. He'd have to stay away the main roads. Best to stay put until dusk and then he could walk through the night. The dirt track that way? He went over and over his route until he fell back into an exhausted sleep helped by the painkillers.

Six hours later, it was nearly dark and getting cold again. The pills had worn off, but the pain had lessened. He still grunted with discomfort as he got to his feet. Floyd stumbled off in the direction of the dirt track making west to Woosterville. "Only twenty miles away?" he grunted sourly to himself.

The journey was a nightmare. He fell several times in the night when he lost the trail. Floyd panicked at times and became convinced he would fall down a hole and die. After a few hours the moon rising in the night sky gave him some light and his walking became more productive. The ground glittered with frost and that helped him to make out the surrounding countryside.

Once he heard a car in the distance and froze. He didn't want anyone to see or find him. The solitary sound of its engine faded away and he began to walk again. "Gotta do about fifteen miles..." he thought to himself. "And I need hot food... cold food, any food..."

By early morning he had walked another ten miles. He had no idea where he was. "Have to get somewhere to sleep... must be a barn or old place I can get a break in?"

But there was nothing, as far as the eye could see. He had to keep walking.

By late morning he saw the small house with scattered farm buildings in the distance and he slowed to check it out.

"No smoke..."

There were many abandoned farms in the area. Floyd just hoped this was one too.

He was cautious about being seen and took his time. There was no sign of movement and he grew more confident. Floyd used the outbuildings to hide his approach. The place looked neglected. "Must be abandoned?" he thought.

The farmhouse had seen better days. Paint peeled everywhere and a few windows were cracked or broken. "Can't be anyone livin' here now?" Floyd said to himself.

The front door was locked, but the door frame was rotten. After tugging at the door handle a few times, the door opened. The room was cold and damp. The place really was empty. He knew that he couldn't light a fire as it might be noticed. The place was way off the beaten track but still...

Floyd realised there was no chance for food, but still he looked over the house. He walked into the kitchen and through the cupboards, but there was nothing. He spotted a can of insect repellent, picked up the can, shook it and pressed the nozzle. It was stiff but after working it a few times, the spray came out. Its contents make him cough. "That's bitchin' strong stuff. Maybe good for repelling more than a few bugs..."

So he put it in his pack.

He also found an old road atlas for the Medusa area and a mark about twenty miles west of the town. "Ten miles to go...?"

He ached with hunger.

Floyd found a corner of the living room and curled into a ball. He was quickly asleep again.

He awoke as it was getting dark. He consulted the road atlas again. "Five miles to Masefield. Must be stores there? I'll have to get there by dawn and hide out until dark."

He loaded everything back into his backpack. Sole contents: water, bug spray and road atlas. His entire possessions apart from the clothes on his back. Floyd tried not to the think of the money. Mom and Masters' money.

There was nothing else. He checked the room to see if anyone could tell he'd been there. "Some scuff marks, but nothin' too bad. Have to take my chances." Battered and bruised and starving Floyd might be, but he was determined to get away from Medusa and the cops.

The dirt trail seemed to carry on forever. The moon was high again and its light gave him just enough of an idea where he was and where he wanted to go. It was trudge, trudge, trudge for the rest of the night, mixed in with stumbles and another fall which knocked the breath out of him.

Every time he faltered, he set up a litany of cursing "Screw you, Sanchez, you prick... Screw Medusa... Screw those jerk-off cops...! Screw everyone in that fuckin' shithole!" And off he went again, stumbling and raging into the night.

He was a mile from Masefield when the dirt track turned into a proper metalled road. There were houses in the distance, lit up in the night. Floyd welcomed the light after so much fumbling about in the near-darkness. But he knew he would have to watch out for people.

Floyd heard a dog began to bark in the distance. Then another.

"Shit, I wish they'd shut their Goddamn yap."

There was no point in continuing on the road. It was too well lit with people and cars about even before the dawn and the dogs would continue to bark as he got nearer. He didn't want locals with guns thinking he was a burglar. He'd have to make a detour out into the countryside again. It was back to falling and stumbling in the darkness.

The street lights had affected his night vision and he had a difficult time going back into the pitch blackness of the surrounding scrubland. After a while, Floyd began to see more clearly and he made quicker progress. He was at the outskirts of Masefield by dawn. It was there that he made his first mistake, driven by hunger.

The craving for food consumed him. It felt like his stomach was eating itself. The discomfort was nearly as bad as the bruises ⋅ and pain. He just had to eat…

"I can't wait until night…" whimpered Floyd. "I need food and I need it now…" So instead of trying to hide, he headed for the centre of the town.

There was a general store, lights on and a young guy moving about, opening up. The smell of fresh bread was maddening, so Floyd went straight in.

He quickly found the bakery, grabbed a sandwich, some chips and a bottle of water. There was coffee brewing so he helped himself to a paper cup and lid. He walked up to the counter with his purchases.

The young guy spotted him. "Hi, good morning how can I help you?" he said cheerfully, but he faltered when he saw Floyd's face with the bruising and black eyes. "Dude, are you OK?"

Floyd tried to smile. "Yeah, thanks. I just need these," and he placed the food on the counter with a twenty dollar note.

"Yeah, sure. Do you need a bag?" The guy tried to smile, but it didn't quite reach his eyes.

"I'm OK, dude." motioned Floyd to his backpack, quickly putting the groceries in.

"There's your change. Have a nice day." Floyd noticed the fake smile again.

"Thanks and you," muttered Floyd as he left the store. An instinct made him look back and he saw the young guy pick up the phone and start dialling. "Time to get out of here…"

As soon as he was out of sight, he began to run, cutting down side streets. Floyd found a small park with a bench. He stopped and opened his bag, stuffing himself with the food until he began to feel full. After the sandwich and coffee, he almost felt human.

"Where to next?" he thought. "If that guy in the store spoke to the cops, I'm screwed."

He grabbed the road atlas out of his bag. "There... here's the park... freeway a mile thataway... maybe I could hitch a lift?" He quickly packed his bag and started towards the road and out of Masefield, keeping a watchful eye out for police cars. For anyone.

It was nearly light when he got to the freeway. The occasional truck went by. Floyd stuck his thumb out to try and hitch a ride. This was Floyd's second mistake.

Twenty cars later, Floyd had no ride. He began to walk again down the highway. It was risky, especially if the local cops had put an alert out for him, but Floyd wasn't he'd survive another five mile walk. He was exhausted and at the end of his tether.

A few cars stopped, but when they saw his face and the bruises they accelerated off. Floyd was beginning to think he would never get picked up. One guy stopped and offered to 'take a young guy like you anywhere you want to go...' Floyd declined. He didn't want a ride that bad.

Back in Medusa, the Sheriff in Medusa had received a phone call from on old pal. "Thanks, Tex. If I can ever return the favour? You know I will..."

He shouted through his office door. "Guys? Guys? We have a lead. A suspicious teen, looked like he'd been fighting. Outskirts of Masefield. Yeah, from Tex."

One of his deputies came in. "So we doin' this 'official' or as a favour...?"

The sheriff grinned. "A favour, this time. We don't want anyone getting in the way of justice for that little prick, do we, Larry?"

"We sure don't, Boss. Is this a 'resisting arrest'?"

The Sherriff smiled. "Sure is."

Larry smiled back. "Good, we can have some fun... I'll get the guys together."

"About thirty minutes? Remember, plain clothes?"

"Sure, Boss. We'll get back into uniform when we've grabbed him."

Thirty minutes later, the Sheriff and his deputies were off, eager for the chase.

Chapter 9 – So Near and Yet...

Floyd found it easier to walk than hitch. The food had boosted his energy levels. He was focused on getting to Woosterville and just disappearing. He was too tired and still struggling with the after-effects of his beating to think about getting off the highway. It was his third and final mistake.

He spotted the signpost. "Woosterville... one mile." Floyd let his hopes get up. He'd stopped hiding from the passing traffic. "Nearly there... what I wouldn't give for a good meal and a good sleep..."

Floyd walked slowly, limping along the side of the road, counting his steps. His enthusiasm rising as he passed the city limits sign:

Welcome to Woosterville

Dare to Dream

Floyd didn't notice the car speeding up behind him.

Floyd halted. "Which way to go?" he mused. The roar of the car engine made him turn and he saw the Medusa plates. Before he could think, he was running. Down the side road and over the nearest fence. He vaulted each fence he saw and was soon running across lawns and around swimming pools to get away from whoever was in that car.

The Sheriff was furious. "I told you to take it nice and easy! You have to go screeching up to the boy. We coulda had him in the street. Now where do we find him?"

"But Boss…"

"Don't. Just don't," growled the Sheriff. He pointed at two of his men. "You, Larry! You, JJ! Get going after him on foot. Brandon, drive down this road and make the next left. We can cut him off there."

The deputies looked at the Sheriff dully. "Well move, you idiots. I want that kid here now."

The two deputies jumped out and began running down the side road after Floyd and the car roared off. "Ted will kill me if we don't catch the little bastard," thought the Sheriff.

Floyd was out of energy. He'd climbed over three sets of fences and dragged himself over two more. He couldn't run any more. He tried to find somewhere to hide but there was no shelter he could immediately find. Floyd didn't see the old couple looking through their kitchen window. Seeing the wild looking boy in their garden, they immediately phoned the local cops.

"There's a boy in our garden. It looks like he's been beaten up. No, he's not caused any damage… he looks like he's trying to hide. Hey! There's two men here now. They've spotted him. They've got guns. Yes, OK. I know. Our bedroom has a lock. I have a gun too, but you better get here soon…"

Larry and JJ wearily climbed another fence. They were tired and angry. The Jensen boy would get it worse for this. The Sheriff would be furious if they didn't get him soon. And God knows what Sanchez would do to them all.

"Larry," called JJ. "I see him over there!"

They ran over to where Floyd was trying to hide, behind a log pile. "Come out, you little fucker. Come out now and we'll make it easier on you."

Floyd refused to move. He recognised the deputies and he knew that if he went with them, he was as good as dead. As the two men approached, he prepared to fight back. He grabbed the bug spray out his backpack.

It was a one-way battle, but Floyd got his licks in. Kicking, punching, scratching, biting and flailing, he poured all his remaining energies into resistance. He managed to get the bug spray in JJ's eyes and a punch to Larry's crotch which made them back off for a second.

All the hate of Medusa and its cops Floyd could muster kept him going, at least for a few minutes.

"You little bastard," gasped Larry, nearly doubled up in pain. "I'll kill you, you little shit!"

JJ paused, wiping his eyes with a handkerchief, cursing Floyd and threatening the boy with all the things he was going to do to him. It took a minute for Larry and JJ to recover and move again against Floyd. This time they punched and kicked the boy, rather than restrain him. Floyd was too drained too resist and his weak movement were not enough to stop their attack. He could only try to shield himself from their blows.

It took a few minutes, but Larry and JJ gradually battered Floyd into submission. Larry grabbed him by his legs and dragged him out into the garden.

"Let's get movin', JJ," panted Larry. "Get him back to the car. Then we'll have some fun back at the jail."

JJ chuckled. "We'll make this one squeal, Larry. Take turns... let's go down the side of the house."

They roughly picked up Floyd by his arms and legs, half carrying and half hauling him onto the side-road and down to the main road where they hoped the Sheriff would be waiting. They had got to the main road, when they heard the police siren.

"Shit. It's the local cops. You got your badge, Larry?"

"No! You better not have yours. We can't get caught by the local law."

The Woosterville patrol car saw the two men with Floyd and were quickly in pursuit as they ran away, leaving the boy in a heap on the sidewalk. Larry and JJ spotted the Sheriff's car, but it was quickly speeding away. They had no way of escaping the local cops.

Two Woosterville uniformed cops got out of the squad car, with their guns pointing at Larry and JJ.

"On the floor! Hands on heads. Move!" one commanded. The Medusa cops quickly complied.

Larry and JJ were quickly handcuffed and their pockets searched.

"Well, what have we got here?" said one of the local cops. "A police badge from Medusa. Where did you get that from?" He turned to his colleague. "Jeff, check on the person they were carrying."

"JJ, you fool. We're as good as dead," cursed Larry.

The local cop gave a bitter grin. "Well 'JJ', well 'John Doe', we'd appreciate it if one of Medusa's finest and their friend came with us to the station to explain what they are doing in our city."

Larry pleaded. "Come on man, we only wanted to arrest the kid. He killed his own mother. It's a clear case of homicide. Just let us go with the boy and we'll be no trouble to you."

The local cop grunted. "If you are Medusa cops, you'll get nothing from me. I know what the law means in that backwater shithole."

The cop turned and shouted down the road. "Jeff, what are we dealing with?"

"It's bad, Mason. A kid, in his teens, these guys have beaten him up real good."

Mason shouted back, "Ambulance first. I'll let the precinct know we have special guests from Medusa. One's a cop."

"Medusa? One of those guys here? Let me get my licks in now?"

Mason laughed. "Maybe..." He turned to the two handcuffed men. "See how we feel about your brand of justice in Woosterville? It might pay you to cooperate?"

Larry and JJ lay there, silent and sullen.

"Have it your own way, guys," responded Mason cheerfully. "Car 245, we have an assault out on Route 34. Male, teen, about sixteen or seventeen? Perpetrators with me. In cuffs. One of them's the law in Medusa."

And then he laughed. "You know I can't comment on that. I sure would like to, though?"

132

"Officer Dobbs is seeing to the kid, but he needs an ambulance. Medusa law isn't saying much. Oh yeah, another car, heading east, no time to get plates. Blue sedan. More Medusa cops? Maybe. Yeah, too quick. OK, on our way in with our 'special guests'.

Mason laughed again and turned to the Medusa cops. "Course if we do find that you've beaten up an innocent kid, we'll have strong words, won't we?"

"He's a murderer," replied Larry. "We was just apprehending him. Honest, guys."

"Murderer or not, you aren't beating any kid up here in Woosterville. We'll have words with you about staying in your jurisdiction too..." Mason grinned. "I'm looking forward to that."

"Right, on your feet..."

Mason pushed the pair into the police cruiser. "Get ready to answer questions when I get back guys?"

Mason walked over to Jeff with the boy. "Christ, he's been worked over good, Jeff."

"Yeah, fresh beating. But look at him. He's been beaten more than once before. Breathing and steady heartbeat, but not recovered consciousness. I'll feel better when this kid's in hospital."

133

"Has he got any ID?"

"No, but he's got a letter. A reference. You might find the name on it interesting..."

Mason took the letter. He went pale. "This is way above our pay grade, Jeff."

"I know. What're we going to do, Mason?"

"How do I know? Let me think..."

Floyd groaned, distracting their attention for a moment.

"Kid? Kid? How are you doing?"

Floyd moaned again and fell back into unconsciousness.

"At least he's with us. Look Jeff. You never saw this letter, OK? Neither did I. I'm gonna use my own cell phone to call the number, but you keep out of this."

"Whatever you say, Mason. I don't want no trouble..."

"Give me a few minutes to phone. You never saw or heard anything. Right?

"Yeah. Sure. Do whatever you've got to do, Mason."

Mason walked away, dialling the number off the letter on his cell phone. "Hi, may I speak to Alvin McCall? I'm a police Officer. Mason Lewalski. I've got a kid assaulted out on Route 30. Names 'Floyd', I'm guessing from the reference letter from you. No sir, but I've got two suspects. One seems to have a badge from Medusa. No, sir."

Mason listened intently and then responded. "Ambulance should be here shortly. The two guys? Yes, sir. I understand. I'll let you know where the boy ends up. No, sir. Thank you."

Mason put his phone in his pocket and walked back to Jeff. "Whoever did this is in serious shit, Jeff. We don't ever tell anyone anything about this."

"You know it," Jeff nervously replied.

Five minutes later they heard the wail of sirens. The medical staff were efficient and soon had the boy in the ambulance and off to the hospital.

Mason walked away from the police car and made another call.

"Mr McCall? Yeah, Mason Lewalski. He's going to Woosterville Mercy. Yeah, I gave them Floyd's details. No sir, you're welcome. No, we know. I have no idea what this is about. No, it will stay off the record. No, we know when to mind our own business. Yes, sir. Goodbye."

135

Mason walked back to the patrol car. "Let's get back to work, Jeff."

Chapter 10 – Medical Marvels

Floyd gradually awoke. Groggy, confused and bewildered. His head and body dully ached. He groaned, groggy with sleep and medication.

"Hi kid, how are you doing?"

Floyd thought for a minute. "Alllvinnn…?"

"That's right, Floyd. I heard you were here and that some guys had done a number on you. This is becoming a bad habit, kid."

"I…don't… remember…"

"Give it some time, Floyd. I want to know all about it. And I'll make sure those people never hurt anyone again."

"Yeah… that would be good…" And with that, Floyd fell back asleep.

He was like that for several days. Waking, confused, but Alvin was usually there.

"You OK, Floyd?"

"Yeahhh… think so. Don't hurt so much." But he yelped as he tried to stretch. "Fuck, what happened to me?"

"You tell me, kid?"

"I dunno… I was gettin' away from Medusa… then the night out sleepin' in that bush. Then the farmhouse… I can't remember after that…"

"You were heading west to Woosterville, kid. Ring any bells?"

"Ummm… not sure. Remember leaving the farmhouse. Then walked. Oh, yeah those goddamn dogs in Masefield. Yapping and tapping. So I cut round… yeah, that's it. Then… dunno."

"You had a can of bug spray, the remains of a ham and cheese sandwich. Bottle of water in your bag too."

"I did? Oh. The store. I got the food and saw the guy who served me make a phone call. Got away from Masefield as soon as I could. That's the last I remember. I think?"

"It'll come back, kid. Now take it easy." Alvin could see just remembering the last two days was exhausting Floyd

"OK…." whispered Floyd.

That was the last peace Floyd got. The next day, Alvin was there again, but this time accompanied by a young cop.

"Mornin' kid. How you doing?"

Floyd scowled. "OK. Sore, but... I'm hungry."

Alvin laughed. "Great, back to normal? By the way, this is Officer Goldman. Eric Goldman. He's going to be around to make sure you're OK."

The older man could see the boy's resistance.

"I don't need no cop as a guard. Ain't I had enough of cops?"

Alvin sighed. "It's for your protection, kid."

"I don't want any cop protection' me neither. I hate those mother-fuckers. Get him outta here!"

Alvin grinned. "You act like you've got choice, kid. You're actually under arrest. The Officer is here to make sure you don't abscond and become a threat to the community."

"Threat to the community? Me? You gotta be jokin'?"

Alvin suddenly looked serious. "You've been accused of murdering your Mom, Floyd."

"What?" Floyd sat up in the bed. He immediately regretted the sudden movement as the room spun around him, but he gritted his teeth and continued.

"It's the Medusa cops, ain't it? Doctor Masters said they were gonna set me up. He knows Mom had cancer."

Alvin tried to soothe the boy. "Look, Floyd, I know you wouldn't hurt your Mom. Just lie back and relax."

"I don't wanna relax. I want you to know what happened..." Floyd suddenly became very pale.

"Shit, my head..."

Alvin moved over to the bed and pushed the boy back to a lying position. "I don't think you're ready for this yet, Floyd. Eric here will see to you. I'll be back tomorrow."

"Yeah... OK, Alvin. I... need some more sleep... but I don't want no cops here..."

Alvin ignored Floyd's protests and turned to the cop. "Let me know if anything comes up, Eric?"

"Will do, sir," came the reply as the young cop stood to attention.

"Hey," laughed the older man. "I'm just Alvin, y'know? Just a diner owner. No 'sir' for me. Understand?"

"Of course, sir. I mean, Alvin."

Alvin chuckled again. "See you in the morning..."

The next morning Floyd was feeling much better. The nurse arrived early and wanted to give him a bed bath. Floyd was mortified. She was close in age to him and very pretty. He could see Eric the cop checking her out too.

"D'you think I could do it myself, nurse?" he asked.

"Call me Debbie, Floyd. You really don't have anything to be embarrassed about. I do this all the time. "

"I bet you do..." Floyd thought to himself. "I'd sooner do it myself, if you don't mind."

"That's fine with me, Floyd. We just need to get you to the bathroom." And with a sudden movement the nurse pulled the sheets back covering him.

Floyd tried to grab the sheets back. Debbie smiled again. "I'm sure you've really got nothing to be ashamed of, Floyd."

Despite himself, the boy grinned in embarrassment.

"That's better Floyd. You have a nice smile you know? Now let's get you into the wheelchair."

Five minutes later, the boy was seated. There had been much grumbling and cursing from Floyd as Eric and Debbie got him out the bed. He resented his weakness and having to use the wheelchair. He sat there, hunched and surly. "Like an old guy... why does he have to be here?"

Eric looked pissed. "I'm here to make sure you remain safe, Jensen. Like it or not, here's where I am and here's where I'm staying. Sulk like a child if you feel the need."

Debbie pushed him down the hall into a shower room with Eric following. "Bath or shower, Floyd?"

"I'd give anything for a shower."

"Shower it is then..." and Debbie and Eric helped him out of the wheelchair.

"I'll wait outside," said the young cop, smiling at Debbie and she smiled back. Floyd felt a quick pang of jealousy. Why was that dipshit cop still here?

He stood there, a little unsteady and looked at Debbie. She stared back.

"Well...?" said Floyd.

"Well what, Floyd?"

"Well ain't you gonna leave?"

Debbie smiled again. "No, Floyd, you need to get a shower and I need to be here to give you a hand if you need it."

Floyd blushed again. "I'd sooner do it myself, Debbie."

"No can do, Floyd. Now get out of your gown and get showering…"

"You can't make me do that?" said Floyd.

"I can take them off you if you like?" smiled Debbie.

"You wouldn't?" said Floyd, completely aghast, but she quickly came up to him and began pulling at his gown.

"No! You don't have to… I'll do it. I'll do it…"

"Good. You need a good shower, Floyd and I need to make sure you're safe in there."

Floyd quickly stripped off his clothing and turn to hide himself.

"God, Floyd. Who did this to you?" asked Debbie, eyes wide at his injuries. He was covered nearly from head to foot in bruises and abrasions.

"A bunch of guys, a few times."

"No wonder you've got a police guard. OK, let's get you showered. Over there, Floyd."

Debbie pointed at a cubicle with a small shower curtain and Floyd stumbled into it. He started the shower and yelped as the water started. "Jesus, it's freezing!"

Debbie just giggled.

Floyd was mortified and stayed quiet, pleased the nurse could not see his embarrassment.

The water began to warm and soon Floyd was relaxing as he washed himself.

"How are you doing, Floyd?"

"Can't I have another minute?" he pleaded.

"Nope. I think you're clean enough by now, Floyd."

Floyd turned off the shower. He felt much better and less sore. He pulled back the shower curtain. "Have you got a towel?"

"Of course, Floyd. But you'll have to come out the cubicle first."

"No! Gimme the towel."

"Out first, then towel."

Floyd refused to move.

Debbie spoke again. "I can wait all day. You need to come out and get dried. Stand there getting cold if you like. You seem like a nice kid, but you've sure got a big chip on your shoulder. Both shoulders."

Floyd shook his head. He hated being at her mercy. Although she was attractive, he just didn't like how she looked at him. Like a piece of meat. He'd had no real experience dealing with the opposite sex and being checked out like this made him embarrassed and resentful.

"I'm still waiting," came her voice once more.

With a sigh, he pulled back the shower curtain and walked out of the cubicle.

Debbie stared at him. Floyd felt it was like being sized up for dinner. She was in charge and he hated it.

"Here's your towel, Floyd. You get dried off and I'll get you some clean clothes."

Debbie was soon back with a fresh pair of shorts and t-shirt. She made him get back into the wheelchair, despite his protests. They were met by Eric outside and he helped her get Floyd back into bed.

"I don't need no help from some dumbass cop!" he snapped, but they ignored his complaining.

"Thanks, Officer," replied Debbie, happily. The young cop smiled back.

"You're welcome, nurse. Call me Eric."

"Call me Debbie, Eric" she said, returning the smile.

Floyd watched them flirt and felt jealous again. He wanted her to smile and talk to him, not some jerk cop, even if he thought she was a weirdo.

"Can I get a drink?" Floyd asked.

Debbie turned back to him. "Of course you can. What would you like?"

"Can I get some juice?"

"OK. Anything for you, Eric?"

"No, I'll have something later. Thanks, Debbie."

After delivering the juice, Floyd and Eric were left alone in the room. Floyd was still feeling jealous and the cop had little to say. Floyd's stomach began to rumble. Loudly...

Eric grinned. "Hungry, Floyd?"

"Just a bit."

"Let me see if there's any food for you."

"Thanks, man."

Eric was back a few minutes later. "No food for you til after your examination."

Floyd groaned.

"Which is in about 30 minutes."

The time passed slowly. Hospital entertainment was awful. Just chat shows and soaps and advertising. Floyd had never been a big tv fan as he spent most of his days out and his Mom couldn't afford what passed for cable in Medusa.

Debbie came back with the wheelchair. "Off we go to your examination," she said cheerfully.

"When am I gonna get somethin' to eat? I'm gonna starve at this rate."

"After the examination, Floyd. I promise."

The examination room was two floors below Floyd's ward. An older man in a white gown greeted them. "Hello, you must be Floyd. I'm the consulting physician here, Dr Bennett. I'm appointed by the police department to examine you. If you can take off your t-shirt and shorts, we can begin. There's a gown over there."

There was a flicker of defiance, from Floyd. He was still feeling the effects of his beating, he felt intimidated and resentful all at the same time.

"Everything, Floyd. Shorts too."

Floyd stood there with just a hospital gown on in front of Dr Bennett and Eric, head bowed, but his hands clenched in fists.

"Right... Floyd, can you lie back on the examination table?"

"Whatever..." sighed Floyd.

He heard Bennett speak formally. "Beginning recording at... 11.30am. Subject is a male, seventeen years old. Looks a little malnourished. He has been subject to a beating..."

The Bennett's voice started to sound far away as Floyd began to fall asleep, despite the poking and prodding. The voice droned on untll...

Suddenly Floyd was suddenly awake and started up from the couch in pain.

"Whoa! Hang on Floyd. I was examining your torso. Sorry son, you have a few cracked ribs. Lie back down. I promise to be more careful."

Reluctantly Floyd lay back. His examination resumed.

"Significant bruising to the abdomen. Looks like someone kicked you in the nuts, Floyd. Any pain?"

"No... don't think so. Not compared to the rest of me anyhow."

The Doctor smiled. "Good. Any passing blood?"

The boy looked puzzled. "How do I pass blood?"

"As in peeing it, Floyd."

"Oh. Not so I noticed."

"OK. Just an examination to check..."

Floyd began to get off the couch again. "You want to feel me up? I ain't puttin' up..."

"Floyd, lie back. I have no interest in your genitalia apart from seeing if they were damaged in the attack on you. Lie back, son."

Floyd reluctantly lay back on the examination table again. It was the ultimate insult. Some old guy playing with him. "When will this end?" he thought.

"Now, how about your stools?"

"My what?" said Floyd. He had no idea what the physician was talking about.

"When you shit, Floyd. Does it look normal? Any blood?"

Floyd was embarrassed. "Not so I noticed. Been a bit busy to look at my own shit lately, y'know?"

The physician laughed. Even Eric smiled.

"Fair point. Your legs are OK but lots of bruising, especially around the knees. Care to explain?"

"It was all that falling over in the goddamn dark when I was on the run. If it weren't for the moon I'd 'a broke my neck for sure."

The physician smiled again. "OK, over on your front. Shoulders extensively bruised. Don't like this around your kidneys? Painful?" And he pressed the area.

"Jesus Christ! What are you doing?" yelled Floyd.

"Hmmm... Whoever did this used your kidneys like a soccer ball. Very badly bruised. I'm surprised you aren't passing some blood. Let me make some notes..."

Floyd tried to relax again, but it was impossible. He dreaded what the physician might do next.

"Last thing, Floyd. You're not going to like this much, but I have to do it."

"Do what?" Floyd's voice began to rise.

"If you can bring your knees up..."

"What for?"

"A rectal examination."

"A what???"

"It's routine. Floyd, can we get this over with?"

"Is this the very last thing?"

"Physically, yes."

"For fuck's sake," muttered Floyd, "what next?"

"We'll get to that. Now, knees up."

Floyd complied but yelped when he felt something cold on his back passage. "You ain't gonna start fiddlin' with my ass, now? Jesus Christ, how does anyone put up with this?"

Eric spoke up. "You get used to it, Floyd."

"It ain't the sort of thing that I'd like to get used to!" Floyd snapped back.

"No-one likes it Floyd, but it needs to be done." came the reply.

Floyd continued to grumble. "Finger up my ass. Fiddlin' with me. Pokin' and proddin' me. Be easier to die... yow! What the hell are you doin' now?"

"That all seems normal. Prostate OK. I think a check-up in a few days would be a good idea, though. I'm going to get a scan of your kidneys to make sure."

"Oh sure, that sounds great. More fingers up my ass. Won't that be great fun?"

"OK, Floyd. You can get up now. Get dressed. Once you've stopped complaining of course."

Floyd sullenly pulled his t-shirt and shorts on, glaring at Bennett. When would they give him a break?

Bennett looked at him and smiled to himself. Despite the beating and being clearly exhausted, the boy still had spirit in him. "A good sign," he thought. "He'll need it in the next few months..."

"Take a seat, Floyd" the physician motioned to a chair opposite his desk. Floyd sat with a grunt.

"Son, this is a brief psychological check about your mental and emotional state. How you feel about your situation, Floyd?"

"How d'you think I feel...?" Floyd snapped back

"I have no idea until you tell me."

"So what do you want to know?"

"Tell me what's happened to you and how you feel about it, Floyd."

"What's happened to me? I've seen my Mom die. I've had the shit kicked out of me by those dickheads in Medusa, on the run cuz of being framed by the cops, arrested here and being poked and prodded by you up the ass and God knows what. Is that enough?"

The physician scribbled on his pad. "Angry then?"

"Angry? You bet!"

"Anything else?"

"Like what?"

"Anything else but anger?"

"No... That's what's keepin' me goin'. It's what always keeps me goin'. And to get even with that fucker Sanchez and every one in Medusa."

Bennett looked dispassionately at Floyd for a moment. Then nodded his head.

"That's fine, Floyd."

"What's fine?"

"You being angry. It's a perfectly natural response to what's happened to you. I suspect you've subject to abuse for a long time?"

"Abuse? You don't know the half of it."

"What does that mean, Floyd?"

Floyd's anger deflated. "Ever since I can remember I've been 'Marlene's Bastard'. Treated like shit in school. Treated like shit in the street. And my Mom too..." At the thought of his mother, tears came to Floyd's eyes. "I... I never had anyone treat me like I was anything. Apart from Zeke and he's gone."

"Who is Zeke, Floyd?"

"He was my pal, from when we started. Me, 'the bastard' and him 'the nigger'. We were friends... until he disappeared last year."

"Where did he go, Floyd?"

155

"I think he's dead. He had an argument with Sanchez's goons and next thing he was gone. I asked around but no-one would say. They all looked frightened. Mom said Zeke was likely buried outside the town. Zeke's folks vanished too."

"Do you know what Zeke's parents were called?"

"No, they were private. Kept to themselves. They were treated bad too. The only black family in the town."

"What was Zeke's surname?"

"Zeke? Zeke…" Floyd thought for a moment. "To me he was just 'Zeke'. Zeke… Jefferson. Yeah… that was it."

"Thank you Floyd," said Dr Bennett, writing still. And then he paused. "How do you feel about what happened to Zeke?

"Me? I think how he must have felt. And wonder what happened to him. Really happened. I want those bastards to pay for what they did. Sanchez and the rest of them."

"Anything else?"

"I'm sad… I don't really know why… he deserved a lot more than he got. And I got. And Mom. We all deserved somethin' better. But everyone in Medusa made sure we got nothin'. I sometimes wonder maybe we don't deserve anythin'…? I don't know…"

Bennett paused. "Floyd... Floyd. Look at me." Floyd continued to stare at the floor. "Floyd. Please look at me..."

The boy reluctantly looked up. "Floyd, you need to understand that you and Zeke and your Mom were treated terribly by everyone in Medusa. From Theodore Sanchez downwards. None of you deserved what you got or deserved to be treated as you were. It wasn't normal. Do you understand me?"

Floyd returned to looking at the floor. "I... I guess so..."

"Floyd. Look at me." Floyd's head went up again and he stared at the physician. "Can you look me straight in the eye and tell me that any of you deserved to be treated the way you have been?"

Floyd looked away again. "I don't know. Hell, what do I know?"

"Then that's something you'll need to work on Floyd. You blame yourself because you've been made to feel like that. You never deserved that. Neither did your Mom or Zeke."

Floyd looked at Bennett again. "Shit! I don't know what to say... we were like punchbags for anyone who felt like it. Worse than dirt... the cattle and the dogs were better than we were. I can't say I liked that. We were made to feel that's all we were due."

And then he looked away again, visibly battling with his memories and his feelings.

After a few minutes, Bennett pressed Floyd again. "So... what do you think?"

Floyd hesitated again. "Well... I... we didn't want that. Who deserves that?" And then his anger returned. "Ah screw it! No-one deserves that. Not me. Not Zeke. Not Mom. Not anyone."

The physician smiled back. "Well done Floyd. And quite right too. No-one deserves to be abused like you were. Zeke because of the colour of his skin. Your Mom because she had a child without being married. Or you because you don't have a father."

"Thanks... I guess."

"Now... one more question."

"OK," said Floyd hesitantly

"How do you feel about your Mom?"

"I don't feel anything about my Mom."

"Not angry? Upset? Sad?" goaded the physician.

Floyd wavered. "Sad... I guess. I dunno...."

"That's OK, Floyd. Remember that you might feel angry, or sad or upset in the next few weeks. Or all of those feelings together. That too is perfectly normal."

"Maybe," replied Floyd.

"Anything else you want to say?"

"No. Yeah, maybe... I don't know how to say it. That nurse... Debbie. She's pretty... real pretty. But I don't like her."

Bennett looked interested. "Oh? In what way?"

"She looks at me like I'm a slab of meat. Keeps lookin' at me. It makes me uncomfortable. No privacy."

The Doctor turned to the cop. "Eric? Any comments?"

Eric shrugged. "Seems a little bit taken with Floyd here. Nothing sinister. I wouldn't mind if she looked at me to be honest, but that's another story. It might be those pretty eyes of yours?"

Floyd looked insulted. "I do not have pretty eyes!"

"They are unusual, Floyd. Striking. Lots of women will notice them."

"I ain't no friggin' pretty boy!"

159

Eric and Bennett laughed.

"No, that's for sure," said the cop. "You aren't 'pretty', not even by a stretch of the imagination. But girls, and some guys are going to love them eyes of yours."

"See how it goes, Floyd. If you are still unhappy with the nurse... 'Debbie'? Just tell Eric. OK?"

"OK, Doctor Bennett."

The physician smiled back. "You're free to go, Floyd. Remember you can see me any time you like."

"No offence but I'd sooner not..."

"I promise it won't need to be like this again, Floyd."

"Not sure I believe a word of that..."

"Oh! I need a DNA sample."

"What do you need my DNA for?"

"Standard procedure Floyd. Technically you're under arrest. That means I need to take a sample of your DNA."

The boy looked suspicious. "How do you do it?"

"A swab from your cheek is enough."

Floyd still looked untrusting as he opened his mouth. The swab was quickly done.

"Is that it?" he asked.

"Enough for our purposes, Floyd. Off you go with the Officer here."

"Come on Floyd," interrupted Eric. "I'm sure Doctor Bennett has some more people to torture. Isn't that right, Doc?"

Bennett grinned. "Go on, get out of here."

The boy was quickly to his feet and out the door to the hospital food hall.

Doctor Bennett finished writing and then made a call. "Alvin? All done with Floyd. Come and see me."

Floyd wolfed down another helping of lasagne, and grabbed another few fries which he stuffed in his mouth.

"You like the food here?" asked Eric, grinning.

"No. It tastes like shit..." mumbled Floyd around the next mouthful. "But I'm starving."

"Take it easy kid, don't make yourself sick. I'm not going to clean up after you if you puke, you know?" laughed the young cop.

"I promise... not... to..." Floyd stuttered. And then let out a huge belch. "That's better..."

"Had enough?"

"Not just yet." Floyd took a swig of his coke. "Maybe another plateful?"

Thirty minutes later, Floyd sat on his bed, groaning. "I think I overdid it..."

Eric laughed. "I did warn you, Floyd."

"I know, but I've lived on nothin' for days, I couldn't stop myself."

"Let nature take its course, kid. "

He got no reply. Floyd, despite his full belly, had fallen asleep.

The next few days were a bore as the boy healed. Breakfast followed by some light exercise. Then back to bed and napping. Then up at lunch and some more exercise. Floyd was starting to go out of his mind.

"If you don't let me out of here soon, I'm gonna find a way out," he snapped at the nurse. He was royally pissed and everyone who saw him got the full force of it, especially Debbie who wouldn't stop with fussing and flirting. It still made Floyd uncomfortable and she wouldn't stop.

The young nurse grinned, ignoring his temper. "I think it's time you went home, Floyd." But she paused as she saw the even darker look that passed over his face.

"Floyd, what did I say?"

"It's nothin'. I ain't really got a home now and I ain't got nowhere to go neither."

The nurse protested. "You must have somewhere, Floyd?"

Eric, the cop interrupted. "Debbie, Floyd can't discuss his situation with anyone. I hope you both understand that?"

"But where's he going to go?" asked the nurse.

"I don't know, but he's under protective custody. That's why I'm here."

"But what's he done?"

"Debbie. I can't say. Neither can Floyd, until his case is resolved. But now he's feeling better, it may be time for him to move on. Give me a few minutes to make a call."

The cop left the room and found a quiet place to make a call. "Hi, is that Alvin? Yeah, it's Eric. Our chick wants to fly the nest. Yep. Stubborn little son-of-a-bitch. Bad-tempered too. Yes, I think it's time he left hospital. OK, see you shortly."

Alvin turned up a few hours later. Floyd cautiously greeted him. "Hey, Alvin."

"Hi kid, how are you doing?"

"OK. But I want to get outta here now."

"I'll see what I can do. Doctor Bennet says you're OK, but you need a scan of your kidneys."

"Yeah, he said."

"He also said what a stubborn little bastard you are too, Floyd."

Floyd looked resentful but said nothing. Alvin smirked back. "If you check out you can be out of here tomorrow."

Floyd looked unsure. "Where am I going to go?"

"You'll stay with me and Janie, but first the local cops want to speak to you."

"Are they going to put me in jail?" Floyd looked alarmed.

"Doubt it kid. But you will be staying with me 'under police protection' while your case is assessed."

"Then they throw me in jail?"

Alvin laughed. "No-one is throwing you in jail, Floyd. Now, go and get your scan and we'll go and see the cops tomorrow."

"But what if..."

"No buts Floyd, see you tomorrow." Alvin nodded at Eric and left the room.

The scan went quickly and Doctor Bennett came to see Floyd later. "Your kidneys are bruised Floyd, but you should be OK. Just watch out for passing blood. You'll be released tomorrow."

"Thanks, Doctor Bennett. I'm sorry if I've been a pain in the ass."

"You're a surly young brute, Floyd, but it's not a problem. I see a lot of guys like you. Take care of yourself and best of luck."

Bennett shook his hand and left the room.

Debbie came to see him an hour later. She seemed distracted. "I hear you'll be released tomorrow. Floyd. It's the end of my shift now, so I won't see you again..." She looked unhappy.

Floyd feigned disinterest. "Yeah..." he drawled.

Debbie bustled around the room, ignoring Eric's obvious interest and closed the curtains around Floyd's bed. She sat next to him.

"Here's my phone number. I expect to hear from you."

"Hey I don't think... said Floyd but he was interrupted by Debbie's attempted kiss.

Floyd was taken aback but was soon yelling. "Get off 'a me!"

The curtains were suddenly pulled back and there stood Eric, looking very annoyed.

"Just coming out, Eric!" said Debbie, with a smirk as stood up and left the room.

There was silence in the room and Floyd had just began to calm down when Eric spoke again.

"Did she try it on with you, Floyd?"

"Yeah. I didn't ask for this, Eric."

"I know. Do you want me to report this?"

"I... I don't know. Will she get into trouble?"

"I'd think so. What did she do?"

"Tried to kiss me. Gave me her phone number."

Floyd looked at the piece of paper and tore it up. "I told you she was a screwball, but you wouldn't believe me."

"I'll report it to Doctor Bennett. Just forget about it kid. You'll be out of here tomorrow. I'll make sure she doesn't come back."

Floyd suddenly felt alone. Uninvited attention from a nurse who turned out to be a nutjob was a fruitcake and an uncertain future ahead. It wasn't that he didn't trust Alvin, but he wondered who the so-called diner owner really was, with the local cops jumping to attention whenever he made an appearance.

Maybe he'd learn more tomorrow?

Chapter 11 – Alvin Unleashed

The morning came too soon. Floyd had a poor night with little sleep. He worried about what was going to happen to him, convinced he was going to jail and going over and over Debbie's unwanted attentions in his mind. He realised she was attractive but there something about her, now proven, that gave him the creeps.

A new nurse came to see him at 7.30am. "Time to get up, sir," she said. The formality was welcome after the over-familiarity of Debbie. He was soon on his way to the bathroom for a shower. Floyd noticed the whiskers on his chin. The lines of tiredness made him look gaunt and strangely older. It was a harder-faced Floyd than from a few days before. Floyd approved. "Got so far, just keep goin'..." he muttered to himself.

Breakfast came and Floyd hoovered up the food like the proverbial condemned man. Eric watched amused as the 'Black Hole' absorbed another meal. "Such a skinny kid, yet you eat for three..."

The nurse came back an hour later. "We need to discharge you and you'll leave with the Officer here." Floyd nodded his agreement and after signing a few incomprehensible forms, he was out the door, into Eric's car and on the way to the local precinct. The boy began to become anxious again.

Eric drove into the parking lot, found a space and began to get out the car. He saw the look on Floyd's face.

"Floyd, you look like a man waiting for the firing squad. It won't be anything like that."

The boy shrunk in the seat. "You don't know that. Anything could happen."

Eric shook his head. "Floyd, I've known you for nearly a week. I know you're decent. You're an aggressive prick at times, but knowing what I've heard? I don't blame you at all. I don't believe you killed your Mom. And no-one believes anything from Medusa's cops. You get me?"

Floyd shook his head. "I can't believe they'll just let me go..."

Eric interrupted. "You've got Alvin, Floyd. Anyone who has him on their side has nothing to fear."

Floyd looked at the young cop and paused in thought. "Who is he, Eric? You jump to attention when he's mentioned, like you half want to mess yourself. He's just a diner owner, right?"

Eric looked serious. "I've said too much, kid. Whatever you do, don't mention anything I've said to you about that man. Taking him at face value is the safer option. I don't want any attention on me or my career, you understand me?"

"Yeah... yeah, course not, Eric. I would never do anything to hurt you. You've been a buddy to me this last week." And then Floyd smirked. "You're not bad for a cop."

Eric chuckled. "And you aren't too bad for some skinny kid with a massive chip on his shoulder who's been on the run and beaten to a pulp either, Floyd."

Floyd grinned back.

"Come on Floyd, time for you to face the music."

Floyd followed Eric into the main entrance and up to the desk. Eric talked very quietly to the desk sergeant, who was quickly on the phone. A few minutes later they were collected by another sombre looking cop.

Before they entered the room, Eric stopped Floyd. "This is where we part company, Floyd."

Floyd looked at him with dismay, but said nothing.

"Floyd. Look at me, man. You've got nothing to fear. Now get in there and take them on. Head held high, kid."

With a shake of hands, Eric was gone.

Floyd entered the room. There were two chairs and a table.

"Take a seat," he was ordered.

When he sat down, the cop left the room and shut the door behind him. There was the sound of the door being locked. It felt like a literal cell door closing to Floyd.

The boy sat there for ten minutes and then became restless. He got out the chair and began pacing about the room. He spotted the mirror on the wall and boredom morphed into Floyd's trademark mischief. "A one way mirror?" he thought.

He walked straight up to the mirror and began examining his face, as if looking for zits. He picked his nose, made faces and generally showed his contempt for whoever might be watching. He was so busy goofing around he was taken by surprise when the door opened. It was Alvin.

"You can stop fooling around now, Floyd," the older man said seriously.

"Hi Alvin," replied Floyd, trying to be cheerful. Alvin did not smile back.

"Take a seat, kid."

Floyd did as he was told.

"From the beginning, after I last saw you, tell me what the hell did they do to you?"

Floyd told him. He told about the trip home, his Mom's sudden illness, the beating he received from Sanchez's goons, going to Doctor Masters, finding his Mom dead and going on the run. Alvin stayed quiet throughout, only nodding occasionally. When Floyd had finished, Alvin sat and stared at him.

Floyd tried to stare back, but there was something in Alvin's eyes. Something cold and calculating and intimidating. And there was anger. A furious boiling rage. Floyd had to look away. Anywhere but at the older man, finally settling on staring at the table.

Alvin continued to stare.

After what seemed like hours, Alvin finally looked away. "Thanks, Floyd. I wanted to hear it first from you. You're going to have to tell this again, many times. It'd better be the truth, kid."

Floyd looked back at him and with a hint of defiance said, "I ain't one to bullshit and I've never lied to you!"

Alvin looked back, still stony-faced. "And you better never lie to me, kid."

The older man straightened himself in the chair and looked again at the boy. "First thing, kid. You're safe here. No-one from Medusa can touch you. Second. I have some 'associates' who know about you and Sanchez and what's going on in Medusa. You might be a breakthrough for us... for them."

Floyd paused, summoning up his courage. He then spoke.

"Alvin, who the hell are you?"

Alvin smiled. "I'm just a guy who runs a diner, kid." But his face grew hard once more.

"And it's best for you and Janie and everyone else I care about to think the same. I hope that's clear, Floyd?"

Floyd sniggered. "You can't fool me. There's something about you, Alvin. You ain't no diner owner. Or you ain't just one." Floyd smirked at the older man. Another mistake...

Floyd didn't even see Alvin move, but he was suddenly face down against the table with an arm painfully high up his back.

"You listen good, you little bastard. I'm just a diner owner who occasionally helps out punks like you outta the goodness of my heart. Understand?"

Floyd gasped with the pain and surprise at Alvin's strength. "You can't do this to me! I have..." But his complaint ended as his arm was forced further up this back.

"What am I?" Alvin commanded.

"You... you're Alvin."

"And what am I?"

"You're a crazy son-of-a-bitch... aaaah!"

"Wrong answer. I can do this all day, Floyd." Alvin's voice was cold. This wasn't the easy going guy the boy thought he knew.

"Aaaah!" groaned Floyd again. "Stop it!"

"Then what am I?" Another wrench on Floyd's arm.

"Shit! You're... a diner owner. Please stop!"

"Without the cussing. What am I?" repeated Alvin again.

"You're a diner owner."

"Well done kid. What do I occasionally do?"

"Beat people like me up?" came Floyd's sarcastic reply. "Ahhhh! Stop it. Stop it!"

"When you answer the question properly. What do I occasionally do?"

"You... you occasionally helps out punks like... like me out of the goodness of your heart!"

"Good boy. Now answer the questions like you mean them... who am I?"

"Alvin."

"What am I?"

"A diner owner," said Floyd dully.

"Like you mean it, Floyd..." said Alvin with another jerk of Floyd's arm.

"You're a diner owner."

"And what do I occasionally do?"

"You occasionally helps out punks like me out of the goodness... the goodness of your heart!"

"Well done, son."

The pressure was off Floyd. Alvin grabbed him by his shirt and dumped him back in his chair.

Floyd looked up at Alvin with fear in his eyes. The older man scowled back.

"You're frightened now, Floyd, aren't you? Of me and the situation you're in? Aren't you?"

At this stage, the terrified Floyd would have agreed to anything. "Yeah... yeah... I am. I don't know who you are, but I don't want to get on the bad side of you again."

Alvin laughed. "It's never a good idea to get on the bad side of any diner owner, kid. Understand?"

Floyd had no hesitation in replying. "No, sir. I never will."

Alvin hesitated. "Floyd, you don't have to 'sir' me. But let's make it clear. This conversation never happened. OK? If I ever get to know that mouth of yours has yapped I'll get to know. And you'll be sorry. Understand?"

"Yeah... yeah... I get you Alvin."

Alvin grabbed Floyd again and hauled him to his feet. He spoke quietly but firmly. "And if you ever mention any of this to Janie, no-one will ever see you again. Do I make myself, clear?"

There was a sudden harsh stench of urine. The bewildered Floyd's bladder had cut loose.

Alvin let go of Floyd and stepped back. "Hell, kid. You don't have to be that frightened..."

Floyd said nothing, but his pupils were dilated black with shock.

"OK Floyd. This never happened. We'll get you cleaned up and some food in you. Then some friends of mine want to talk to you."

At Floyd's continued look of anxiety, he carried on. "They won't hurt you Floyd. But they do want to know anything and everything you know about Medusa, Theodore Sanchez, his men and any other things you might know about that goes down in in that shithole."

"OK. OK!" said Floyd, hastily. "I'll say anything you want me to..."

Alvin's face softened. "Floyd. What we want... that they want, is the truth. What you've seen. Who is involved? Who was hurt by those scum in Medusa? They don't want any tall tales, understand? What you know is enough to bring Sanchez to justice, I'm thinking. So just the truth, kid."

"What do I know that could bring Sanchez down?"

"Enough. We'll see. I have confidence you'll say what's in your heart. And that's good enough for me. Now, clean clothes. Give me ten minutes."

Alvin was up and banging on the door. Floyd couldn't help himself recoil slightly at the older man's sudden movement.

"You haven't any reason to believe I'll ever hurt you, Floyd. Except for what we discussed earlier…"

"That never happened," Floyd blurted back,

"Good job, kid" smiled Alvin. This time, the smile reached his eyes.

The door opened and Floyd was left in the interview room, sitting in his piss stained clothes.

Ten minutes later Alvin was back with bundle of clothes accompanied by a young cop. "These should fit. Even for a skinny guy like you. Here…" Alvin put the clothes down. "This cop here is God, Floyd. Are we clear?"

"Yes, Alvin," responded Floyd.

"Good. He will take you to get a shower. You will shower and put some clean clothes."

"Yes, Alvin," Floyd responded meekly again.

"Then you'll meet with my associates."

Chapter 12 – Floyd, Grilled

Twenty minutes later, Floyd was delivered back to the interview room. Alone again. He began to feel sleepy when the door re-opened.

Several men came in. They were all big guys with hard faces. Suits. Sunglasses. Last in was Alvin who gave him a quick smile. "Clean, kid?"

"Yeah..." replied Floyd warily. He looked nervous.

"Good. These are a few 'associates' of mine, Floyd. What I spoke to you about earlier also refers to them. Get me?"

"Yeah... sure... it never happened... I don't know who anyone is..."

Alvin laughed and one of the big men smiled too. "Looks like you got this kid well trained, Alvin?"

"Maybe," laughed Alvin. "He wasn't the most able student at the start, but he soon got how it needs to be. Got a stubborn streak, but he wouldn't be the first, would he?"

The man looked lost in thought for a second and then smiled back. "You'll never let me forget, will you, old man?"

"You wish," Alvin replied with a grin.

Floyd was curious. Who were all these men? They were deferential to Alvin as well?

"OK, Floyd. These guys want to ask you some questions about your life in Medusa. Tell them what you know. You don't need to fear these men, but you do need to be straight with them. OK?"

Floyd nodded.

"OK kid, tell us about life in Medusa from whenever you can remember."

He hesitated. "In what way?"

"Just home and your Mom and school for start with."

"OK. Well I'm known as 'Marlene's Bastard' in Medusa and we always got treated bad. Both me and Mom. By everyone. I hated it and everyone there. Mom just seemed browbeat and a bit frightened. The only friend I had was Zeke..."

An hour later, Floyd had pretty much told the story. The regular visits to his home by Sanchez. Zeke and his folks disappearing, Mom's acceptance of insults and slurs, his hatred of school, work and everything in Medusa. All of the men asked questions or asked Floyd to repeat something for clarification. They smiled at the story of Sanchez's face and the baby Jesus in the crib, but they grew stern when he repeated what had occurred the night his Mom died.

"Thanks Floyd. Anyone got any more questions?" asked Alvin.

One of the stern men replied. "Just one or two more?" Alvin nodded.

"What is your relationship with Theodore Sanchez?"

Floyd faltered. "Relationship...? What do you mean?"

"You seem to have crossed him a few times, Floyd. So why aren't you dead? From what we know, no-one upsets Theodore Sanchez more than once?"

"I... I dunno... I never tried to have anything to do with Sanchez. If he was about, I stayed outta the way. Mom always told me to avoid him. I always kept out the way."

"How close was your Mom to Theodore Sanchez?"

Floyd began to get sore. "What are you implyin'?"

"I imply nothing, Floyd," said the big man, his eyes cold.

"Just answer the question, kid," interrupted Alvin.

"Well… she seemed to hate him. I've told you about his visits. What he did to her. The bruises. When she warned me away Sanchez, she said she 'didn't want to lose anyone else'. She wouldn't tell me what that meant. I guessed it was a boyfriend, maybe?"

"A sweetheart?"

"I don't know. She said he'd 'have made a good father to me…' Sanchez is somewhere in the middle of it, I'm sure."

"A name?"

"No… no. She never said."

The big man turned to Alvin. "That's me done, sir."

"OK guys. Floyd will stay at the diner with me," and he turned to Floyd and grinned. "Where I can keep an eye on him. I take full responsibility for him. No foster homes and all that shit. Check my credentials if you guys need to. They should still be up to date"

The group of men shook their heads, as one. "No sir'. 'There's no need'. 'We know the score.'

"He's my nephew if anyone wants to know." He turned back to the other men in the room. "If you have any more questions, let me know? Otherwise I'm gonna let this kid have a break?"

"OK, Alvin", "Yes sir", "Will do Alvin" came the replies. And with a nod to Floyd, they all left.

"So, kid," asked Floyd. "Are we done?"

"I hope so, Alvin..." replied the boy tiredly. "Or should that be 'Uncle Alvin?'"

"Not quite, kid..."

Floyd groaned. "Not more questions?"

"Just a few, Floyd."

"Shit, more 'just a few'."

"Shut up, Floyd!" growled Alvin.

Floyd sat sullenly.

"OK. Explain why it looks like you have been fighting."

Floyd looked confused. Alvin pointed. "Your knuckles."

"What about my knuckles? Ain't I been poked, prodded and asked enough?"

"I know you never hit your Mom, Floyd. But tell me about your right knuckles?"

Floyd looked at his hands. "I think it was that scrape I got into when I first saw you. Then when I got beaten up by Sanchez's gang in Medusa, I might have got a shot or two in. I dunno? "

"Anyone else?"

"The Doctor. Doctor Masters. I hit him. So that he could say I stole his wallet. He gave me his ATM number to get cash to help me. I forgot! Someone threatened him and his wife and kids to get him to say I hit Mom!"

Alvin sat quietly. "That fits with the pile of cash you had in your bag. Where the heck did you get ten grand from, Floyd?"

"It was Mom's. Taped to the bottom drawer. Doctor Masters saw me get it. Two thousand of it is his."

"Anything else?"

"No! Alvin, you gotta help him. I'd be dead by now if it was for Doctor Masters. He helped me get away. Please, he could be in trouble. And his family!"

"We'll take care of it, Floyd. But let's get you sorted first."

"I ain't important! Doctor Masters and his wife and kids first."

Alvin smiled. "You're loyal, I see that. OK we'll help, but we won't jeopardise bringing down Sanchez. OK?"

"But… but… I'd love it if you could get to Sanchez, but not over innocent lives."

Alvin smiled again. "Natural sense of justice. Protect the weak. Why you could be a cop, Floyd!"

Floyd looked horrified. "A cop? No way. I'd sooner…" and then he stopped, seeing the look on Alvin's face.

Alvin looked grim. You'd sooner what, Floyd?" he said quietly.

"I meant nothin' by it." Said Floyd, defensively.

"I understand kid. What would you sooner be?"

"I'd sooner be anything than be like the cops in Medusa. Sanchez's ass-kissers. Bullyin' and intimidatin'. You just said 'justice' and 'protect'. They'll never know what that means."

Alvin smiled once more. "Good. I want to know where we stand, kid. I've had some… 'dealings' with crooked cops. I feel the same. Sometimes death is what they deserve."

Alvin stood up. "Come on kid, let's get you home."

"Home?" Floyd looked suspicious.

"So you can become my new kitchen worker, kid."

"For free?" Floyd looked even more wary.

Alvin smirked. "No, not for free. Minimum pay. But you get bed and board too. Can't say any fairer than that."

Floyd hesitated. "All that? For me? But why...?"

"Because you've got potential kid. In what I don't know, but I think you'll do OK. Deal?"

"Deal," said Floyd spat into his hand and put it out for Alvin to shake.

Alvin eyes danced with amusement. "I admire that enthusiasm, but you don't spit in your hand in the food retail trade."

"Oh!" Floyd looked mortified.

"Don't be sorry, kid. Just go and wash your hands and then I'll be happy to shake it."

As they left the precinct, Floyd watched as Alvin talked to the uniform cops, who were stood to attention. "Like they were on parade…" Floyd thought. He couldn't hear what was being said, but they all listened politely and nodded. Who or what Alvin was still interested Floyd, but he understood now that it was dangerous to think about that too much.

"Come on Floyd, time to get going."

Floyd jumped. He had become lost in thought. "I didn't see you!"

"You're tired, kid. Come on let's get going." With a wave to the uniforms, they were gone.

Alvin pointed to the battered four wheel drive in the station parking lot. "Get in, kid."

Floyd stayed quiet and began to fall asleep as Alvin drove. He was still sleeping when they arrived at the diner. Alvin gave him a gentle shake. "Kid… Floyd… we're here…"

Floyd woke suddenly, but did not move. He wasn't sure where he was. But he was prepared to fight!

Alvin spoke gently. "Floyd… Floyd… it's Alvin. We're here. At the diner… OK?"

Floyd started awake, suddenly sitting up in the passenger seat. "Didn't know where I was. Thought was back... back in Medusa..."

"No, Floyd. You'll never be going back to Medusa again. There's a world out there to discover, kid. Me and Janie and others will help you find it."

"Yeah, sure..." mumbled Floyd, like he didn't really believe it.

"Come on Floyd. Let's get you moving."

With a grunt of effort, Floyd began to move out the seat and open the passenger door. He wavered for a minute and stood up, hanging onto the door frame. Alvin watched but made no effort to help.

"Just a bit further, kid."

Floyd followed Alvin through the diner door and inside. Janie was behind the cash register. She saw Floyd. "Floyd! Oh my God! What's happened to you?" and she moved to hug him.

Alvin intervened. "Janie! Take it easy. He's been badly beat up. No hugging tonight, baby!"

"What happened to him, Alvin?"

Alvin looked around the diner. There were a few people there, but all of them were intently watching.

"Folks, don't let your food get cold," he called out and turned back to Janie and Floyd. "Later..." he mouthed.

"Come on, Floyd." Alvin guided the boy to the stairs and up them. Floyd stood at the top and looked confused. "Out of it again," murmured Alvin.

"Turn left, kid. Same room as you were in before. That's it."

Alvin guided the boy into the room and went to the bed, pulling back the covers. "Get your sneakers and jeans off, Floyd. You'll manage as you are."

Floyd sat on the bed and fumbled with the laces. After a minute he was no further along. Alvin kneeled down. "Let me do it, kid. You start on your jeans."

Alvin eventually got Floyd lying on the bed and pulled the covers over him.

"I'll leave the light on kid. You're OK here. I'll get you water."

When Alvin got back, Floyd was fast asleep. He watched the sleeping boy for a moment. "Get a good night, kid. Tomorrow is a new life. A good life. I promise you that..."

Alvin moved quietly to leave the room and closed the door. He walked down the stairs and fund Janie waiting.

"What's going on, Alvin? What happened to him?"

"Baby, where to start?"

"Who beat him up?"

"This is all I know. Walt...! Let me talk..."

"OK, Alvin."

"Floyd was beaten up in Medusa. His Mom was found dead and the local cops believed Floyd was involved..."

Janie looked shocked, hand to her mouth. "Floyd?" she said incredulously. "I can't believe Floyd would ever..."

"Janie, baby. Let me finish..."

"Sorry, Alvin."

"That's OK. I was shocked too. But I don't believe Floyd could hurt his Mom either. The Woosterville cops picked Floyd up. He was in a bad way and they found my reference letter on him. So I went in and they released him on bail to me."

Janie stared at him. "Is that all, Alvin?"

Alvin stared back, looking innocent. "Yeah, sure, baby? What else could I tell you?"

Janie frowned at his pretence. "You aren't telling me everything, Alvin, that's for sure."

"That's all I know, Janie. I swear! He has to stay here and they will question him later."

Janie still looked doubtful. "I believe you," But then she glared at him. "Millions wouldn't. I'm not a dummy you know?"

"The most beautiful dummy I ever met, Janie!"

She smirked. "Now this is classic distraction techniques..." but her words were halted by a kiss.

When she got her breath back, she looked at him again. "I consider myself distracted. For now. I may need more distracting later, you big jerk!" And she pecked him on the lips. "But let's get through the evening first?"

Alvin smiled. He hoped Janie would stay distracted. "Mothering Floyd should do it too?" he thought.

"OK, evening customers, where are you...?"

Chapter 13 – Floyd Catches His Breath

Floyd woke slowly in a comfortable warm bed. Daylight flooded through the window. He slowly took in his surroundings. He wasn't sure where he was, but he felt safe. The room was very feminine, with lacy curtains and bright pastel colours. "Mom would like this sorta stuff..." he thought. But then the memories started to come back as he realised Mom would never like anything ever again. His mood turned more sombre.

He lay there quietly for a while longer, picking over what had happened in the past few days. He was still sleepy and sore, so the memories came slowly. His musing was interrupted by a knock at the door.

"Who is it?" called out Floyd.

"It's Janie, Floyd. Can I come in?"

"Sure. Just give me a second." Floyd hauled himself out of the bed with a groan. He quickly found his jeans but couldn't find his socks and sneakers.

"You OK, Floyd?" came Janie's voice.

"Yeah, sure. Just give me one more second." Floyd walked to the door and walked barefoot to the door. Janie smiled as she saw him.

"It's 11am, Floyd, we thought you should get up?"

"11am? Holy shit! I never sleep this late. Honest!"

Janie grinned at him. "A kid your age. Up early? Yeah, sure Floyd!"

Floyd couldn't help but smile back.

"Are you hungry?"

"Yeah, starving," replied Floyd.

"Alvin is making you a late breakfast, so you've got about fifteen minutes.

"Oh! I forgot! We got you some t shirts and underwear and socks. You can get some jeans later. There's a clean towel in the bathroom, with the clothes. I'd get moving if I was you?"

Floyd got to the bathroom, found his new clothes and the towel, got out of his dirty clothes and into the shower. The hot water soothed him and he was soon feeling clean and relaxed.

There was a sudden knock on the door. "Floyd, it's Janie. Breakfast in five!"

"Thanks, Janie!" he shouted back. He reluctantly got out of the shower, dried off and dressed. He still couldn't find his sneakers so he walked in his socked feet down the stairs.

He heard Alvin's shout: "Out the front, Floyd!"

He found Janie and Alvin tucking into a meal. The smell made his stomach grumble, but he was relieved the sound was not too loud.

"Hi Floyd," smiled Janie.

"Hi Floyd, come and eat," greeted Alvin. "Where's your sneakers, kid?"

"I dunno I couldn't find them. I can't remember what I did with them last night."

"Did you try looking under the bed?"

Floyd reddened. "I'm ain't sure. I'll take a look after I eat?"

"Eat first, sneakers after," agreed Alvin.

"We need to feed you up, Floyd," said Janie.

The boy remained standing, warily looking at the couple eating and longing to fill his belly, too.

Janie spoke first. "For God's sakes Floyd, sit down and eat!"

The boy quickly sat and soon was inhaling the best breakfast he'd had in his life. "Coffee, eggs, bacon, hash browns are the best..." he thought.

Alvin and Janie watched him in fond amusement. "He's gonna choke, Alvin?"

"He's fine, Janie. All kids his age are like that. He'll stop when he wants."

Floyd did not seem to want to stop. After his third helping, Alvin intervened. "Kid... kid... Floyd. "Enough. You've eaten for three or four big guys. Time to stop!"

Janie started to scold Floyd too. "There's no good you eating so much in one go! It isn't good for..."

She was interrupted by a huge belch from the boy.

"Floyd you're a pig!" Janie said, revolted by his grossness.

"Sorry," the boy replied, not looking one bit apologetic, a big grin on his face.

"So, Floyd. What do you plan to do with yourself?" asked Alvin.

Floyd paused. "I ain't really had time to think. "I thought I was gonna help you in the kitchen?"

"You are, Floyd. But I want you to have a few days to relax. You've just got out of hospital. So I don't want to work you too hard." Alvin gave an evil grin. "In three week's time, however..."

Floyd looked warily as Janie and Alvin smiled at each other.

"Looking anxious again, kid. You're perfectly safe here."

Janie smiled encouragingly. "We want you to be happy here, Floyd."

"Thanks guys. But what am I gonna do for the next few days? Am I allowed out?"

Alvin looked thoughtful for a moment. "Leave it for a few weeks. Get bored. Then you should be OK to explore the city. But I want to know where you are. I'll get you a cell phone."

"I want to get out today!" Floyd whined.

The grim look returned to Alvin's face. "In your position, what you want and what you don't doesn't hold a lot of water, kid. I want you to get out and see Woosterville without worrying about anything else. When you look better. Have you seen the bruises? You sure should be able to feel them, kid."

A look of amusement crossed the older man's face. "Oh, yeah. I heard all about Debbie. The very pretty nurse who made eyes at you?"

"She was a nutcase!"

Janie began to smile too. "Floyd, who is this Debbie?"

Both Alvin and Janie looked puzzled at Floyd's scowl.

"She was too interested in me that I'd like. Even Eric the cop noticed in the end. Gave me her cell phone number. Tried to kiss me too. Plain crazy!"

Janie tapped the table with her finger. "Then until you get fit and can avoid being bothered by weirdos, I guess you'll have to stay here for a while. Won't you Floyd?"

Floyd became embarrassed. "You... you guys... always teasin' me."

"Floyd. You'll get to meet people, but not just yet. Wait a while. Depends how you are physically and how you feel? Let your bruises fade. You look awful, son. So, relax. Get out of here and take in the city when you're up to it."

Floyd looked stubborn. "I want to go back to the gallery."

"Oh yeah. That guy Sean. What if he's there?"

"I... maybe I should apologise. He didn't mean nothin' by it, at least I don't think so."

"Get to know the city first, Floyd. Go and see this Sean later."

Floyd hesitated. "I'm still beat so maybe I shouldn't?" He let out a huge yawn.

"More sleep, Floyd?"

"I think so... I hate being like this! Like I'm an old guy."

"Kid, if you need it, go and do it. We'll yell you for lunch." Alvin looked at his watch. "A late lunch. We need to get to work, Janie?"

Floyd walked back up the stairs, yawning.

"What we gonna do with him, Alvin?"

"Not sure baby. I said we'd keep him safe until everything calms down. Then I'll think of what we can do for his future."

Janie smiled at him. "Mr Tough Guy has a soft heart?"

Alvin smiled back. "You're a bad influence on me, baby. All that 'help unto others' garbage. I love you too much, you know that?"

"And I love you. But I need to start the lunch menu first."

"I'll be in the kitchen in ten minutes, Janie. I just have to call a supplier."

When she was gone, he picked up the phone and dialled. "Hey it's me. Yeah… yeah… retired me. What's the news? Nothing yet? OK. There's a Doctor Masters in Stone City you should take a look at. The kid says he's legit but got pressure put on him by those fuckers who work for S. Yeah, the Sheriff."

Alvin pulled the phone away from his ear. "Don't shout at me, dickhead! There's no way that kid hit anyone deliberately. He admits to hitting the Masters guy. The kid says Masters' wife and family have been threatened. You know S, he'd off them without a second thought."

The voice on the phone got quieter. "Yeah? Get Masters' statement for yourself. Does it stink? I betcha fifty bucks it stinks to high heaven."

Alvin chuckled, "I'll look after the kid. You dig. I'll email anything I got when I get it? OK? Don't drag the boy into anything until you've got stuff yourself OK? He's been through enough from living in that backwater hole. OK? Love to Elaine… I know that. But she can always come here and we'll cook for her… yeah, sure. When I mean 'we' I mean 'me'. And you too. Take care of yourself, buddy. Bye."

Chapter 14 – Boredom Strikes

Floyd had a few long and tedious days upstairs at the diner. He tried to avoid Alvin and Janie as much as possible. He liked Janie a lot, but he wanted some time to himself. He was still very wary of Alvin. He spoke little and huddled in his chair when he was with them.

Sometimes he was just in a rage, though he kept it to himself. An elemental and angry rage. He wanted to fight, he wanted to hurt the people who had hurt him. He sometimes thought he'd like to kill them. Kill all of them in Medusa who had crossed him in one way or another. Make them suffer. When he felt like this, he sat there, teeth and jaw clenched and tried to relax.

If Janie or Alvin bothered him when he was like that he would shout at them in frustration, cursing their interference. "Why can't you leave me be? Why do you have to meddle the fuck out of everything I do or say?"

They were patient, but sometimes the darker side of Alvin would come out too in response. "Say what you like to me, you little bastard, but not to Janie. You'd better remember that if you know what's good for you. What helped you in Medusa won't help you here. Do I make myself clear?"

Alvin still frightened Floyd and the boy knew that the older man could easily beat him up. Or worse. So he'd apologise and retreat to his room. Floyd could see how his comments hurt Janie and he resolved to be calmer. Sometimes it worked.

202

The fits of anger lessened over the weeks as Floyd healed physically, mentally and emotionally, but the quietness of the apartment upstairs had started to drive him crazy.

He fell asleep in the big armchair in the corner of the den, bored stiff of daytime TV. When he woke, it was dark outside, but there was a lamp lit in the corner. Floyd found a post-it note stuck to his seat. 'Thought you might be hungry but you were fast asleep. There's a sandwich in the fridge. Love Janie."

He smiled. Janie seemed to want to look after him and seemed to like him, too. He still wasn't sure why. No-one in Medusa had shown him much kindness, even his Mom as he got older.

Janie was at times cheerful and tired and sometimes bossy, but always interested in his welfare. He just didn't get it. She was so different from every woman he'd ever met. He didn't get how Janie and Alvin seemed to love each other so much, either. Their continuous flirting, the mock arguments, the embarrassing affection. He thought the kissing was gross, was gross, especially for an old dude like Alvin. He'd never seen anyone in Medusa behave in that way, young or old.

The thought of Medusa made him gloomy again, reminding him of what had happened to his Mom and his worry about Dr Masters and his family.

He sat in the chair a while longer until he felt the pangs of hunger. He got out the chair and walked into the kitchen.

Floyd was soon tucking into a huge sandwich and a large glass of milk. The food was welcome. He was warm. Clean clothes.

Somehow, there were people that cared about him.

He felt safe. For the first time in his life, he began to relax and his rigid body language began to loosen up.

An hour later, Janie came into the kitchen looking frazzled.

"Hey Floyd, how are you feeling?"

Floyd smiled back. "I'm good, Janie. You look tired. Can I help?"

"No, your job is to relax. We've got a lot of customers at once. It pays the bills, but sometimes it's too much. Alvin made me take a break."

"I don't mind helping. I'm so bored anyway."

Janie smiled at him. "You might be sorry you said that, Floyd?"

"If Alvin's OK, I'll be happy to help."

"Just give me a minute to sit. My feet..." she groaned.

"Do you want a drink, Janie?" asked Floyd.

"My angel! A tea. In the top cupboard. Yes, the breakfast tea. Make it strong."

As Floyd prepared her tea, she talked to him, despite his reluctance to answer, so she spoke about her own life. She had been pretty, but from a poorer background and treated badly by everyone, especially by men. "Some guys think a pretty face makes a girl easy. Don't be like that, Floyd."

There was a note of bitterness as she described her father and mother. "If she saved, he stole it, if she hid it, he beat it out of her. We were always one step from the street. It was a mercy when he died. With a bottle in his hand. If Mom had more confidence, she would have took off with me and my two brothers and never looked back."

Janie smiled at Floyd. "There's me, laying all this on you, when you've seen enough trouble."

"I don't mind Janie. I always thought it was just me, but there's more than just you and me, ain't there?"

"It's true, Floyd. And a shame. So many like us with potential and it just gets crushed. By the time Dad died, I was eighteen and out on my own. Men never left me alone, so I had to have a man to protect me. That didn't work so well either," she said wistfully.

"What happened?"

"I exchanged one loser for another. My Dad got replaced by a local gang boss. He protected me, but he made me almost like a slave. But he tangled with a rival gang and he ended up dead."

"What did you do?"

"I lived on my own for years. I kept out of sight. Then I met Alvin." A smile came to her face. "He was funny and kind and gentle. And he stayed that way. He might not be the prettiest guy around and he's older than me, but what's not to love?"

The other 'Alvin' appeared in Floyd's mind. Cold, forceful and casually violent. But he treated Janie well and she knew nothing about that side of him. "Best keep it that way for her sake as well as my neck," he thought.

"He seems like a nice guy..." said Floyd hesitantly.

Janie smiled. "He is. But he'll be hard on you, Floyd, when you work for him. It's not that he won't care about you, but he will always expect you to try your best. If you fail, fail trying hard. Alvin won't give you many chances if you don't try hard."

"Thanks Janie. I'll remember that. The tea!"

She smiled again at his concern. "Strong tea Floyd, not stewed to within an inch of its life?"

Janie gulped the tea and grimaced. "Yuck! But it has caffeine and that will do the trick..."

She stood up. "Give me a minute to talk to Alvin."

"OK, Janie."

Ten minutes later Alvin came into the room.

"So, kid. You want to help?"

"Sure, Alvin."

"You up to it?"

"We'll soon see?" quipped Floyd.

"OK, we got a deal. You stay out of sight in the kitchen. Washing up. Tons of it. Think you can handle that?"

"If it helps you guys, I'll do anything."

Alvin smiled back. "Thanks, kid. OK, let's get to it."

An hour later, Floyd was tired. The mountain of plates didn't seem to lessen. He swore it was growing. But he kept at it. He didn't notice Alvin and Janie watching him.

"Stubborn little devil, isn't he?"

"You say that like it's a bad thing, Alvin?"

Alvin chuckled. "Nope. It's helped that kid in the past and it will help him now."

"So he's starting early?"

"No. Let him have his days free. If he's fit he can work evenings. But in three days, he's full-time. Till he drops."

"Are you sure he's up to it, Alvin?"

"Till he drops, Janie. I know he can take it. We've already seen it. Soon he'll have a job and his own money in his pocket. Then he needs to get and meet other teenagers. What more does a kid of his age want?"

"Or kids your age too, Alvin?" smiled Janie.

Alvin smiled back. "Sure. But old guys usually don't get as lucky as me, do they?"

"Why don't you guys get a room?" came Floyd's voice. They suddenly noticed he was watching them. He was trying to look disgusted, but they could see he was amused.

"Hey, haven't you got a ton of crockery to wash?" said Janie sternly, but her smile broke through too.

"Kid's getting cheeky already, Janie?"

Floyd's face fell but the response was sniggers from the couple.

"Got you, kid!"

Floyd shrugged. "I'll get back to it, then."

"See that you do, Floyd!"

Floyd slept well that night. He was exhausted by the physical hard work and relaxed enough to fall asleep easily. A sleep that was mercifully dream-free.

Chapter 15 – Alvin and Sean Scheme

The next day, Janie and Alvin were working together in the kitchen, when Alvin suddenly stopped work and swore.

"What's wrong, Alvin?" asked Janie.

"I forgot about that guy Sean Lynch, at the gallery. Meant to see what he was like. Floyd wants to go and see him."

"Go and find out, Alvin."

"I can't leave you to manage on your own, Janie."

"It's Wednesday. What happens on Wednesday afternoon?"

Alvin paused. "I dunno?"

"Exactly. Nothing happens. This place is a graveyard. So get out and see who and what this Sean guy is?"

"You sure, baby?"

"Sure I'm sure! Now get..."

He came up to her and kissed her. "Thanks, Janie. Can I make it up to you later?"

Janie affected non-interest. "You might be able to. But it will take a lot of work to persuade me."

Alvin moved closer. "I can be very persuasive when I want to," he said softly.

"I'm counting on it, Alvin... now, off you go!"

Alvin made his way downtown to the City gallery. He wasn't sure what he was going to say to this guy until he got there. "Size him up and see how I go?"

He spotted the security guard at the entrance. "Buddy, do you know a guy called Sean Lynch?"

"Professor Lynch? Yeah, he's the boss here. Who's asking?"

"My nephew Floyd came in here a couple weeks ago. Got real upset. Said he was talking to this Sean Lynch around the time it happened."

"I'll see if I can get ahold of Sean. Do you mind waiting?"

"Sure. I'll sit over there and have a coffee."

Alvin sat with his latte admiring his surroundings. "Sure is swanky. But this coffee tastes like sh..."

"Excuse me sir? Professor Lynch will be down in about thirty minutes. Would you like to wait here or take a look around?"

"Based on your coffee, I'll do the tour... thanks, man. Have you got a guide book for art dummies?"

Alvin lost track of time as he walked around. He couldn't make any sense of the modern stuff, but he did like the older paintings. He smiled to himself. "Maybe a couple of these for the diner. That should do it... or a better class of customer, with more dough?"

He spotted the security guard with an older man.

"Hello, you must be Floyd's uncle?"

"Yeah that's me."

"It's a pleasure to meet you. I enjoyed talking to Floyd, but he's a strange sort of boy. Very insightful and intelligent, but quick to take offence when I told him that. Is everything OK at home?"

Alvin looked around the room. "Is there somewhere we can talk privately?"

They were soon sitting in Sean's office.

"Can I offer you a drink?"

"Thanks, but based on your coffee, maybe not?"

"Not the first time I've heard that. A tea man myself but even that..." Sean made a face. "Wish I knew someone who could help us with that."

Alvin handed over a business card. "Here you go. I run a diner. I'd be happy to help you."

"Thank you, Mr...?"

"Just call me 'Alvin'."

"Thank you, Alvin. Please call me Sean."

"Will do, Sean."

"So... Floyd. May I speak frankly, Alvin?"

"Sure. I hope the boy hasn't been a nuisance?"

"On the contrary, Alvin. He made my day. Such an intelligent young man. Perception. Insight. Thoughtful. So rare. Although rather sensitive. I may have frightened him off with my enthusiasm?"

"Floyd can be quick to temper. It's his age. He's had a tough time lately, too."

"I could see that in his reaction. But it was his notebook. I'm afraid I had a look. Once I started reading I just couldn't stop."

"Wait a minute, Sean. You went through a teenage boy's diary?"

"No. Of course not! It's not a diary. Except it is a little."

Sean paused, not knowing what to say. "Oh, I'm talking nonsense here."

Alvin scowled back. "It sounds like it, Sean."

"How to start? This notebook is very personal to Floyd. I'm not really sorry I read it, because there's so much potential in him."

"What do you mean, Sean?"

"Alvin, your nephew is a first-class observer. He writes what he sees. But then he seems to make a huge leap into analysis of what he's seeing."

"In what way?"

"It starts very crudely with just his feelings. It's a simple reaction to the world around him. But it gets more sophisticated as it goes on along, over time. He's trying to understand the nature of people. It's very crude and very undisciplined. He's seeking to understand people in what he writes and he's developing his own ideas how he would represent them to others. There are notes and sketches about what he thinks is going on around him and how he can tell their story."

"You've lost me, Sean. I run a diner..."

"Floyd appears to have a natural desire to create based on experience and observation. Some people call it 'art'. He's neither a great writer nor a great artist at the moment, but there's things in here which are intriguing and unusual for a boy of his age."

"His Mom would be proud, Sean. But what can we do to help that? Although he's a nice kid at heart, I often only see an angry, confused young man."

"Please get him in to talk to me. I think he could apply for a small scholarship that would pay for some classes at the local college. Part-time of course and he'd have to fund everything else. If he does well, we'll see about university. But doesn't he live in Medusa?"

"Yeah, he did. But now he's living with me."

"Could you support him, Alvin?"

215

"Sure I would, but… look Sean, Floyd has been through hell the past few weeks. He's lost his Mom, but finally got away from Stone City. We'll do anything we can to help him."

"Oh, the poor boy! Give him my best. To lose his mother so young? If there's anything I can do to help, please ask him to contact me."

"Thanks, Sean. Can we leave it a few months? He's my kitchen slave. I want him busy and distracted. Let's get him settled and working and a steady life first?"

"Of course Alvin. Here's my card. Contact me whenever you think fit."

"Sure. Do you want to keep the notebook?"

"I think I will, if you don't mind? It will help me plan what classes Floyd should attend. He has a lot of catching up to do."

"That's OK by me, Sean. Keep this to yourself? I want Floyd to have a break."

"Of course. Happy to keep this in confidence."

"Thanks, Sean. Now about your coffee…"

Chapter 16 – Master and Slave

Janie and Alvin gave Floyd a few more easy days. They fed him, let him nap. Let him lie in if he needed to. Let him help in the kitchen if he wanted to. Floyd wasn't at all surprised how well Alvin understood how to recover from his injuries.

"You never forget how kid, when you've needed to," but he wouldn't say any more about it. Floyd knew better than to ask.

They talked to him when he wanted to talk, which wasn't much, so they left him alone when he needed to think. When they thought he was brooding too long, they talked to him or sometimes at him. Floyd began to feel they were fussing.

"Not again! I don't want to talk. I just want to be quiet. To be left alone."

Alvin pressed. "You need to talk, kid. To get it out your system."

"Please, honey," said Janie. "We just want to help?"

Floyd tried to relax. "I know that and you don't know how much I appreciate it. But you keep asking me and asking me 'How are you?' How do you expect me to be? Mom is dead and I'm on parole to Alvin here."

Floyd's temper rose: "I can't leave this damned diner and walk the street like a normal guy. How do you think I feel?"

With that, he got off his seat and stormed upstairs.

"That went well, Alvin...?" said Janie.

"Janie, we just got him to get angry... that's the best thing he needs. Get angry and get it out of his system. And tomorrow he starts being our kitchen slave."

"If you say so, Alvin. But shouldn't he have a few more days?"

"No... he's young. He's moving around better, so he's healing. He's a young guy: part gorilla and part hormonal dickhead. He'll come around. But tomorrow I'm going to push him."

"You sound like you're going enjoy this, Alvin?"

Alvin smiled. "I always was mean to new recruits. They hated me. But they all did OK when it got tough. Floyd will be no different. He just has a lot of catching up to do."

"Get teaching, you big bully!" laughed Janie.

"I will. You can be good cop, baby..."

"Are you trying to charm me again?"

"Why certainly, Janie! Same time and place...?"

"You bet! Dirty old man!" and with that she kissed him and moved off to the kitchen.

The next day came as a shock to poor Floyd. Alvin banging on the door. It was still dark.

Alvin crashed through the door beaming with enthusiasm. "Up and at 'em, kid!"

"Whut th..." mumbled Floyd. "Whut time's it?"

"Time for you to get out of that bed and cleaned up and in my kitchen in about 30 minutes?"

"You kiddin' me?" mumbled Floyd as he pulled the bedclothes back over his head.

Alvin silently counted to ten. Then with a parade ground bellow, he let into Floyd.

"Shift your ass, you little shit! You think we're here to serve you and wait on you?"

Alvin grabbed the bedding and dragged it off Floyd. "Move! Two minutes and it's a bucket of water. Don't try me, boy!"

And with that, Alvin dragged Floyd off the bed and on to the floor.

"You can't do this...?"

"Do what, kid?"

"Drag me outta bed like I was no-one."

"You are no-one! I'm shielding you from the cops and Sanchez's thugs. So get real, Floyd. I own you until this is sorted out. I'm the master here and you, kid, are my slave. Well?"

Floyd was shocked by Alvin's words. He barked like a sergeant-major. "Just... just give me a minute..."

"You got two minutes, kid. Then it's the coldest bucket of ice water I can find. Well?"

Floyd grabbed his clothes and stuff and headed to the bathroom.

"And don't use all the hot water. Janie will kill you and then me..."

The bathroom door slammed shut and Alvin heard the click of the lock. He'd deliberately pressed a few of Floyd's buttons, but it got him moving. "Who wants to be seventeen and up at 5am? Not without some motivation..."

Whistling to himself, Alvin walked down the stairs and into the kitchen. "What to start the kid on? Fried eggs. Toast? Bacon. And coffee. Yeah, that will do for now."

Twenty minutes later, Floyd came into the diner kitchen, sullen and looking like death warned up.

"Hey Floyd," greeted Alvin cheerfully. "Want some food?"

"Yeah," grunted Floyd.

"Well there you go. Bread. Eggs. Toast. Coffee. Get to it. And make some for me while you're at it."

The boy looked dumbfounded. "Me? Cook? And for you too? You've gotta be kiddin' me. I ain't ever cooked, Mom always does it. She usually made microwave meals." He stopped, realising what he'd said.

"Floyd, everyone should be able to cook. Guys who can't support themselves in the kitchen are wimps. Don't let any macho tell you otherwise. The way to everyone's heart is through their mouths and stomachs. You're going to learn how to make people love you."

"But I don't know how to start?"

"OK. So what takes longest to cook?"

"The bacon. I guess?"

"Then bacon it is. Get to it. Fetch the griddle..."

"The griddle?"

"Kid, haven't you ever cooked?"

"errr... no. I tried. Mom shouted at me for an hour."

"Your Mom, God rest her soul, should have done something about it. "

"Don't you badmouth my Mom!" snapped Floyd.

"Floyd... I apologise. But there's the griddle. Put the bacon on it. Yes, that one. No, in strips. How can it cook in a lump?"

Poor Floyd struggled as he individually put the strips of bacon on to the griddle. He cursed under his breath as he dropped a strip on the floor. He picked it up and went to put it back on the griddle."

Alvin immediately stopped him. "Jesus, kid, where's your hygiene?"

"It's only been on the floor for second. Here, I'll wash the dirt off."

"Almighty God! Didn't they teach you anything at school?"

Seeing the storms clouds in Floyd's eyes, Alvin hastily continued. "Forget I said that, kid. Look, the rule here is if you drop food on the floor here, you throw it away. Understand?"

Floyd was astonished. Nothing was wasted at home and food dropped anywhere was washed under the faucet and still eaten. His Mom had constantly drilled it into him

"I couldn't waste food like that? Mom used to say it was a sin!"

Alvin laughed. "Noble sentiments, Floyd, but remember I have customers here who I can't poison. It's easy to get a bad rep and if the sanitation people get onto me I may as well close down. By the way, did you wash your hands when you came in here?"

"No... I just had a shower, why wash them again?"

Alvin grimaced. "I can see we've got some ways to go, kid. I'll write you a list. You always wash your hands when you come in this kitchen. Get me? If I catch you once I'll be angry. Catch you twice I'll kick your ass out the door, down the street and half way back to Stone City. Is that clear, Floyd?

"uhhh...yes sir!"

"Then what are you going to do now?"

Floyd hesitated. He still hadn't quite woken up. "Wash my hands?"

"Fantastic. You can learn?"

"Gee, thanks," mumbled Floyd as he walked to the sink.

"Not that sink!"

"What?"

"That's the food prep sink..."

Floyd looked at Alvin in amazement. "How many friggin' sinks do you need?"

Alvin put his head in his hands. "Enough to keep you scrubbing for the next three months if you don't shut your yap?"

Floyd took a deep breath, then exhaled. "Why more than one sink?"

"Hygiene again. Your worst enemy and your best friend. Sinks for washing vegetables. Sinks for meat and sinks for washing hands. Then big sinks for washing everything afterwards? Make sense?"

"Sorta...?"

"Well done, kid. Now the hand washing sink is over there. Far from everything else."

Floyd quickly washed his hands.

"Now back to you cooking me a hearty breakfast, Floyd. Bacon first…"

An hour later Floyd was done. In every way. The bacon was burnt but cold. The eggs a mess, neither scrambled nor whole. The toast was like soot. But Alvin forced himself to eat it and he made Floyd eat it all too. The coffee that washed it all down was like bitter oil.

"Well, son, that wasn't the greatest meal I've ever had." Alvin saw Floyd's face fall.

"But you cooked me and yourself your first meal. It's always good to get that one out the way. Now, it's time to for you to help me get started."

Floyd looked terrified. "No, I won't make you cook for my customers. But you can watch me and help fetch what I need. OK? I don't expect perfection, but you better jump to it, kid."

"Yes sir…!" joked Floyd, performing a sloppy salute.

"You'd have been kicked out of any unit I ever heard of with a salute like that, you young idiot!" the older man laughed.

The boy suddenly looked extra interested. "You were in the army?"

A look of discomfort passed over Alvin's face. "No, Floyd."

"Musta been the navy then? Air Force. Did you fly planes? Wow that would be somethin' else..."

"No, Floyd. We'll talk about this another time. We need to feed our customers. Over there. See? The refrigerator? Fetch me a dozen eggs. See in the corner? There's the napkins and fancy stuff Janie deals with. Lay them out over there to help her get started.

"uhhh...OK."

"Then hop to it...?"

Five hours later, Floyd was drained. He'd never stopped. He thought it might never end. But Alvin kept up with his patter: barking orders, asking Floyd questions and telling him where he got it wrong. After some bumbling mistakes, the boy usually got it right.

He was so tired he didn't noticed that Alvin had been watching him. The older man approved. Floyd had no confidence and always approached a task like he might fail. When he failed he usually got angry at himself and anyone within his view to hide his embarrassment, but he always tried and often succeeded.

"I'd better let the dozen eggs go" he thought. "He was ashamed enough and cleaned it up as quickly as he could. We've all done it sometime…"

The older man continued to muse. "A good worker. Thorough. He's got some brains. Gets it wrong once and never again. Just needs building up… educating? Absolutely! That hole of a town kept him back for too long. No confidence. Too angry. How do we overcome that? Janie will have some ideas too… hmmm…"

At 11am things began to be quiet. The mountain of dishes and cups and plates and cutlery were washed and put away. Floyd's mouth opened wide in a jaw cracking yawn.

"Kid, go and have a break. I'll shout you for lunch."

"OK, Alvin."

Two hours later Alvin found Floyd asleep on his bed. Dead to the world. He looked so peaceful and he'd done much better than Alvin ever imagined. He silently left the room, down the stairs and into the front of the diner. He saw Janie working at the till.

"So. Stealing from me again, Janie…?" he joked.

"Why of course. How else can I live? And anyway I'm going to run off with Floyd when he's older."

"Cradle snatching, baby?"

"He's seventeen... lots of energy... you know?" she smirked at him. "Although you aren't too bad for a man of your vintage. I could trade you in, though?"

"Our trainee, with 'lots of energy', is fast asleep."

"Did you wake him?"

"No, I hadn't got the heart. He worked hard this morning, He has no skill at cooking though..."

"How bad was it? He didn't even see me when I came in earlier."

"Could be better. Burnt and cold is a polite way to describe it. He'll learn. At least I hope so."

"OK, I'll stick with you for now. You can cook and you've got more energy than Floyd. But that might change, Alvin?"

"And on that day I'll weep. Now, what's the takings this morning...?"

Floyd eventually woke at two pm. He was embarrassed as he stumbled down the stairs. Janie and Alvin greeted him with a smile.

"Hey, sleepyhead," called Janie.

Floyd glowed with embarrassment.

"Don't feel too bad, kid. You'll get used to it. In a year or two..."

Chapter 17 - Gwen

Floyd did as he was told. Mostly. He was slow to trust Janie and Alvin even though he genuinely liked them. He still railed angrily at them on occasion, but their response was to encourage him and keep him busy. They piled work on him until he wanted to drop.

Both of them teased him about his posture and nickname him 'The Little Storm Cloud'. His hands were still clasped in fists, his fixed gait like someone too used to trouble and he always looked fierce. His defensiveness was always on show. It took time, but he began to relax, smile more and walk easier, not so tight and tense. That tension that had filled his entire life was ebbing away. Some days Floyd was a mess: he knew he was free, but he still wanted to keep his guard up. He willed himself to relax, but it was tough.

Alvin fascinated Floyd. The boy knew that violence was part of the older man's nature. He'd seen it at the precinct, but there was another Alvin: easy-going, good-humoured and strangely cultured. There was always classical music or opera playing in the kitchen and Alvin would sing along, sometimes in German, Italian or French.

His language was mixed with snippets of Shakespeare and poetry and other writers Floyd had never heard of. There was another person behind Alvin's mask, Floyd was sure, neither brute, nor diner owner. Who he really was interested Floyd, but he knew better than to show too much interest.

Janie just smiled at Alvin's antics. It was if she had no idea who she was really dealing with. Floyd found her naivety and good-nature equally baffling and fascinating.

She was his saviour. Janie was always patient and kind. Alvin often got in a temper at Floyd's moods, but she was always there: tolerant, supportive and good-humoured. She got him to relax, to talk and got his mind away from Medusa. She was the glue that kept the diner and everyone in it: Alvin, Floyd and the customers. She made them all feel valued. Janie was the one who cared about everyone around her. That didn't mean she didn't tease him, or give him a hard time when he needed it

She was the first woman he'd had any sort of relationship with and he loved her in a starry-eyed way. He knew he'd do anything for her. She had become special to him. He spent a lot of time trying to hide it, but it was apparent to Alvin and Janie.

"He's sweet on you, baby."

"I know, Alvin. It's just a crush. That's all."

"I know. But the kid's had no-one for a long time. His Mom was a case, from what he's said. Not her fault, but you're more like a Mom to Floyd than she could be."

"Like a sister too."

"Sure. He's a lucky guy to have a sister like you."

Janie smiled back at Alvin. "He's lucky to have you too."

The older man loomed thoughtful. "Hope it can stay like that, Janie."

"What do you mean, Alvin?"

"He's a decent kid, but rough around the edges. I wouldn't take him at face value. He's had to survive by his own wits in Medusa. He's no saint, Janie."

"He wouldn't hurt us, Alvin."

Alvin paused. "No? Maybe so, but he has a hard edge to him. Jesus, how could he not where he's grown up? He needs a lot of managing, baby. Maybe years. He might have to get counselling. Who knows?"

Janie looked determined. "Whatever it takes, Alvin. I want to see him have a normal life."

Alvin smiled back. "Good. I feel the same too, but he responds better to you than me. You need to tell me if it gets too much?"

"Whatever it takes, Alvin."

"Have it your way, Janie. How's about we get to bed?"

She smirked back at him. "I can be persuaded, Alvin."

A few weeks later, Floyd had the beginnings of being a competent cook. He woke at five am, worked until eleven, had a nap and up again at one pm to help with lunch. At four pm he was given time off, but at seven pm it was back to work. He was utterly exhausted all the time and couldn't understand how Janie and Alvin managed their days.

"You get used to it, kid. You're doing better than a few weeks ago and you'll be better again. We're glad of the help though, aren't we, Janie?"

"Floyd, you're a life saver. Alvin and I have so much more time for each other..."

"I have no idea what you mean, Janie," Floyd grinned.

Alvin turned back to Floyd. "We think you need a reward, kid. How about a day out in Woosterville?"

Floyd looked bewildered. "I can? I thought you'd never let me?"

"Not today," Alvin called out. "There's a cell phone in the kitchen. It's yours. Get out of here for the day, but be back for seven this evening?"

"Now?"

"Yes, now. Would you like a written invitation, kid?"

"No, I'll go now." Floyd rushed to grab his coat.

"Got money, Floyd?" interrupted Alvin.

Floyd hesitated. "No..."

"Alvin took his wallet out. "Here's fifty bucks. Spend it wisely."

"I can't take money off you like that. Alvin?" protested Floyd.

"It's a loan against your first salary here, kid. No charity here. You owe me that fifty bucks out your pay next week. Understand?"

"Yeah, sure. I'll see you guys later?"

"Bye Floyd... Enjoy your day!" Janie called out.

The first thing Floyd did was buy a new notebook to replace the lost one and he started again as he did with his old one: scribbling away with his thoughts about the people and places he observed and ideas about their stories as he wandered aimlessly around Woosterville. There were little sketches of people's features and clothes with notes about how they moved and talked.

Floyd deliberately avoided the main bust terminus and the gallery. He wanted to see Sean Lynch and apologise, but he didn't know how to do it or what to say.

After a few hours of the streets and stores, he headed for the city park. Strangely, he felt lonely for the first time. Surrounded by so many people, but no-one of his own. No-one to share these experiences with. He thought of how happy Zeke would be to explore the city with him: his excitement and his need to experience everything.

He suddenly missed his Mom very much. He'd had little time to think of her and suddenly it was all there. He'd hated her sometimes, but it had never lasted. He'd never see her again. That was it. No family. No real friends. Nothing.

He sat there on the park bench, fighting his emotions. Tears fell, alternating with fits of anger at what had happened. He didn't notice the older lady sit next to him until she spoke.

"Are you well, young man?"

Floyd started. "Sure, I'm... I'm OK thanks, ma'am."

"You don't look 'OK', young man. In fact I don't see many people that upset in this park."

The lady was small, with grey hair and her voice was cultured and imperious, as if she was used to being obeyed, but there was a twinkle of amusement in her eyes.

Floyd sniffled and wiped his eyes with his sleeve. "I'm just getting over a bad time. You don't need to worry yourself about me."

"I can't help but worry when I see a young man sitting here all alone, upset. You look like you've been in an accident, darling."

"It's nothin, ma'am..."

"My name is Gwen. Please don't call me 'ma'am', it makes me feel old. And you are...?"

"Floyd, ma'am... I mean... Gwen."

Gwen stuck her hand out. "Pleased to meet you, Floyd."

Floyd shook it. "Pleased to meet you too, Gwen."

"Can you tell me what happened to you?"

"I can't, Gwen. My Mom died, but I can't say no more."

"Oh Floyd, I'm so sorry. You're very young to lose your mother, dear boy."

"Thanks. I've been busy for weeks, but now it's hit me." Floyd began to blubber again. He was embarrassed but just couldn't help himself.

Gwen put her hand on around his shoulders. "Time will heal, Floyd. Have you got family?"

"Yeah. I've got my Uncle. He's a great guy and keeps me busy."

"But it's not like having your own mother, is it?"

"No... no, it ain't."

"I'm here most days, Floyd. You can talk to me any time. I'd be happy to listen to you."

"What do you do, Gwen?"

"I'm retired now, but I used to work at the university. A Professor in the Sociology Department. I still like to watch people and see they do. That's why I visit the park. I haven't learnt to shut off the academic part of me yet."

Floyd smiled in agreement. "I like to people watch too. Just to get to understand what makes them tick. What I see sorta makes me want to write."

"A writer? How wonderful, Floyd! Have you ever submitted any of your work?"

"Hey, I didn't say I was any good?"

"Floyd, you'll be the last one to know that. Others are the best judge of what's good or not. Keep writing and writing and writing! Some of it will be garbage, but some of it will be good. A tiny percentage might be wonderful. When you're ready, I'll be happy to read some of your work and give you feedback. Do we have an agreement?"

Floyd smiled back. "It's a deal, Gwen."

"Good. I notice your tears are gone, dear. Talking to others helps, doesn't it?"

Floyd smiled at her. "Yeah, it sure does, Gwen."

They sat for an hour, watching the people come and go in the park. Observing, sometimes commenting. Gwen often made him laugh with her pithy comments about the foibles of humanity, especially her scathing comments about the guy with the toupee.

"It's so obvious... What does he think he's doing? That girl is half his age? Probably needs viagra just to talk to her..."

Floyd laughed until the tears nearly came again. He opened his notebook and wrote down some ideas, inspired by Gwen's monologues.

Gwen suddenly got to her feet. "I'm late for lunch. I must go. I'd rather stay and chat, but I have a tedious lunch appointment with an old student. It's been a pleasure to meet you, Floyd. I rarely get to talk to anyone intelligent these days, so you've made my day."

"Awww you don't need to..."

Gwen interrupted, the imperiousness returning. "Floyd, if a lady pays you a compliment, take it with grace."

Floyd smiled and then spoke formally back, but he couldn't quite hide his cheekiness. "Why, Gwen. It has been a pleasure to meet you too. I don't often spend time with attractive ladies and I have enjoyed our conversation too. I don't feel lonely like I did."

Gwen laughed at his antics. "It needs some work, but you could be a real charmer if you wanted to, young man. And don't think you're the only one who feels lonely. Thank you for your company, Floyd. See you again some time?"

She gave him a brief nod and was gone. He sat a while longer, enjoying the view of the park of the people, especially the girls his own age throwing a Frisbee around. Every time they looked back at him, he looked away shyly. He went over the conversation he had had with Gwen in his head. He felt better and more peaceful.

He wandered aimlessly back through Woosterville until it began to get dark.

Back at the diner, Floyd was greeted by Alvin "What did you get up to kid?"

"I got talkin' to a lady in the park."

"Oh? Young and pretty?"

"No. She was an older lady. Retired professor. Nice, though."

"Were you careful, Floyd?"

"Yeah. I said my name and I'd lost my Mom. That was all."

"What did she say about herself?"

"Gwen's a retired sociology lecturer. We sat and watched the people. She's funny."

"Good. It's great that you are starting to meet people. You seem to like academic types, though?

Floyd frowned. "Seems so. Ain't nothin' wrong with that, is there?"

"Not at all, kid. You have a brain, so use it. Do you plan to see her again?"

"She said she was there at the park most days. Is that OK?"

"Of course it is, kid. I wish you could just get on with your life and not tell me anything at all. Hopefully you can have secrets of your own again soon?"

"I wish. There were some really pretty girls at the park…"

Alvin grinned. "Go for it, kid. Just remember the rules. Don't get any of them pregnant, or I'll be very angry with you. Get me?"

Floyd was immediately indignant. "Holy fuck, I just want a day out with some people my age. Hell, anyone of any age. What makes you think it'll go that far?"

"Kid, I've seen the way our female customers look at you. Young and old. Hell, I've seen Janie checking you out too. I bet your friend Gwen is charmed by you too. 'Older' or not."

Floyd flushed with embarrassment. "I don't know why?" and then he grinned. "Maybe I just got it?"

Alvin laughed. "You little prick, 'course you got it! You aren't that good-looking, but everyone notices those eyes of yours. You can charm when you can be bothered. But you be careful. Don't get too involved with anyone. First our friend in Stone City needs to be taken care of. Second you're only seventeen. Third I think you're going to have some new options in the next few months…"

Floyd looked puzzled. "What do you mean...?"

Alvin got out his seat. "Time for the evening shift, Floyd."

Chapter 18 – A Near Miss

Floyd continued his regular trips out around his new city home on Wednesdays and Sundays. Sometimes he met Gwen twice a week, sometimes just once. There were always new distractions and things to see in Woosterville. He still got upset and angry, but just being out and about and talking to Gwen helped.

On this particular Wednesday afternoon, he was exploring the area around City Hall.

Floyd spotted Debbie before she could see him. He paused for a moment. She looked beautiful. She was so out of his league! What did she see in him? She seemed older than she looked in her nurse's uniform, but that didn't make her any less attractive.

"She's still a nutjob," he thought.

Before he could get away, she saw him and walked quickly towards Floyd giving him a radiant smile. Floyd felt a rush of attraction in return. "Why would a woman as beautiful as this like this be so pleased to see me?" he thought.

She gave him a hug. "Floyd, how are you?"

Floyd remained shy. "OK, thanks, Debbie."

She smiled again. "You look good, Floyd. You look better than good…. What are you doing here?"

"Just wanderin' about. Day off, so go-as-I-please."

"So where are we going?" she asked, staring at him intently.

Floyd stepped back, stuttering in response. "W…we? I don't think that's…"

"How about some time with me?" she interrupted, grabbing his hand.

Floyd came to a stop. "I… I can't, Debbie."

Debbie looked puzzled. "Why not?"

"I can't say, but I ain't allowed to get too involved with anyone."

She pouted. "I was hoping that we could spend some time together, Floyd?"

He stuttered, trying to think of excuses. "I can't, Debbie, I have to work. Maybe another time?"

Debbie, however, was insistent. "How about tomorrow night?"

"I can't, I'm working."

"Friday?"

"I work Friday evening too."

"Saturday?"

"Same."

"Sunday."

"It's my day off."

"You don't want to spend your day off with me?"

Floyd didn't know how to respond. He'd only just met her again and she wanted to take over his life? He began to feel frustrated at her strangeness.

"I can't spend time with you, Debbie. I have to work and sort out a life for me."

Debbie scowled. "I want to spend all the time with you."

"Well I ain't gonna be able to do that, Debbie."

Her sudden anger caught Floyd by surprise.

"I like you. I want to spend time with you. I want to spend the night with you. Do you like me or not?"

Seeing the doubt in his eyes was enough. "Fine!" she snapped. "What made me think that a limp-dick faggot kid you like was good enough for me?"

She stormed off without saying another word. Floyd was too shocked to know how to reply. When he got back to the diner his surly mood was noticed by Janie and Alvin.

"Floyd, what the hell is wrong with you, kid?"

"Nothin'," was the boy's reply.

"Can't fool me, kid. We've seen you moping since you got back from town. Care to say what it's about?"

"We're worried about you, Floyd," said Janie. "Is it something we've done?"

Floyd's face softened. "Awww Janie it ain't you. I came across Debbie near City Hall."

Alvin interrupted. "What did you do, Floyd?"

"She wanted to spend all her time with me." Floyd looked flustered. "Wanted me to… to spend the night with her."

Floyd went red. "I ain't ever… you know… with a girl. I only just met her. She was pissed and walked off. I told you she's a screwball!"

Alvin sighed. "Come and sit down, Floyd. You too Janie."

They sat in a booth out the front.

"You know I told you about not getting too involved, Floyd?"

"Yeah, I know, because of what happened to me."

"Sure. That's right, kid. But I gotta say this. Janie, I'm sorry baby if this offends."

"Say it Alvin, I won't be."

"Kid, I told you that've 'got it'. You know that don't you?"

"Sorta. I don't know why, Alvin?"

"Tell him Janie."

"Floyd. I see the customers react to you. Woman and men. You aren't pretty, but you get a reaction. The guy who usually sits at table 17? His eyes pop out his head! He always leaves a bigger tip when you serve him."

"You're kiddin' me, Janie?"

"No. I'm not, Floyd. Sometimes he looks like he wants to own you. It's sort of creepy. But he's never done anything so I've let it go. And it sounds like Debbie wanted to own you too."

"I was gonna say that too, baby."

"I know you were, Alvin. I'm not blind, am I?"

Alvin smiled at Janie. "You've got the brains too, baby."

"You're just a guy, Alvin. And you too, Floyd. Women usually know what's going on."

Janie turned back to Floyd. "Some women and some guys when they see what they want, they'll do anything to get it. Remember what I told you about Dino? He thought he owned me. I don't know if Debbie is like that. But alarm bells are going off from what you've said about her."

Floyd still looked puzzled. "I sorta like her, Janie. But I couldn't spend all my time with her or any one person. I have work. I like meeting Gwen. I like working with you guys. I want to explore the city and see new things. To spend all my time with one person? Because they want it like that? It would just be like Medusa where I only had Mom and nobody else."

"We wouldn't argue with that, kid. You need to build a life for yourself. Be your own guy. When you meet the right girl, she'll know that. And she'll appreciate that."

"Girls like Debbie ain't for me, that's for sure."

Janie smiled at him and patted his hand. "She wasn't, Floyd. They'll be others. Lots of others, I think."

Alvin chuckled. "And there's the guy at table 17 if you get stuck?"

Janie snorted with laughter and Floyd joined in too.

"I don't know what you'd do without you guys?"

Janie looked pleased. "We only told you what you knew already, Floyd. You know we're always happy to listen."

"It's true, kid. You pretty much got there yourself. We're just here to give you a nudge. I'll mention it to the hospital if you want?"

"I'd prefer to forget about her, Alvin."

The older man nodded. "Sure. But any more problems and we need to act. OK?"

Floyd nodded, absently. His mind was in a whirl trying to understand Debbie and her motivations, but he knew he had Alvin and Janie for support. He still wandered around Woosterville on his free Wednesdays and met Gwen in the park on Sundays. Although he wouldn't completely forget the Debbie experience, the way she had treated him faded from his memory.

He still kept an eye out for 'the fruitcake' while he meandered around Woosterville. Just in case. Floyd was beginning to understand that some people in life don't make any sense at all.

Chapter 19 - Brains and Beauty

After a few months Floyd had got into a routine. Medusa was a lifetime away. He had this new life and it was good. Alvin had stopped teasing him about being 'so intense'. He was relaxed. Sort of. But… he couldn't say anything to the guys at the diner, but he had begun to feel restless. Just a desire to do more. He was still writing and sketching ideas, but he was hitting a brick wall.

On the next Sunday, he spoke to Gwen about his frustrations. "I sorta want to do more. I've got ideas, but I don't know how to express them. It's gettin' frustratin'. I don't want to keep doin' the same thing."

"What would you like to do, Floyd?" Gwen asked. "Art? Writing? Sociology? I think you have a mind to do any of them, if you want to."

"I don't have any qualifications, Gwen."

"None?"

"No, the school couldn't wait to get rid of me."

"More fool them. They sound like idiots."

"Idiots is too nice, Gwen."

"Let me have a think. I know a Professor Lynch. Sean Lynch. He might be interested in talking to you. Don't get your hopes up, though?"

Floyd froze at the name, but tried not to react. "Yeah. Don't do it now, I need to think about it."

"When you want to Floyd, just tell me. Now, what do you think of that tree over there?"

"You mean the one with the girls over there with the frisbee?"

"Yes, that's the one. Notice how they all keep looking over at you. Why don't you go over and chat?"

"Ah, no, Gwen, I couldn't."

"Heaven's sake, why not? I'll get them over here if you like?"

"No! I have no time with work and I don't want to get too involved."

Gwen gave him a puzzled look. "No? It would do you good to spend time with people your own age, Floyd. Not with an old lady like me."

"I like talking to you, Gwen. What would they have to say that's more interesting?"

"Don't you find them attractive, Floyd?"

Floyd frowned. "I ain't gay, if that's what you're thinkin'!"

Gwen smiled back at him.

"I kinda met a girl here, Gwen. Debbie. I liked her, but she wanted to take over my life. I think she's crazy. When I wouldn't, she cut me off."

"Oh, Floyd! That isn't the experience I'd wish on anyone. You should still go over there. Play frisbee. Learn to be with girls your own age. Just as friends. It would be a new experience for you, don't you think? What have I said about writing and life experience?"

"Yeah... yeah. I know. OK, I'll do it. I don't like leaving you on your own, though."

"I'll be perfectly fine, Floyd. I'll watch you enjoying yourself in the company of a group of attractive young women. Look up the word 'vicarious' when you get home. It will remind me of my younger days. Watching you and them will be a treat for me. Now. Off you go!"

Floyd hesitantly approached the girls. "Do... do you mind if I join in?"

They all turned as one and most of them smiled back.

"Sure, why not?" said one

"You bet!" responded another.

"We were hoping you'd come over!"

"Cool. I'm Floyd, by the way..."

"Hi Floyd," they chorused back at him.

As they tossed the frisbee back and forth he learned their names. There was Marla, who Floyd couldn't fail to notice: tall, busty and athletic. She flirted outrageously with him. Her friend Julie looked stern and studious and made barbed comments at Marla whenever she focused on Floyd. He almost thought she looked jealous.

Ella was an aggressive player who flung the frisbee with energy. The gorgeous black girl seemed liked she wanted to take on the world, but went shy when Floyd caught her checking him out. He saw Trinity look at him too. He couldn't fail to notice how beautiful she was, but there was something about Trinity's manner that Floyd didn't like. She had contempt for him. He didn't know why, but he was wary of her.

There was Morgan, who was dressed in all the latest fashions. Floyd was attracted to her too, but she was plastered in make-up and lipstick. Everything was so perfect to the extent she didn't seem real at all.

Lastly there was Mary. She was plain looking, but her face lit up when she smiled. She blushed and looked away when he smiled back at her. She seemed to like him and he thought he quite liked her too.

Floyd occasionally looked over at Gwen and she gave him a wave when she saw him. The last time he looked, she was gone and being distracted he didn't see the frisbee which hit him in the back of the head. The girls squealed in concern as he fell to his knees, seeing stars.

A babble of voices surrounded him.

"Oh my gosh, are you OK?"

"He wasn't looking, I didn't mean it."

"Are you OK, cutie?"

"Yeah. I think so," Floyd gasped. "Just give me a minute."

The girls helped him sit down on the grass and they were around him, rubbing the back of his head and making sympathetic noises. After a few minutes, Floyd began to recover, although he still felt woozy.

"I'm OK, but I'd better get home"

You don't look OK, let us take you home."

"Julie can drive us."

"Yeah we can do that..."

"As long as she drives like she's got a brain..."

"Hey! At least I've got a licence!"

The chatter made his head spin, so he found it hard to disagree.

Floyd gave Julie directions to Alvin's Diner.

"I've heard of that place. It's old-fashioned," said Trinity, scornfully.

"Hey! The food is great!" replied Floyd defensively.

"Maybe but it's the sort of place my parents would go to. It's not for guys our age."

When they arrived, Floyd invited them in.

Janie watched in astonishment at the group of girls fussing over Floyd as they came in the diner door. She called through the kitchen door.

"Alvin, get out here! You'll love this! Our lover boy strikes again!"

Alvin was soon watching with a big smile as Floyd tried to explain what had happened, with the girls butting in with their own comments.

"Ladies! Ladies! Give Floyd a minute! What happened kid?"

"I was playing frisbee and I got it in the back of the head."

"Look at me, kid. Hmmm... your eyes are OK. No concussion, I don't think. How's your head?"

"A bit sore. I'll live. Got some tylenol?"

"Sure. Janie, got some under the counter?"

"Here you go, Alvin," she said, handing him the bottle.

"Thanks, baby. Can we get you ladies something to eat or drink while I check Floyd is OK?"

The girls found a table and had a Coke each, resuming their usual banter.

Ten minutes later Floyd came back down. The girls invited him to sit and he was soon interrogated about how he felt. Alvin and Janie continued to watch, amused.

Floyd suddenly looked up. "Hey Alvin. Can I pay for some food for these guys? They think this is a diner for older people!"

"We do great food here, ladies. What will you? It's all on Floyd, apparently?"

Alvin laughed at the look on Floyd's face. "Kid, I'm happy to do it to for free to say thanks to these ladies for looking after you."

The girls shrilly protested.

"No, we can pay"

"If it's good, I'll pay…."

"Don't be so mean, Julie. If you eat it, you can pay up!"

Alvin watched, still smiling. "Here's the menu. Let me know when you're ready?"

Floyd's head continued to spin. Surrounded by pretty girls who continued to talk amongst themselves relentlessly. He had no idea what was going on as they jumped from one topic to another, from the menu to Floyd, to the 'cute guys at the mall' to their schoolwork to 'that bitch Imelda' to the menu and back to Floyd again, round and round. Their perfume. The way they touched his shoulder and rubbed against his leg. It was all becoming a bit much for him.

He looked up helplessly at Janie and Alvin for help, but they just grinned back.

"Hey, Alvin! Do you need some help in the kitchen?"

"No, kid, you enjoy being with your new friends. Janie and I will be fine."

"But..."

"No, it's OK, Floyd. Janie, can you give me a hand?"

Janie smiled back. "I'd be delighted to, Alvin. Have fun Floyd."

The girls turned their attention back to him. There was more cooing as they asked him how he was. Yet again! Floyd forced himself to smile. He really didn't want the attention, but at the same time he loved it.

"I'm fine, thanks, guys. Have you decided what you'd like?"

There was more high-pitched chatter as they asked Floyd and each other what was the best meal. After ten minutes. Floyd decided he'd have enough and interrupted them.

"Why don't we all get something different and then share?"

"That's a great idea..."

"But I don't like tomato..."

"Well then don't eat tomato, Julie..."

"I'll eat the tomato, Julie."

"You'll eat anything, Marla..."

"You bitch! Wait 'til...."

"Guys! Guys!" interrupted Floyd. "I'm just gonna order, OK?"

The girls suddenly went quiet. Floyd caught Janie's eye and she walked up to their table.

"What can I get you guys?"

Everyone looked at Floyd. He was embarrassed at being the centre of attention again.

"Let's have the ribs, two of the triple burgers and lots of fries. Can we have the pulled pork sandwich too?

"Sides?" asked Janie, scribbling on her pad.

"Yeah. The coleslaw."

"I hate coleslaw!" interrupted Julie.

"Extra coleslaw for Julie" quipped Marla.

Floyd smiled. "Lots of coleslaw then."

Julie stuck her tongue out at him and he laughed back.

"Can we have some barbecue chicken as well, Floyd?" asked Erica.

"Sure! BBQ chicken too, Janie?"

Janie quickly wrote down their order. "Thanks, guys. Any more drinks?"

Once Janie had gone, the table went quiet. All the girls were looking at Floyd. The girls began to giggle at his discomfort.

"So are you guys all at school?", he asked, in desperation.

"Yes we're all at St. Vincent's. We graduate in September next year."

"What are you guys studying?" asked Floyd.

"I want to be a writer," replied Julie.

"You hate writing!" interrupted Marla.

"But the tutor is cute..."

"He's sooo cute..." agreed Marla.

"How about you, Marla?"

"I want to be a physical ed teacher."

He found himself staring at her again and quickly looked away. Marla smiled back and the others giggled.

"Looks like you like physical ed teachers, then Floyd?" said Julie.

Cue more giggling.

Floyd laughed too. "I ain't got much practice being with so many beautiful ladies."

There was a sudden silence and Floyd's heart dropped. Had he said the wrong thing?

Then the babble stared again.

"'Beautiful' he calls us..."

"Beautiful ladies...."

"We're going to keep this one..."

"'Ladies' he called us..."

"Not you, Marla. You're no lady..." interrupted Julie.

Marla looked furious. "You bitch! I'll..."

Ella raised her voice. "Stop it! Don't be so mean, Julie. Marla's beautiful. Both of you are ladies. When you feel like it."

"You're all beautiful," said Floyd.

"What, even Mary here?" said Marla.

Mary looked at the table.

"Mary too." said Floyd. "You're all beautiful in your own way."

Mary looked at him like a rabbit in the headlight. Then she looked at the table again.

"She is..."

"She's lovely..."

"You're so shy, Mary. Why don't you look up?"

Mary looked nervously around at them all.

"We all love you, Mary..."

"We love your eyes, Mary."

"Floyd likes you too...."

Floyd and Mary looked at each other and both looked at the table. Then shyly back up at each other.

"See? Made for each other..."

"Awww young love..."

"Does that mean you're boyfriend and girlfriend…?"

"Marla! You'll be marrying them off, next…"

"Just because I've got a boyfriend, Julie."

"How many hundred boyfriends have you had now, Marla?"

"Guys! Guys!" interrupted Floyd again, before the next outbreak of war. "Mary isn't my girlfriend, but I'd be happy to go and see a movie with you, Mary. If you want?"

Mary looked terrified. In a small voice, she spoke. "I'd… would you? I've never… you don't want to really. Do you?"

"Of course I do. Are you free Wednesday evening?"

"I… I think so. Have you got time? You might be busy? I don't want to waste your time."

"You ain't wastin' my time, Mary. Wednesday. Seven pm. I'll meet you at the Multiplex?"

"Say yes, Mary…."

"Hot date for Mary and Floyd…"

"Shut up Marla…"

"You shut up, Julie, at least Mary is having a date…"

Fortunately at this point, the drinks arrived.

Mary kept glancing at Floyd. When he saw her, she quickly looked away, but she had a faint smile on her face.

"It's like watching tennis," said Marla.

"Love-fifteen!" cackled Julie.

"Advantage, Floyd!" laughed Ella.

They all laughed, including Mary. She looked direct at Floyd and he looked back. "She really does look nice when she laughs," he thought.

"What are you studying, Floyd?"

"I ain't."

"You must be studying something, Floyd?" asked Marla.

"No. no… my Mom died a few months ago and Uncle Alvin let me live with him here."

A chorus of concerned coos started again. They hugged him and caressed him. The mention of his Mom made him feel down, but the girls' touches made him feel something else entirely. His mind began to wander.

"Where are you from, Floyd?" asked Julie

"Oh, a small town about seventy miles that-a-way," replied Floyd, vaguely.

"What's it called?"

"Do you mind if I don't talk about it?" Floyd said. "I'd like to forget it for now."

"Oh, Floyd. I'm so sorry for being nosey." said Julie.

"Nosey bitch!" said Marla.

"Marla! Don't be so nasty!" said Floyd.

Marla suddenly looked contrite. "Sorry Floyd. Sorry, Julie."

"So will you go back to school?" asked Julie.

"I don't know. I'd like to study, but I didn't like school much."

267

"What do you like doing, Floyd?" asked Mary quietly.

"I sorta like writing. But I like drawing, too." He pulled the notebook out of his back pocket and opened it.

Floyd passed the notebook around. "Hope you don't mind. I saw the four of you with the frisbee and I did some little sketches."

"That's you, Julie! Look, he's got you smiling! How did he do that?"

"You've made me look good, Floyd. Look at you, Marla. But your boobs aren't as big as that!" said Julie.

"Yes they are! Floyd's got them just right" and she gave Floyd a smouldering look. "Perhaps I could get you a closer view sometime?"

Julie laughed. "You're such a tease, Marla. Don't frighten off the artist!"

Floyd was relieved when the starters arrived.

The girls continued to talk as they ate, but thankfully for Floyd, not so much. He began to relax and enjoy their company. For the first time he had female company and he found that he liked it.

Janie walked back to theit table. "How's the food, guys?"

"It's really good!"

"It's delicious..."

"Not as delicious as Floyd..." flirted Marla.

"Stop being such a tease, Marla..."

"I can tease Floyd if I like..."

"We like him without wanting to jump his bones, Marla!"

Floyd just sat there, smiling. They enjoyed the food and they liked being with him. That pleased him. They liked him for who he was, so it didn't matter what anyone else might think. Even himself.

"Would you come back here?" asked Floyd.

"Sure, but we want you with us..."

"It wouldn't be the same without you, Floyd..."

"I'd like him to serve us..."

"He'd look cute in an apron..."

They all laughed. Floyd felt bolder. "If it takes an apron, I'm happy to get you back here. This place needs more beautiful girls, so I expect you back next Sunday!"

The girls giggled again.

Alvin and Janie watched from the kitchen with a mixture of pride and some concern.

"He's a flirt machine, Alvin."

"I know. Charming as hell. A dog! What do we do, Janie?"

"Let him flirt. Look what it's doing for his confidence. But you need to give him the talk again. Nothing wrong with a few dates, but keep his feet on the ground."

"That Marla doesn't know how to keep her feet on the ground at all, baby!"

"Dirty old man!" laughed Janie.

"Hey! I was a dirty young man once. I can spot 'em and she's trouble."

"I know, Alvin, but we can only warn him. And get him some condoms."

"Why me?"

"Well. 'Uncle Alvin', you're his closest relation, so it's your job, buddy!"

Alvin scowled. "I thought we'd be giving him a job and a place to stay, not managing his sex life too, Janie!"

Janie laughed. "We never had any kids, Alvin. But we've got one now."

Alvin's face softened. "Yeah. We have. Could be worse. He's a good kid. Even if he might be a teenage Casanova in the making?"

"Condoms. And 'the talk'. As soon as they're gone. OK?"

Alvin sighed. "OK, Janie."

The girls loved the meal and said they would be back.

"Meet us in the park and we'll come over here, Floyd."

"Can we bring some friends?"

"We'll invite some cute guys too!"

"Invite who you like, Marla," replied Floyd.

"Marla will invite the whole swim team!"

"Shut up Julie, you can't even get a guy!"

"Ladies! Ladies! Let's not spoil the meal!" said Floyd.

Mary just looked at him and smiled.

"I'll see you, Mary, next Wednesday at the Multiplex."

The other girls whooped.

"Mary's got a hot date! Mary's got a hot date!" they chanted.

Mary was scarlet but laughed too. She looked again at Floyd like he was the centre of the whole universe.

Floyd sighed at the teasing, but forced a smiled back. He knew that was it was all in fun. He hoped?

"Hey guys, I've got to go." said Julie.

"Julie's got a hot date too?" joked Marla.

"Sure have! Just not with the whole football team."

Marla shrieked with indignation.

"Guys! Guys! The bill?" interrupted Floyd.

The girls went quiet again, sorting out their money. When they saw Floyd open his wallet they protested.

"We'll pay for you, Floyd!"

"Yeah we've had such a great time!"

"Let us pay for you, cutie..."

"I couldn't let you all pay for me like that." he protested.

"We'll sulk...!"

"We won't let you play frisbee again..."

"We'll sulk for weeks..."

And suddenly Mary spoke up. "If you don't let us pay, no hot date on Wednesday!"

The whole group erupted into laughter and Floyd conceded. "Ok! Ok! I know when I'm beat! Just this once."

Janie came over with the bill and the girls paid up, one by one.

"Thanks guys, was everything OK?"

"It was great Janie…"

"Thanks Janie, we'll come again…"

"We'll tell everyone about the food here…"

Janie was delighted. "Thanks, everybody. See you again soon?"

"See ya Janie…"

"Next Sunday for sure…"

"Make sure cutie has his day off…."

"Yeah we want Floyd for frisbee and food…"

Janie left them to it as they left the diner in an excited babble.

Floyd followed them out and each of them gave him a hug. Marla gave him a kiss on the cheek. "More where that came from, Floyd. If you want?" she whispered.

Then they were gone. Floyd came back inside looking very tired.

"Well done kid," said Alvin.

"Some new customers for us, Floyd," added Janie.

"I know! But I'm beat. They are all great guys but I can't keep up with them..."

"Welcome to the world of guys, kid. Women are beautiful but they make our heads spin!" laughed Alvin.

"That's what you're there for, Alvin" smirked Janie. "And you are for them, Floyd."

Janie turned back to Alvin. "Time for 'the talk', big goof..."

Floyd looked puzzled. "The talk? What's that, Alvin?"

"Let's go upstairs where it's more private, kid."

They settled in the den.

"So, kid. Had a nice day?"

"Yeah sure. I met Gwen and she made me talk to the girls. And here they all are."

"Brains and beauty, kid?"

Floyd flushed.

"What do you mean, Alvin?"

"I mean you seem to be good with girls, kid."

"So…?"

"Good at charming attractive young women, Floyd."

"There ain't no law against me talking to girls is there?"

Alvin laughed. "If there was we'd all be in jail, kid!" But then he turned serious.

"Kid, you're seventeen. You've spent the afternoon with a group of gorgeous young women. You can't tell me that didn't make you… well…"

Floyd tried to look innocent. "Well what, Alvin?"

Alvin laughed again. "You know very well what I mean, you little jerk! Anyhow, play games if you like. Tomorrow, I'll get you a box of condoms. A big box I think?"

"I... you want to what?" But... I... I ain't ever done... you know..."

Alvin tried to look innocent. "Done what, Floyd?"

Floyd hesitated. "You know darned well what I mean, Alvin!"

Alvin smiled. "Whether you have or you haven't isn't important kid. But your chances of whatever it is happening has just gone up six-fold from what I can see."

"But they're just my friends..."

"Friends they may be, but remaining friends? I've seen the way some of them look at you. Whether it's Marla the man-eater or shy Mary, or the others who pretend they don't, they all like you Floyd. And that might not necessarily be as a friend in the future."

"But I'd never..."

"'Never' with a guy your age and a pretty girl? Tell me you aren't attracted to them, then?"

"Well sure. They are all pretty…"

"Not pretty, kid. 'Gorgeous'. Any guy from fifteen to a hundred fifteen would see that. And they like you. So a box of condoms you will get and you will carry a few in your wallet. At all times. OK?"

"Yeah. Sure. But I won't need them. I ain't that sort of guy. I'd want to get to know them first. I do remember what Debbie was like, you know?"

"Good. Debbie isn't all women. They're all different Floyd."

"I ain't blind, Alvin!"

"No you aren't, kid. But you're a bit blind to how women see you. You've joked with me that you've 'got it'. It's not a joke, Floyd. You've got some sort of appeal and it can make your life fun or it can make your life hell."

"I ain't that sort of guy!"

"No you aren't kid. You're a decent young guy. But there's not many young guys who can resist a beautiful women. Most of us don't get that level of temptation. But you're different, Floyd. Women do like you. Young and old. I'd bet that Gwen likes you too."

"Gwen? She's like a Grandma to me!"

"But she's not dead yet, Floyd. She's not as old as you might think. And there's few women who'd say 'No' to an opportunity to talk to a young guy who has a brain."

Alvin grinned. "Don't get ideas you're some sort of pin-up. You really aren't. But looks aren't everything, you know?"

"But we talk about art and writing, there's nothing..."

"Like I said, you've got some brains too. Makes you even more attractive in some women's eyes. Those eyes, decent and brainy too."

"I ain't decent! And I ain't brainy!"

"You're still blind to yourself, kid. Ask Gwen the next time you see her. If she thinks you have potential. How much do you want to bet she says you've got potential?"

"This is ridiculous, Alvin."

"How much, kid?"

"OK, ten dollars."

Alvin laughed. "Ten dollars? You better man up, kid. Hundred dollars. You in?"

"Where am I gonna get a hundred dollars?"

"Your salary. Coming up next week. Missing one hundred dollars if Professor Gwen says what I think she will say."

Floyd paused. "This is stupid. She'll never say that."

"Hundred bucks says she will?"

"OK. Darn it, you're on!"

And they shook hands on it.

"Oh yeah. I forgot. If Gwen thinks you have a brain, Janie and I expect you to use it."

"What do you mean, Alvin?"

"Time you went back to school, kid."

"School? What do I ever want to do that for again? I won't do it!"

Alvin rubbed his temples and sighed.

"When I say 'school', I mean studying at a local college or at university, kid."

"I don't want to, Alvin."

Alvin sighed again. "You're my employee, kid. I want you to go and learn one day a week. I don't mind what you do, as long as you try."

"What would I do?"

"How should I know, kid? Maybe you should go and talk to Sean Lynch at the gallery?"

"But what would I say? I was like an idiot, the way I talked to him."

"Kid, he's a lecturer. He's met lots of idiots before, even worse than you."

Floyd rolled his yes. "Gee, thanks, Alvin."

"Did he say you were an idiot?"

"No."

"Then what did he say?"

"He said her liked the way I thought about things."

"Well there you go!"

"He was just sayin' it..."

"Here's the deal, kid. You ask Gwen and she says she thinks you've got a brain, you owe me a hundred bucks. If you go see Sean I'll let you off."

"Why would you do that for me?"

"Why not? Janie and I know you've got potential. We want to see you get on with your life, but you don't seem to see that potential in yourself."

"But I like it here. You ain't gonna kick me out? You and Janie are all I've got, Alvin."

"Kid. I'll never kick you out. When you want to go, you'll go. There's a job for you here as long as you want it. But both Janie and I know you've got more to you than being a kitchen worker."

"OK. I'll do it. I'll ask Gwen."

"Go for it, Floyd. Now get back to work! We've got a ton of washing up and cleaning for you to get on with."

Chapter 20 – Girls, Dates and Being Primitive

Floyd messed around with his hair, yet again. It still didn't look right. He'd had to shave (Alvin's suggestion), but mercifully without cutting himself. Why was he so nervous?

It was Wednesday and he had a movie date with Mary.

He wanted to chicken out. He didn't know who she was, or what she liked or what was her favourite movie and what to say at all. When he got downstairs he asked Alvin.

The older man looked incredulous. "You want me to tell you what to say? No way, kid."

"But what do I say?"

"You just told me what you don't know about her."

"Isn't that the problem?"

"Then ask her, dummy? 'What's your favourite movie, Mary?' 'What do you like doing, Mary?' 'What are you studying, Mary?'"

"It can't be as simple as that, Alvin."

"What...? Simple? Taking an interest in someone else means asking questions and appreciating the answers! It's how people find out if they have things in common. It isn't simple at all. Floyd. But you've got to do it. So get!"

As he grabbed his coat, Alvin spoke again. "You look like a storm cloud. Fists. Scowl. Like you're going to a brawl."

"Shit," Floyd mumbled to himself, willing himself to relax. Alvin was a pain in the ass, but he had a point. He turned to Alvin, with a cheesy, glassy-eyed grin.

"See? Happy? Relaxed?"

The older man gave a huff of laughter, shaking his head. "Yeah, sure. Oscar material, Floyd. Enjoy yourself, OK? Now get lost."

She was in the lobby of the movie house and waved at him.

"She's got a great smile," he thought. So he smiled back and it didn't hurt. He was surprised how pleased he was to see her.

Floyd kissed Mary on the cheek and she reddened, but immediately kissed him back.

"What are we going to see?"

"Why don't you decide, Mary?"

"I've heard things about that one?" Mary pointed at the signs for 'Wearing Her Shoes'. "Can we see that tonight?"

Floyd groaned inwardly. "A chick flick...", but he smiled. "Sure. Let's go..."

Two hours later, he was free and they walked together along the sidewalk.

"What did you think, Floyd?"

"It was good. I liked it."

She smiled. "You hated it really, didn't you?"

Floyd hesitated. "Uh... yeah. I did. Do you mind?"

"No, not at all. I thought it was pretentious and boring. Let's try a boy's movie next time?"

"There's gonna be another time?"

"Of course. I like being with you, Floyd. Why wouldn't I? Can we get something to eat?"

It was just a burger in a McDonald's, but they were in there for the next hour, Floyd carefully asking questions about Mary: the scholar, the would be scientist, her aim to be a biologist and her dreams for the future. Floyd felt his answers were drab in comparison.

"Just because you aren't at a school doesn't make you a dummy, Floyd."

"Compared to you, I'm a dummy, Mary."

"That's not true, Floyd. You've listened more about what I want to do than anyone I've ever met. Most people are bored by me. That's why I'm quiet, in case I bore others."

"Mary! You ain't boring. I've had a great evening with you. Getting to know you has been fun."

Another smile lit up her face as she hugged him. "You mean it? Thank you, Floyd!"

He hugged her back. Mary sounded as unconfident as him, in her own way. She was clever and thoughtful, but she thought of herself as boring?

Suddenly, she sat up. "The time? It's 10.30pm! I promised Mom and Dad I'd be back at 10!"

"Jeez, Mary, you better get gone."

Mary kissed him again on the cheek as they hailed a cab. Quickly she got in, leaving Floyd to walk back home, alone.

Janie and Alvin were closing up the diner when he got back.

"A hot date, kid?"

"Alvin. Don't embarrass him. It's his first proper date. How did it go, Floyd?"

"It went fine. We saw a movie. We both hated it, though. Then we went to McDonald's and we talked."

"Is that all?" said Alvin suspiciously.

"Yeah. That's all. I like her. She likes me. I like her company. Is that OK?"

"That's perfectly fine, Floyd. Is it going to stay like that?"

"I dunno, Alvin. I'll... we'll take it as it comes along."

"That sounds great, kid. Mary is a friend and that's the best thing for you both at the moment."

"Do you guys want help cleaning up?"

"Thanks, Floyd. Can you help Janie clear the tables and get everything into the kitchen? Then there's lots of dishes to wash, as usual."

"Just give me a minute, Janie."

Floyd stood in front of the sink washing dishes, but his mind was elsewhere. He thought of Mary: her face, her laugh, her affection for him and her clever mind. But she thought he was clever too? Normally, he'd reject praise, but she really seemed to believe it.

It made him think again about Alvin's bet. A hundred dollars? Maybe he might lose it?

The next Sunday, Floyd met Gwen in the park as usual. The girls were already there, throwing their frisbee around. They waved when they saw him.

"You've made some friends then, Floyd?"

Floyd grinned foolishly. "I seem to have, Gwen."

She smiled back at him. "What I wouldn't give to be their age again..."

Floyd's smile faded. He didn't know how to respond.

Gwen gave a little cough and sat upright. "Anyway, how are you besides, Floyd?"

"I'm OK, Gwen. The diner keeps me busy. But Alvin wants me to ask you a question."

"Oh?"

"Yeah. He thinks I'm smart and should go to college. I thought he was makin' fun of me. I ain't smart."

The old lady looked shocked. "Floyd! How could you think that?"

He paused. "I guess that sorta answers my question. He wanted me to ask you if you thought I had any brains."

"Floyd. Look at me. I have met many students over the years. I've met a handful or two I've enjoyed seeing learn and become something useful. Someone important. It's in you too, Floyd."

"You can't mean that, Gwen?"

"Then why am I saying it, Floyd? You may have noticed I don't suffer fools gladly. If that's so, why am I still talking to you every Sunday?"

"I ain't a fool?"

"Precisely!"

"So you think I'm clever?"

Gwen smiled. "You have a natural, raw talent for observation, writing and drawing. Quite honestly, you're rather primitive. A rough diamond. But you can learn the disciplines to improve and be something special, I think."

Floyd raised his eyebrows. "Primitive? Gee, thanks, Gwen."

"You are rather raw and untrained, Floyd. You need a good patron. I think I have someone in mind. His name is Sean Lynch. He's..."

"I've met him," interrupted Floyd.

"You have? How wonderful! He's such a great advocate for the arts. He must have seen something in you too."

Floyd hesitated. "Well... it... it didn't go very well."

"Sean is a darling man. What happened, Floyd?"

"Well... he saw me in the gallery lookin' at the pictures. It was the 'Venus of Urbino'. I was writing notes. He came over and talked to me."

"What did you do, Floyd?"

"He said he liked how I thought about things and I told him I was a fool. That's what they called me in Med... at home. And I got angry when he praised me. I ain't never had anyone talk to me like that before. I... I thought he was hittin' on me. Gwen, I'm such an idiot!"

Gwen looked at him for a moment in complete astonishment, then gave an unladylike snort of laughter. "Oh Floyd, what a character you are. Sean would have been horrified at the time, but he'll see the humour of it, now. You must go and see him. I'll happily write a letter for you."

"But what if he doesn't want to see me?"

"But me no buts, Floyd. He'll see you. If he saw something then, he'll see it now."

"You sure?"

Gwen gave Floyd one of her impatient glares. He put his hands up in defence. "OK, OK, I'll do it! Just no more death ray looks?"

Gwen laughed at him. "Only if you deserve it, Floyd. Now, tell me what you're thinking when you see the park. This time, ignore the people. You're good at observing humanity, now shift your attention to..."

An hour later, Floyd was tired. Gwen pushed him and challenged everything he said. Not to criticise, but to get him thinking. "It's 'The Socratic Approach', Floyd," she explained.

"What's that?"

"You've heard of Socrates I hope?"

Floyd frowned. "Greek guy?"

"Any more…?"

"Wrote stuff?"

Gwen sighed. "You'll have to do better than that, Floyd."

"I dunno. Phil… philosopher. He thought about things a lot."

"Better. But still not enough. I'll get you a book."

Floyd looked at her in horror. "Me? A book? Reading?"

She grinned back at him. "Yes. You. Reading. How else will you learn?"

"I'm too stupid, y'know."

Gwen pulled a face. "We've discussed that, Floyd. Now back to Socrates. He said 'I'm not here to teach you, I'm here to make you think'. What do you think about that?"

"You're doing it to me?"

"Precisely! Clever boy! I'm trying to make you think."

"But why?"

"Floyd, everything you do is instinctive. 'Primitive' as I said. You lack knowledge and structure. You lack even the knowledge to create a structure for you to learn. You've never learned how to learn. Does that make sense?"

"Yeah, sure. No-one ever taught me to learn. They just ignored me or shouted at me."

"So my task is to give you some knowledge and tools to help you know how to learn."

"How long will that take?"

Gwen began to laugh. "How long is a piece of string, Floyd? I'm still learning. I'll never stop learning. Until I die. Neither should you."

"No, I get you. So always learning? I can do that!"

"I'll get you some books."

"More books?"

"Yes, Floyd. More and more and more books. Now go and meet your friends and enjoy yourself."

Floyd gave her a hug. "Thanks, Gwen! See you next week!"

Gwen smiled sadly as he walked away. "Oh, to be seventeen again... never mind about that you silly old fool! What books does he need?"

She admired the young people for a while, as they ran around throwing the Frisbee: their beauty and their enthusiasm. She couldn't quite shake a feeling of jealousy.

Chapter 21 – Revelations

Floyd had another enjoyable Sunday talking to Gwen and then with the girls for the rest of the afternoon, then back to the diner. Janie was her usual friendly self, but Floyd noticed that Alvin was 'off' with him and everyone else. The older man was distant and distracted. The girls started their latest mock fight, so Floyd thought no more about it. It had become his job on Sunday's to referee Marla and Julie's arguments.

When they'd all gone, Floyd was in the kitchen helping. Alvin came in, looking even more serious.

"Kid, I need a word. Janie, can you manage by yourself for a while?"

"Sure, Alvin."

"Let's go upstairs, Floyd."

They sat in the den.

"They want you back at the station, Floyd."

Floyd froze. "For what?"

"More questions."

"Fuck, not more? How many more? Just when I started to get a life!"

"I'll be with you, kid. Every step of the way. I'll make some calls. Might just be routine. But we need to get there tomorrow morning, early. OK?"

Floyd looked sullenly at the floor. "Yeah... sure."

"Just one thing, Floyd."

"What?"

"Don't think of running away. We'll get through this."

Floyd tried to look innocent. "Why would I do that?"

Alvin gave him a grim smile. "One, because I've seen you run before and two, I've seen other people look just like you do now and run. Far too many. So don't do it, kid. Don't even think about it."

"I don't want to go to jail, Alvin."

"You won't, kid. Let me call my contacts."

The night was misery. Floyd was moody and withdrawn and Alvin was distant. Then the normally good-humoured Janie flew into a temper.

"I've had enough! What is wrong with you two guys? All evening, you in a mood and you with your mind somewhere else. I can't work like this! I need my two guys with me this evening, not you two losers!"

She stormed out of the kitchen and up the stairs.

"I'll handle it, kid."

Floyd looked defiant. "No. This is about me. I'll talk to her."

Alvin hesitated. "Go on then. You better do it right, kid, or you'll answer to me."

Floyd looked scornful. "As if I'd ever hurt Janie?"

"Good. Remember that. Tell her I'll speak to her later."

Floyd found Janie in the den, sitting in her favourite armchair staring into nothing.

"Hey," he called.

"What do you want?"

"To say I'm sorry. From Alvin too."

"Why are you both being like this? You know I depend on both of you. We make such a good team, but this evening... what's going on?"

Floyd sat on the arm of the chair and put his arm around her. "It's not you. It's me. I've gotta see the cops again tomorrow. I thought it was all over. Alvin will come with me."

Janie hugged him back. "Oh, Alvin, what do they want?"

"More questions, Alvin said. There's always more and more friggin' questions."

"Alvin and I will do anything to help you, Floyd."

"I know you will. I'm just hoping that's enough."

"You've never told me what happened, Floyd."

Floyd paused. He didn't know how to say it. "You know my Mom died?"

"Yes, Alvin told me."

"The local cops said I did it. I killed her."

Janie looked horrified. "Alvin told me that, too. I can't believe you'd ever do that, Floyd."

"You know?"

"Of course I know. It's my job here to manage you and that big goof downstairs."

"I didn't do it. The local doctor was pressured to say I killed Mom. I didn't. I couldn't. The cops here believe me, but they have more questions."

Janie hugged him again. "When I said we'd do 'anything' to help you, Floyd, I meant that. Alvin and I will help you. No matter what anyone else might say. We know you could never do such a thing."

"Thanks, Janie. I'll get back to work. And I feel better too!"

"Go on. Tell him in the kitchen I forgive him too."

"He's worrying about me too. You know what he's like."

"Tell him I love him too."

Floyd smirked. "'I love you, you big goof' might be better coming from you, Janie?"

Janie laughed. "No, I want you to do it. Tell me how he reacts!"

Floyd went back down the stairs and into the kitchen. Alvin was busy preparing food.

"I love you, you big goof!" said Floyd.

Alvin froze and then turned. "You do, do you?"

"Oh yes. Janie loves you too."

A smile crossed his face. "Good. I love you too, you little jerk. Now those vegetable don't prepare themselves, so get on with it!"

When Janie came back down the stairs, the two guys were back at work and the atmosphere was much better. She soon joined them and their usual banter resumed.

The evening flew as usual and a tired Floyd got to bed late, but he found it hard to settle to sleep.

It was a worn out Floyd that woke to Alvin's regular knock on the door. They prepared the daily breakfasts and were busy until ten am. Floyd's apprehension grew as the morning rush slowed.

"We'd better go, kid."

"Yeah, I know. When do you want to leave?"

"Get your coat. We don't need anything else."

They were soon in the car and driving downtown.

"It's the same guys you met before, Floyd."

"What the hell more do they want?"

"They aren't regular cops, so they won't be throwing you in jail. I'm not entirely sure what they want. We'll soon know."

The desk sergeant spotted them and made a call. Floyd and Alvin were rapidly taken back into the interview room they had been in before and they waited. The same group of hard looking men came into the room. They nodded briefly at Floyd but looked with respect at Alvin.

"Floyd, this is Saul Hanser. You don't need to know who anyone else is."

Saul nodded at Floyd, who nervously nodded back.

"What's going on, guys?" said Alvin.

"We're a go with Medusa. Our guys are ready. FBI too. We couldn't get in direct contact with the Dr Masters that Floyd mentioned. His wife and daughters are still at home. We'll make sure they are safe."

"Good news, Saul. When?"

"Three days. We want Floyd out of the way so we'll put him in a safe house."

"The kid is safe with me."

"Alvin, he's a main witness. We can't afford..."

"He's safe with me. End of conversation."

Saul sighed. "OK, but you know what will happen if we don't get this right?"

"You know I know. Anything else?"

"We wanted to talk to Floyd again about Medusa."

Floyd groaned. "I think I said what I wanted to say. About a million times?"

Saul ignored Floyd. "Alvin, we need to check."

"I wish I had my old notebook," said Floyd.

"Notebook. Why?" said Alvin.

"Sometimes I saw things I didn't understand. I know now what was going on. But I lost the notebook when I first came to Woosterville."

Alvin laughed. "Get me a phone, guys."

"What? Why do you need a phone?"

"Sean Lynch has your notebook."

"He does? How do you know? You've met Sean? What's going on?"

"Later, Floyd."

"No! Not later! Now! What's goin' on?"

Alvin hesitated. "I met him to find out who he was. We discussed your potential. He read the notebook and he likes the way you think. I told him to leave it until all this was over. Is that enough for you?"

"You did all that behind my back? You've got no right..."

The older man scowled at Floyd. "Shuddup, kid! I've got every right to keep you safe!"

303

"I'm not a child! You can't..."

"Enough!" roared Alvin. "Remember what I said about you doing what I ask? This is one of those times."

"You can't just..."

"Yes I can! So can these guys! You have the life they and I make for you until that son-of-a-bitch Sanchez is down. Do you understand?"

Floyd froze. He was completely at the mercy of Alvin and these men. Once again at the mercy of others. It frightened him but something about it made his blood boil too.

"What do you want from me?" he said quietly.

"The truth, kid. Your observations of Medusa. Who you saw, what happened? Backed up by your notebook. Then you're a free man."

"OK."

"OK, what, kid?"

"OK. I'll do what you want. Then I'll go away and I never want to see you again."

"Is that what you really want? Or is this anger speaking?"

The boy responded quietly. "It's what I want."

"Very well, Floyd. But at home we keep civil. Janie is not to know anything. You still understand that?"

"I understand enough about you now, Alvin."

Alvin turned to the other men. "OK guys, what else?"

Saul looked hesitant. "DNA test results."

Alvin looked puzzled. "Why DNA results?"

"Doc Bennett took DNA samples from Floyd after he was arrested. We got the results."

"Is this relevant to the kid, Saul?"

"I'm afraid it is."

"Then spill the beans!"

"Alvin. Floyd isn't going to like this, but it is relevant to the case and the prosecution. It needs to be managed carefully."

Floyd interrupted. "What's going on?"

Saul turned to Floyd. "We found a match to your DNA."

"Who?"

Alvin looked concerned at Floyd and back at Saul. "Yeah, who? The kid needs to know."

The big guy sighed again. "The closest match to Floyd is that of Theodore Sanchez."

"You've gotta be kidding!" said Alvin.

Floyd just stared. There was a roaring in his ears. He couldn't think at all. "I have to get out..." he said quietly.

"Just a minute kid. So what relationship is Sanchez to Floyd?"

"Definitive result is he's Floyd's father."

"Jesus!" replied Alvin, completely horrified.

"I have to get out of here..." said Floyd, a little louder.

"I know kid. I can't even begin to understand what you're thinking, but can you just wait..."

Floyd began to shout "I have to get out now, let me out..."

He lunged for the locked door, pulling at the handle more and more violently. The men were stunned at his reaction, but then began to pull him away from the door. They realised their mistake as Floyd attacked. Biting, kicking, punching, head-butting and scratching, like he was possessed. Floyd made not one sound apart from laboured breathing as he fiercely resisted any approach.

Floyd made a mess of everyone who came near. All of them became bloody and bruised from his attacks. One of the cops sat doubled in a chair nursing a kick between the legs. It took four of them to restrain him in the end with cuffs. He still tried to bite anyone who came near.

Alvin watched in horror. He'd seen Floyd angry an upset, but he'd never seen the kid like this. The boy was literally possessed with rage.

"Kid. Floyd. Will you stop? Please?", but Floyd continued to resist.

In the end the cops had no choice but to put him in a cell and remain cuffed. Doctor Bennett, the precinct physician gave him a sedative to help him relax. The doctor looked troubled.

"I need to talk to you, Alvin. Don't put me off."

"OK, Doc. Just let me finish with Saul and the other guys."

Alvin and the other men went back to the interview room.

Alvin collapsed into the nearest chair. "Well that went well?"

Hanser looked shocked. "I thought he was a nice kid, Alvin? But he's an animal! Look what he did to all of us..."

"I know. I don't know what to say. I think after the past few months he thought he was safe. Now he knows that son-of-a-bitch Sanchez is his father. Who wouldn't snap?"

"What do we do? He's our key witness. We'll have the notebook, but he's the only one that can tell us the meaning of what he's written."

"Wait until the Doc's report, Saul."

"Alvin, he's too vulnerable. Sanchez's defence will rip him to shreds. They'll ask for DNA evidence too. Once there's a relationship proven they'll play it as a family rift and an ungrateful son. There's no way Floyd is fit to respond to those claims."

"I know, Saul. But I still think the kid is made of sterner stuff than that."

"It also explains why he isn't dead. Even Sanchez couldn't do that to his own son."

"You make him sound saintly, Saul!"

"You know that's how they'll play it, Alvin."

"OK. Here's the plan. Get the notebook. Get your guys working on it with questions for Floyd? We'll assume the kid will come through."

"We'll happily do that for you, Alvin."

"Can you delay the op in Stone City?"

Saul sighed once more. "Difficult. Everything is in place. We've got the Masters family under observation and we can't keep people there for weeks. The entire family are useful witnesses too."

"Due to go in three days."

"That's the long and short of it, Alvin."

"Then I've got two days to get that kid back on board."

"Make it a day, Alvin. We need testimony and a hell of a lot of work to get Floyd's notebook and his comments turned into even basic prosecution material."

"Get the notebook now. I'll phone Sean Lynch. He'll be expecting you."

"OK. Let's see if I've got anyone in one piece after Floyd's rampage..."

Alvin laughed grimly. "If you could harness that anger, he'd make a good cop, don't you think?"

Hanser looked troubled. "With his background? I doubt it Alvin."

"It worked for you, Saul."

"I know. But that was a long time ago. I'll speak to you later, Boss. You need to call your guy. Johnson, Berthoff, get to City Gallery and ask for Sean Lynch. He'll have a notebook. The rest of you, go and see Doctor Bennet to be checked over."

The men were soon gone.

"I'd better see how the kid is, Saul."

"Good luck with that, Alvin."

Floyd was still lying on the cot in the cell. Alvin spoke softly.

"Kid? Floyd? Can you hear me?"

There was no response. Alvin sat on the bed and gave Floyd a shake. "You with us, Floyd?"

"Go screw yourself..." was the slurred response.

"Good. Awake. Much better."

"Go screw yourself, asshole!" this time Floyd's voice was clearer and stronger.

"Much, much better. Almost back to normal, eh, Floyd?"

The boy did not respond.

"OK. This is how it's gonna be, kid. I understand your anger about Sanchez. But it changes nothing, Floyd."

Floyd's voice was eerily calm. "You haven't just found out that the biggest bastard and murderer and source of misery and everything that's bad about Medusa is your father."

"I know it's upsetting, Floyd."

There was a bitter laugh. "Upsettin'? Yeah, it's just like stubbin' my toe ain't it? Upsettin'. What a fucking dickhead you are. Now get the hell away from me..."

"As you wish, Floyd. But you're the only one with the notebook and what's in your head that can put Sanchez away. He's no father to you. You owe him nothing. Think about what happened to your Mom, Zeke and so many others."

"Get the hell away from me, you bastard!" yelled Floyd.

Alvin left the cell in silence. There was nothing else he could do.

Chapter 22 – Rehabilitation and Resolve

"Any luck?" asked Hanser, when Alvin got back to the interview room.

"Not a chance, Saul. Let's leave him for a while. What can you hold him on?"

"What he did to several of my investigators should do it? We'll never live this down. Six of them taken down by that kid of yours."

Alvin sighed. "My kid? He might as well be, Saul. If he gets half a chance in life and manages his temper. Question is, how do we get him to co-operate?"

"What about Doc Bennett?"

"It's worth a try, Saul. I need to see him afterwards anyway."

"Sure, Alvin."

Bennett came into the room ten minutes later. "Got yourself in a pickle with that boy, Alvin, haven't you?"

"Stating the obvious, Doc. Anything we can do?"

"I just saw the boy. I'd recommend the cuffs stay on. He was calm with me, but he got very agitated when I mentioned your name."

"Great. Just great! Did he say why?"

"You manipulated him. Did things behind his back. Made decisions for him. You knew Sanchez was his father. He thinks you're just going to use him to get at Sanchez and then he'll disappear somewhere. Or you'll just dump him like he thinks everyone else has."

Alvin leant on the table, head in hands. "Can this get any be better, Doc?" he asked.

"You're telling me, Alvin?"

"So will he be fit in any way to be a witness at a trial?"

"At the moment? Not at all. In about a week he may be more settled."

"We haven't got a week, Doc."

"I can't change his feelings, Alvin. Right now he hates you with a passion. It won't last, I'm sure of that. But you've got some work to do to restore his trust. Is there anyone else he trusts?"

"There's Janie… but she knows nothing of this. It's my old life. I gave it up for good reasons, Doc."

"I know that, Alvin and I know why you did. But you always wanted to nail Sanchez and clean up Medusa and this could be your one and only opportunity. But you're more involved with that boy's welfare than you realise. Aren't you?"

Alvin gave a grim smile. "To clean out that shithole is the ambition of anyone who's heard of Medusa. But Janie might never forgive me. And there's no guarantees she'll get through to Floyd."

"Any other thoughts on Floyd?"

The older man scowled as he pondered his response. "Where to start? He's funny and charming. When he feels like it. Intelligent too. If he was my kid I'd be proud of him. But when he's angry? We've all seen that temper now. He feels he's no good and that we'll all let him down. Janie and I have encouraged him and he's blossomed here. But can he ever cope with a normal life?"

"You know the story, Alvin. Kick a dog every day and it will be a mad dog. Be kind to a dog and it will be a well-adjusted happy dog. Kick a dog for its formative years and then treat it kindly? It doesn't bode well."

"True. But Floyd's a human being. An intelligent human being. And I've seen him happy with all of his girl friends on Sundays, in the diner, when he tells us what he's been talking to the Professor in the park about and when he's busy working in the kitchen. When he looks all sappy when he's gone on a date with Mary. Hell, all the female customers and some of the guys adore him. He might be a mad dog, but there's another side to him too."

"Then excuse the pun, but Janie will have to be the 'good cop' and you'll have to be the 'bad cop', but play it gently."

"Gently? I was never gentle in what I did. I can play bad cop, though."

"Gently, Alvin."

"Jesus, Doc...! OK. I'll try. Let me phone Janie. She'll have to close the diner. I'll get someone to pick her up."

"You want me to listen in, Alvin?"

"With Floyd, yes. But what I have to say to Janie needs to be private. Until she starts yelling. Then everyone for miles will hear it."

Bennett grinned. "I'll get you some ear plugs, Alvin?"

"Thanks, Doc. I might need them. And thanks for talking to Floyd too."

"Just doing my job..."

Alvin hesitated and then picked up the phone and dialled.

"Janie? It's me. Yeah, I need you to close up. Someone from the precinct will pick you up in ninety minutes. Yes I know it's short notice. Yes, it's about Floyd. No, he isn't hurt, but he's not happy. I can't tell you everything over the phone. I love you, Janie. Don't ever forget that."

After he put the phone down, Alvin put his head back in his hands and sat quietly, thinking about what he was going to say.

Janie arrived an hour later with a uniformed cop.

"Alvin, what's going on?"

"Have a seat, Janie."

"Where's Floyd? Is he OK? I was so worried for him..."

"Janie! Please! Just sit down and listen."

She sat on the nearest chair, looking earnestly at Alvin. "I'm listening..."

"First of all. I haven't told you much about what I did in the past."

"You're telling me! I thought it was a state secret or something?"

"It is a state secret, Janie. Most of it, anyhow."

Janie nervously laughed. "Now you're being silly. I just want to know what's going on."

"Janie. It's. A. State. Secret. I work with the cops here. You remember where Floyd comes from?"

"Yeah. Medusa. He didn't seem to like it."

"Oh baby, what an understatement. Medusa is run by the mayor, Theodore Sanchez. He's been involved in murder and intimidation for years. I... the organisations I've worked with have been trying to catch him out for years. Then along comes Floyd."

"What's Floyd got to do with this Sanchez?"

"I'll get to that. Floyd can testify that his friend and a number of people living in Medusa 'disappeared' including his friend, Zeke."

"What do you mean, 'disappeared'?"

"As in 'dead', Janie. No-one has seen or heard of them again. Given Sanchez's reputation…"

"So what is Floyd doing in the middle of this?"

"He can testify that Zeke tangled with Sanchez's gang and then vanished. As did Zeke's parents. He can testify that he was badly beaten by that same gang when he was looking for help for his Mom, who subsequently died of her illness. He can testify that the town GP was coerced into claiming that Floyd killed his Mom. Do I have to go on?"

"Oh Lord, Alvin. What he's been through. Where is he now?"

"Floyd is a witness to a lot going on in Medusa. He has a notebook with what he's seen. We need his help to interpret it. That's where we have a problem."

"Is he ill? What's going on, Alvin? I want to see him…"

"Janie! Wait! I haven't finished."

"You better have a good explanation, mister."

"I do. But I don't. You know I talked to that guy, Sean, at the gallery about Floyd and his future."

"Yes, it was a great idea."

"I didn't tell Floyd. I wanted him to have a break. Work, friends, fun and a chance to get away from his past."

"Surely he understand that, Alvin?"

"He doesn't. But I haven't finished..."

"Go on, then."

"He was angry about me talking to Sean Lynch without telling him. But that's not the worst of it. Did you know he had to give a DNA sample when he was arrested?"

"No. But how is that...?"

"We found a match."

"Oh. His Mom?"

"No, his biological father. He took it very badly."

"But why? Wasn't he happy to find out who his real Dad is?"

"Not when it's Theodore Sanchez, he wasn't."

"Oh."

"'Oh' exactly. He went very quiet and then he tried to get out of the room through that locked door."

"Oh, Alvin he must have been so upset!"

"Upset isn't half of it, Janie. When my associates tried to stop him, he bit, kicked and punched anyone who came near him. Six of them are having medical treatment now. It took four of them to cuff him."

"Oh my God, Alvin!"

"He had to be sedated for his own safety and he's now in a cell. All I can get from him is 'Go screw yourself.' That's why you're here. I need your help."

"Me? What can I do?"

"Floyd loves you like a big sister. You know he adores you. He'll do anything for you. At the moment I can't get him to cooperate at all."

"But what will I say?"

"Floyd needs to help us build the case against Sanchez. That means notebook, testimony and being in a courtroom to back it up."

"Testifying against his own father?"

"Very likely."

"How can I help him do that?"

"Janie, do you think Sanchez is Floyd's father?"

"You just said he was."

"No, I mean in the way a father should be. Supportive, encouraging, building his children up and equipping them for life?"

"I didn't have a father like that, Alvin. I don't know what that means."

"Neither does Floyd. He only knows his biological father as an enemy. The guy who was the face of extortion and organised crime in his home town. The man who treated Floyd's Mom like dirt. His own personal whore - not that she had any choice in the matter. I don't even want to think about it. A man who has murdered many and there's so much more we'll probably never know about."

"So what do I say?"

"Try and get the kid to understand how much the cops here need him to end Sanchez's reign in Medusa. The chance for Sanchez and his men to pay for the many victims like Zeke and many more. Don't mention me unless you have to."

"He needs to know that you care about him, Alvin."

"You know I do, but it's not the right time or place. Tell him if you have to but be careful. I'm not important now."

"You're an idiot! Floyd needs to know directly from you, not through me!"

"I know, baby. But you didn't see how he reacted to me in the cell. It... it got to me more than it should. It's my job not to get involved..."

"You're a diner owner! It's your job to relate to people! You're usually good at it. This... all this here is your past. When it's done, I don't want you involved in this again."

"Janie, I can't just..."

"Or we're done. Do you get me?"

"You wouldn't just..."

"You just watch me! I'll do your dirty work this time, because it involves Floyd. But never again. This time I help, but then we both step away. All three of us step away."

"I get you, Janie."

"Good! Now, our focus is Floyd and our business. When this is all over that's all there is."

"Sure..."

"Take me to him."

A uniform cop took Alvin and Janie to the cell. Alvin stayed down the corridor out the way.

"Floyd..." called Janie nervously. "Are you there honey?"

"Oh God..." Floyd mumbled. "What are you doing here, Janie?"

"I was worried about you, Floyd."

"Alvin put you up to this, didn't he?"

"We're both worried about you."

"Worried he can't manipulate me anymore? Dance to his tune? Go away, Janie!"

"I can't go away. I care too much about you."

Floyd suddenly moved from the bed and he grabbed Janie violently by the front of her sweatshirt. "Still so sure I'm that loveable?" he hissed.

She looked at him defiantly. "Yes. Yes, I do. You're a good kid who's had a terrible life. But you've seen another life the past three months. We... Alvin and I want this for you. Everything we've ever done was in your best interests."

"Best interests?" Floyd let her go and sat back in the bed. "How do you know what's in my best interests. I'm a monster!"

"You're not a monster, Floyd."

"My father is a monster. You don't know what I did to those cops. I don't properly remember doing it. But part of me enjoyed it, Janie. I enjoyed attacking those guys."

"So after years of being treated like dirt you got a chance for happiness. Then they came and took it away. Is that what you think?"

"What else is there to think? How can anyone be safe if I react like that? Sanchez has a temper too. What I did was just the same as he does. The piece 'a shit that's my father."

"I don't believe that. Where's the cute kid, flirting and charming? Where's that hard worker who is there in the kitchen or out the front with no complaints? Where's that kid who got all embarrassed when he couldn't boil an egg but can now cook most things we ask for?"

"He's not real. It's just an act. I'm like Sanchez and I can't be trusted."

"I don't believe that. Alvin doesn't believe that. Does Gwen? Or those girls you enjoy being with on Sundays? Or Mary who you're so sweet on?"

"I am not sweet on Mary!"

Janie chuckled. "Do you think I can't see it? She's a lovely girl. When she looks at you it's like there's no-one else. And it's the same when you look at her. You can't fool me Floyd."

"When they know about me they'll change. Mary will change. They'll abandon me like everyone does. Mom, Zeke, you and Alvin. Everyone."

"Are you crying, Floyd?"

"No!"

"I think you are."

"Well I'm not."

"The monster who cries when he talks about his Mom and his friends. A friend he's lost and the one's he doesn't want to lose. Even me and Alvin too!"

Floyd was silent, sniffling.

"Need a handkerchief, honey?"

"Yeah. Please."

Janie chuckled again. "There you go. Pretty polite for a monster too!"

Floyd shook silently with his weeping. Janie put her arms around him and spoke softly. "We all love you. In different ways. If I were twenty years younger you can be sure I'd be chasing Mary off. And those hussies you like being with on a Sunday. Especially that Marla! Sticking her chest out at you at every opportunity."

Floyd snorted with laughter despite the tears.

"There. Much better. Monsters don't usually laugh you know?"

"Perhaps... perhaps I'm only a part-time monster, you know?"

Janie chuckled. "I told you about my father. The drinking. Do you think I drink, Floyd?"

"I dunno… I've never seen you drink?"

"Precisely. I tried it and I liked it. I liked it far too much. So I don't much. Who do you think I got it from?"

"Your Dad?"

"Exactly. It ruined his life and it could ruin mine. But I won't let it. I get help. Alvin knows and my friends know. I always get help from them. We can help you too, Floyd."

"I guess…"

"No, my little monster, you don't 'guess'. You should know. There's Alvin, me, the regulars at the diner, those girls of yours on Sunday, Mary and Gwen and there will be so many others. What about Sean Lynch too?"

"But… but I don't want them all to know about this."

"Then we won't tell them. You just say you have a bit of a temper and when you find it too much, we'll find ways to get you out of the situation."

"Yeah… I can do that, Janie."

"Good! Then it's a deal, Floyd?"

"Yeah… it's… it's a deal."

"Time for you to get your shit together, then. What are you going to do first?"

"I need to say 'sorry' to Alvin."

Janie raised her voice. "Hey! Big goof! There's a kid here who wants to say 'sorry'!"

"He's here?" said Floyd.

"Hiding down the corridor. You upset him, Floyd."

"I know. I don't know what to say, Janie."

"Say 'I'm sorry'. That will do for now."

Alvin appeared in the cell doorway looking nervous. Janie smiled at his uncertain look.

"Alvin. He won't bite!" Then she realised what she'd said. "Shit! I mean he won't bite this time!"

"Are you sure, baby?"

"I won't bite, Alvin. Honest," said Floyd, looking unsure.

"I believe you, kid. Millions wouldn't though."

"I'm… I'm sorry Alvin. For saying that to you. I know you always act in my best interest. I'm sorry what I did to those guys. I hope they're OK?"

"Nothing that a few band-aids won't cure. Maybe rabies shots? Look Floyd, I'm sorry I talked to Sean. I wanted to set things up for your future, but I wanted you to have a summer free from worrying about anything."

"I know. I'm sorry."

"You were right to be angry. I won't do things about you behind your back again. I'm sorry I did it, but I want you to have a good life, kid."

"See! Told you he cares!" interrupted Janie.

"Janie! You don't have to tell the kid everything…"

They were stopped by Floyd's snort of laughter. A genuine laugh of affection and amusement at them. It was a laugh releasing them all from the terrible things that had been said and done in the past day.

"A pair of goofs! As if one of them isn't enough!" chuckled Janie.

"I... we need your help, kid. The guys have your notebook. We need you to interpret. Will you do that?"

Floyd looked lost in thought.

"Floyd?"

"Yeah. Why not? Let's take on 'dear old Dad' and make him pay for what he's done. For everyone is Medusa, not just Mom and Zeke and Zeke's folks. And for whoever it was that Mom was sweet on when she was young. Sanchez took him away from her too."

"Do you know who he was, Floyd?" asked Janie.

"No. But let's do it for him and all of them, Janie."

She gave him a hug. "That's the Floyd I know speaking! I'm proud of you."

"Me too, kid. Shall we get started?"

"Yeah," answered Floyd. "Why not? Can you work with me, Janie?"

"Alvin?"

"If he needs you, baby and you want to?"

331

"I want to Alvin."

"Then let's do it."

Chapter 23 - Testimony

Floyd, Janie and Alvin worked together on the notebook for hours. Floyd with his intimate knowledge of Medusa, Janie with encouragement and patience and Alvin with probing questions.

"There's so much, Floyd," said Janie.

"I know. I didn't have much of a life there, so I wrote and sketched about everything I saw."

"On the outside looking in, kid?"

Floyd nodded. "Definitely, Alvin."

Alvin looked thoughtful. "hmmm... I think we might have to think about you being portrayed as 'a troubled teen'. Sanchez's lawyers will get people from Stone City to say that?"

"For sure! They might be right, too. I never fitted in, I was just 'Marlene's Bastard'. School wasn't good for me or working there neither. I had to use my fists a lot, y'know?"

"We can contrast that with what we all say. I'll get the guys in the diner to say what a great kid you are. Would your harem do that?"

Floyd spluttered. "Harem? They're just my friends!"

Alvin grinned. "If you say so, kid."

Janie smiled too. "Harem' isn't a bad description, Floyd."

"Not you too, Janie?"

"They like you, Floyd. It's a fact of life."

"I... I give up with you two..."

"Good. Then you'll do what we say?" giggled Janie.

"Do I have a choice?"

"Don't look at me, kid. You should have figured out by now who runs our lives. And it isn't me."

"And don't you forget it, goofs!"

"So do we all need a break?" asked Alvin.

"Yeah, I think so?" replied Floyd.

Janie nodded. "Me too, Alvin."

"Pizza OK?"

"Yes, please, Alvin!"

"The usual?"

With everything, Alvin. Please!"

"Hungry, but still a polite monster, Floyd?" said Janie.

"You ain't gonna let me forget that are you?"

"No I'm not. Until you realise how stupid you sounded."

"I know that!"

"Maybe. But you just don't know it enough. Maybe another few months?"

Floyd groaned again. "If you say so, Janie."

"I do. So, the usual pizza with everything for the little monster, Hawaiian for me and meat feast for Alvin."

As if on cue, Floyd's stomach grumbled, giving Alvin and Janie another opportunity to laugh at him.

"Better hurry, Alvin, or the black hole will consume us!"

"OK, give me twenty minutes."

After Alvin was gone, Floyd and Janie relaxed.

"How are you doing, Floyd?"

"Tired."

"Me too. Do you want to stop for the day?"

"No. I want to get finished."

"It's nine pm Floyd and you've had a hell of a day already. Don't you think you've had enough?"

"Yeah, I know. But let's keep going. We're half way through. There's some good stuff for Alvin's guys."

"What are they like?"

"Not the sort of guys anyone should cross. Unless they're me and in a temper."

"What about Alvin?"

"They treat Alvin like he's someone important. I promised Alvin I wouldn't talk about any of this, Janie."

"I understand, Floyd. But once this is over, it's really over. If Alvin gets involved in this stuff again, I walk."

"You wouldn't leave him! Would you?"

"Just watch me, Floyd."

"But he loves you. Anyone can see that. I ain't never seen anyone like you two before."

"I know. And if he loves me, all this stops when you're finished in court. And if you know what's good for you, you'll stop too."

"When all this ends I want out too, Janie."

"Are you sure, Floyd?"

"Yeah. I'm sure."

"I'm not so sure you're sure?"

"Teasing again?"

"No. The truth. This Sanchez guy gets put away. You start a new life. Question is, are you ready for it? Or do you want to hang on to what you are now?"

"Is there something wrong with the way I am?"

"If you think you're a monster, then yes. Controlling that temper of yours is another issue, you know?"

"I was upset. I didn't mean it."

"Oh, I think you did, Floyd. That's what really worries me."

"Is there anything I can say that you won't turn back around on me?"

Janie smirked. "Not really."

"Then do I need to say any more?"

"Not really. But I will remind you that you aren't and never have been a monster. It's no joke really."

Floyd scowled. "You're just like a damned Jiminy Cricket..."

Janie laughed. "Yes! Always let your Janie be your guide..."

Floyd smiled. "I can live with that." Then his stomach growled again.

"You won't live long if Alvin doesn't come back soon with that pizza, Floyd!"

Floyd inhaled his extra-large pizza while the others took their time. He let out a large belch.

"Floyd! That's gross! Tell him to stop it, Alvin?"

Floyd smiled with satisfaction. It was his little bit of revenge on Janie for her jokes at his expenses.

"Yes. Don't be naughty, kid. Or I'll tell Mary that you belch like a pig."

Floyd looked horrified. "You wouldn't. Would you?"

"Only if you keep it up."

Floyd muttered under his breath.

"Was that 'sorry Janie for my grossness', kid?"

"Yeah. If you say so."

"Good boy. Now can we get back to it?"

"Yeah. Let's."

By midnight they had gone through two-thirds of Floyd's notebook. The results were frightening.

"By my count that's eight people missing, twelve publicly beaten up and endless intimidation by Sanchez directly or by his goons. You were right about his temper, Floyd."

"Yeah, once he gets going, he'll never stop. That's why everyone in Medusa keeps their mouth shut. His gang seemed to enjoy it, though."

"So this Roland guy? What happened?"

"Gunter Roland? Nice guy. Got frustrated with Medusa. I think he went away and joined the army. When he came back a few years later he started sassing authority. I think he was on leave. He told Sanchez to go and screw himself. He disappeared a few days later, but all of Sanchez's men looked beat up afterwards. A few black eyes. Gunter didn't go with them easily, I don't think."

"Good. I'll check him out. The army won't be happy with the murder of one of theirs. They will give us support. We'll need it."

"Who is this Elsa Dalton? Pretty looking girl. You sketched her more than a few times. Sweet on her Floyd?"

"Yeah. A bit. I wasn't so sweet when I saw what those bastards did to her."

"What happened to her, Floyd?" asked Janie.

"I don't want to say, Janie."

"They assaulted her didn't they?" asked Alvin.

Floyd closed his eyes for a moment. "Yeah. And more. They beat her so badly no-one hardly knew who she was. Her father complained to Sanchez and he got beaten up too."

"What happened to her, kid?"

"I never saw her in the street again. Then she… she killed herself."

Janie's eyes were wide in shock. "Didn't anyone do anything, Floyd?"

"What could they do, Janie? Sanchez is the law: Judge, jury and executioner. He especially likes the last part. I hate the people in Medusa but they were plain scared of him."

"This is first rate stuff, kid. If I… if we can get one of the gang to squeal then we might find out where Sanchez's victims ended up."

"Where they are buried?"

"Correct, kid."

"But how does that help?"

"Let's say that I've seen that people like Sanchez like to have favourite spots. It becomes a habit. Find one body, you'll find a lot more."

"That's horrible, Alvin," replied Janie, white-faced.

"Yeah, baby, I know. I got too used to it. It's why I stopped. But I... we always wanted to get Sanchez. Now I can almost taste it."

"Oh Alvin. You've been carrying this for a long time, haven't you?"

"Yeah, baby, I have. I'm sick of it. But just one more thing..."

Janie turned to Floyd. "See? 'One more thing'. Look at him, Floyd. He's a good man. A decent man. We both know that. But just it's always 'one more thing'. Promise me you won't be like Alvin in that way."

Floyd looked from Janie to Alvin and back to Janie. He didn't know what to say.

"Do as she asks kid. Revenge is great, but it takes a toll. Like a drug, you want more and more of it. Put away one scumbag, you start looking for the next. When you and I help to make give Sanchez what he deserves, you need to stop. I need to stop."

"We're both cases, ain't we," said Floyd.

"Goof and monster?" said Janie.

Floyd smiled, "Maybe we should rename the diner?"

"I think we should get back to work, guys?"

"Yeah, OK, Alvin."

Two hours later they'd all had enough. But they had substantial evidence of Sanchez's activities, the behaviour of his gang and of the Medusa cops.

"Time to stop, Floyd."

"Huh?" said Floyd sleepily.

"We're beat, kid."

"Just a bit more," Floyd slurred.

Janie looked at Floyd in exasperation. "Floyd, I think you need to sleep. I know I do!"

"Me too, baby."

"OK, let's stop."

Alvin arranged for the notebook and their work to be locked away and they took a cab back to the diner. The mailbox was full of notes from concerned regulars.

"They're worried about us, baby."

"That's so sweet. But I don't think we're opening tomorrow. What shall I put up?"

"Say that it's a family illness and we should be back in a few days."

"I'll do it, Alvin. Get Floyd to bed. Look at him."

Floyd was slumped in a chair, nearly asleep. Alvin managed to awake him and get him into his bedroom. When he got back downstairs, Janie had finished the note.

"All set, Janie?"

"Yes. I think so. Shall we get to bed too?"

"Yeah, sure. How tired are you?"

"Not too tired to show you how much I love you, you big idiot."

"That's what I was hoping you'd say..."

Chapter 24 – Arrested Developments

Two days later their work was done. Janie, Alvin and Floyd were back at the diner. Their regular clientele were all curious about where they'd been, so Floyd mischievously told them all that Janie had received a bequest from a rich aunt. "She was worth millions, I tell ya!"

It was less funny when the newly minted 'millionairess' found out. Floyd was condemned to clean out all the fryers for the next week.

"That'll teach you to tell tall tales. I've got all the regulars being so nice to me. One even offered to marry me! You little creep!"

When Floyd laughed, the punishment was increased. "I think the floors need a deep clean too, don't you think so, Alvin?"

"If you say so, Janie. You're the boss."

"I am, and don't you forget it! And you neither, Floyd. Now get to it!"

That afternoon, Alvin received the call.

"Hi Saul. You did? When? How did it... yeah I know. All of them? Fantastic! S? Hope he resisted arrest? Good. Can I tell the guys? OK, tomorrow? See you at 10am? Thanks, Saul. Tell everyone 'good job', from me. OK? Bye."

Alvin walked into the kitchen.

"I got a call. Our 'friend' is in custody."

Floyd looked up from his cleaning. "Good. I hope they gave the son-of-a-bitch a good pasting."

"Floyd! The cops don't do things like that." said Janie.

Alvin and Floyd smirked at each other but remained silent.

"Did you hear about Dr Masters and his family, Alvin?"

"No. Nothing. We have to be there tomorrow at 10am. Looks like Janie has another rich aunt, Floyd?"

"You stop that or you're cleaning up all the nasty stuff for a month, too, mister!"

Alvin held his hands up in defence. "OK Janie. I get you. But with your millions, couldn't we have some more guys working here?"

Alvin got out of the kitchen quickly as the saucepan just missed his head. Floyd looked on amused until Janie spotted him.

"You got any smarted-assed comments?"

"No ma'am!" said Floyd quickly, as he got back to his cleaning.

The next day Alvin, Janie and Floyd were at the precinct. Early. Saul met them at the desk and looked pleased.

"We got them all, Alvin. Every last damned one of them. Come and see!"

They were brought into a room with a window. "It's one way. He can't see you."

And there he was. The master of Medusa and scourge of so many lives. Theodore Sanchez. Grubby and bruised, his head down. Janie, Alvin and Janie could hear the questions from one of Saul's men.

"Sanchez. We've got so much dirt on you. If you don't admit to what you've done, we've got people who'll talk and evidence to back it up."

Sanchez's head stayed down. He had a sneer of contempt on his face, but he stayed silent.

Floyd froze. This was him. Still arrogant. Still defiant. "Alvin. Tell him I'm here."

"Kid, we can't do that."

"Yes, you can. Tell him 'Marlene's Bastard' is here. His bastard is here. And he looks forward to testifying and seeing him rot in jail, for the rest of his life."

"Floyd, he's dangerous, you can't say things like that. Look at him. He's evil." said Janie.

"I know what he is, Jane. But you look at him. He thinks he can get out of it. Knowing that I'm here and that I'm ready to tell everything will put him on the back foot."

"It's worth a try, Alvin." said Saul. "It might crack that facade."

"You're sure, kid?"

"I'm sure, Alvin."

"OK, do it Saul. Kid, we're gonna let him see you. Just for a second. Smile and wave at him. Try to look pleased."

"I don't need to act. Seeing him like this is what I've wanted for a long time."

"For me too, kid. Saul. Let's do it."

Saul left the room. A minute later they saw him in the interview room and he spoke to Sanchez.

"We have a special guest who's delighted to see you here, Mr Mayor. He wants you to know how he's looking forward to testifying. Take a look see..."

When Sanchez saw Floyd, he looked stunned. Then a little frightened. But it was his rage that took over, as he lunged at the glass, so close that Floyd could see his intensely grey eyes.

"You little bastard! I'll kill you! I should have done it years ago..."

Floyd smiled and gave a little wave. It made Sanchez all the angrier and it took two of the cops to get him back handcuffed to his chair. Sanchez now looked less sure of himself, his face contorted in fury.

Saul gave a grin and a 'thumbs up'. Floyd smiled back, delighted to see the effect on Sanchez.

Janie and Alvin looked at him with concern.

"You're enjoying this far too much, kid."

"I think so too," said Janie.

Floyd's smile faltered. "Can't I have just a few minutes to enjoy how much I've managed to rile that evil bastard so much?"

"You can, kid. But not too much. Look, you got him angry and he's not feeling so confident now. Your job is done for now. Keep that in mind."

"Yeah, OK. After all I've seen and had done to me... I want to see him suffer."

"He'll suffer, kid. No doubt about that. But it's not just about you. Or is it?"

"No. It ain't."

"Good. Now let's talk to Saul about what's happening next."

Saul was in good humour. "You provoked him good, Floyd. Good job! He's definitely on the back foot now. But we have to think about how you're going to testify."

"What do you mean?"

"How old are you, Floyd?"

"Seventeen."

"Then you're a minor."

"So?"

"We have several options. Chip in, Alvin. Floyd can testify in court. He can testify live on close circuit tv or he can record a testimony and that will be played to the courtroom."

"The second option takes the heat off you, kid."

"No, I want to be there. In court."

"Sanchez's attorney has the right to grill you, kid."

"That's correct, Floyd," said Saul.

"I don't mind. Help me get the story straight and I'll do it."

"Are you sure, Floyd?" said Janie.

"Yeah, I'm sure. I want to see Sanchez's face. I want to tell the court what I saw and what he did to Mom and everyone else."

Alvin spoke again. "One problem. Sanchez's brief will be to discredit you. Rebellious son. Turned against his father by people with an agenda."

"That ain't true!"

"I know that kid. So we need to push that you've had no contact and that you had no idea of any relationship with Sanchez."

"There ain't no relationship!"

"I know that too. But you said you need help to get your story straight. That's what we're going to do. Janie, you have to help too."

"But what can I do to help?"

"You're the jury. What we decide to say is true but it needs to be convincing. If it doesn't smell right, you say. OK?"

"I can do that, Alvin."

"That's what you guys need to work on today. I need to get back to Sanchez. Any questions?"

"Yeah. I have one. What happened to Dr Masters and his family?"

Saul's face fell. "We got them out, Floyd. But Sanchez and his thugs had their fun with the Doctor and his wife and kids."

"What did they do to them?"

Saul looked troubled. "I'd rather not say, Floyd. It's another testimony we have against Sanchez. Masters will testify on your behalf by the way."

"Can I see him?"

"No, Floyd. It's best you don't. No contact. The family have had a bad time of it and they'll need a lot of help. You can't help them, Floyd."

Floyd stayed silent, but his anger showed. Another family hurt by Theodore Sanchez.

"I know you're pissed, kid. But this is another nail in the coffin of Sanchez. Be patient a while longer. Hey, Saul, any of his gang blabbed?"

"Not yet, but one is close to cracking. Jake Kalb. He knows what we've got on him. White as a sheet. Sweating up a storm. So yes, be patient, Floyd."

"Kalb? He's a little shit who hides behind the rest. Frightened of his own shadow when on his own," said boy replied.

"He'd be easy to bully, Floyd?" asked Alvin. He turned to Saul. "Not that I'd ever suggest that, of course?"

Saul smiled back. "Of course not, Alvin. That would be quite wrong."

Floyd grinned at them both. "He might be open to 'persuasion', if that works for you?"

They both smiled back. "We can work with that, Floyd. Thanks for the insight. Now tell me about the others?"

"The big guy, George? He's stupid. I ain't sure he understands what he's doin'?"

"We think so too. Can barely speak. Completely out of his depth. What was his role?"

"Muscle. If he was told to hit someone, he would. That's all he's capable of."

"OK. How about the big swarthy guy?"

"Tony Moscarra? He's sick in the head. A brute. Pretty sure no woman could be safe from him. He scares me, Mr Hanser. There's nothin' he wouldn't do. Just plain evil. I think he might be related to Sanchez."

Floyd paused for a moment. "Jesus, that means he might be related to me? I'd almost prefer Sanchez. Oh my God!"

"The other one?"

"Sam Dempsey. I think he's a psycho. Just stares. Dead eyes. Says nothin'. Don't often speak. Turned up in Medusa about eight years ago. But when the gang got goin' beatin' someone up, it was like he had a devil in him. The other guys had to pull him away. I know that they all regularly take knives off him.

Even they wouldn't go so far publicly. He scares the shit outta me too, Mr Hanser."

"Lastly. Theodore Sanchez. Any thoughts, Floyd?"

"In my mind he's the source of every vice and crime in Medusa. Money, drugs, prostitution. I wouldn't be surprised if the bastard was involved in slavery. Lots of people comin' and goin' at night. Sometimes big trucks. Everyone pretends they don't see it. There ain't an activity, legal or not, that he's not involved in. Every business. Everything anyone does in that shithole has him at the centre."

"Is that enough for you to go on, Saul?" asked Alvin.

"Yeah. Plenty. Thanks Floyd, thanks Alvin. And thank you too, Janie, for keeping these two on a leash."

Janie blushed but smiled back.

"So, Alvin. You'll have to be patient a while longer. But we'll nail them all. We have enough now to do it. Finally!"

"I guess I'll have to be patient, Saul."

"OK guys, get to it. I'll have our lawyer in here in about an hour and he'll work with our attorney. Do you remember Ron Gershwin, Alvin?"

"Yeah. Bit of a tough nut, but knows his stuff. Pedantic. Doesn't miss anything."

"I think he'll be good for this case. Can you lead on this?"

"Yeah, sure Saul."

And so they set to work.

Floyd hated the next week. Every day he was coached and encouraged to build up his confidence to be able to testify in front of a court and especially right in front of Sanchez.

"Be yourself, kid. Not too cocky, not too angry. What's happened to you personally and your Mom, but also what you've seen happen to others. If you get angry, you fall into their trap."

Floyd was irritable. "I'd be less angry if you hadn't said that to me about a million times!"

Janie watched, amused. She intervened when she thought Floyd's testimony wasn't right, but now she had no more to say. But she could see that her two men had had enough.

"I think it's time for a break, Alvin."

"No, baby, not just yet, Floyd needs to..."

"Floyd is letter perfect. He needs a break and so do you."

"Just a little longer, Janie..."

"'Just a little longer...'" she sighed. "While you're doing that, shall I pack my case?"

"I'd rather you didn't, Janie."

"Then let's take a break, Alvin."

Gershwin watched the exchange. "I think you all need a break. I'm happy so far with what we've achieved with Floyd's assistance. Good job, son. Why don't you get out for the rest of the day? I'll speak with the D.A. and see if she has any more questions...?"

"So where to, Alvin?" asked Floyd.

"How about lunch and then the park?"

"Sound good to me!" said Janie.

"Me too!" agreed Floyd.

The rest of the day was spent pleasantly, enjoying a takeaway and a stroll around the park. Floyd couldn't keep his mind off the upcoming trial.

"So what if Sanchez gets off free?"

Alvin turned to Janie. "Sanchez? Who's that?"

Janie smiled. "I have no idea? Is it a new customer?"

"Maybe, baby. We could sure do with some more of them."

"You guys think you're so funny," said Floyd. "But what will we do...?"

"I don't know about you, but I'm enjoying time with my Big Goof and my Little Monster. In the park, relaxed. That's what's important now, Floyd."

"Yeah, I know, Janie, but..."

"She's right, kid. Let's enjoy the day."

"But I only want to..."

"Kid. Let's. Enjoy. The. Day."

Floyd sulked for a while, ignoring any pleasantries. He spotted Gwen sitting at her favourite bench.

"Hey it's Gwen. Can we go and say hello?"

"Of course we can, kid. But no mention of anything."

"I know, Alvin. I'm not an idiot."

"Never said you were, kid. Now let's meet your Professor."

Gwen was delighted to see Floyd and quickly fell into conversation with Janie and Alvin.

"Floyd has something about him. He has an ability to study and go far. You realise that?" Gwen said.

"Yes, we do. Thanks for encouraging him. We want him to study but we don't know how we can support that."

"Carry on as you are already, Janie. Give him time. Be patient. He has a lot of potential. But he's still primitive."

Seeing the scowl on Floyd's face, she smiled. "You don't like that do you, Floyd?" Even if it's true?"

Alvin was amused. "'Primitive?' I like that. It explains what he looks like first thing in the morning."

"That's true," agreed Janie. "He'd also benefit from speaking a little clearer."

"I ain't gonna change the way I speak!"

360

"'Ain't'. That's one thing that needs to go, Janie."

"'Gonna'. That's another, Alvin"

Gwen joined in. "It's true, Floyd. You speak quite well, but people will judge you on accent and articulation. Less contractions and you'll be a better communicator."

Floyd started to sulk again.

"Little Monster, you need to do this."

"Why? There's nothin' wrong with the way I speak."

"'Nothin'. That's another," said Gwen.

Janie, Alvin and Gwen looked at other, smiling. They all knew Floyd had potential, but could he use his talents?

"Kid, we all think you have brains. Remember what we've been saying to you. Moving on? Learning new things? Forgetting the past? You'll always be 'Marlene's Bastard' if you don't."

"'Marlene's Bastard'? What an awful thing to say to anyone. Who called you that, darling?"

"Almost the entire town, Gwen."

"Idiots. Moronic cretins. Were they jealous or just stupid?"

"I dunno, Gwen. They just liked to treat me bad."

"'Dunno'. That's got to go too, kid."

"Will you stop that?" growled Floyd.

"Not until you stop talking like that, kid."

"Did you speak to Sean Lynch yet, Floyd?" asked Gwen.

"No. But he has." Floyd shot Alvin a dirty look.

"Yes, I did, Gwen. He thinks Floyd has potential too, but it seems that our young man here doesn't feel the same."

"It's not that!" protested Floyd. "I just ain't... I'm just not cut out for studies."

"How do you know until you try, Floyd?" said Janie.

"Because I was useless at school."

"Those fools! You've told me what they were like, Floyd. They ignored your talents and they tried to make you a dummy like they were." said Gwen.

"It's true, kid. You've said the same thing to me and Janie. Time to move on, kid."

"Floyd, you've got an opportunity here, don't waste it," said Janie.

"I need to think about it. Maybe in a few weeks?"

"Why not now?" asked Gwen.

Floyd hesitated. "Well... I just need... I've got..."

"We just thought the kid needed a break over the summer, Gwen. He's earning some cash working at the diner, but he'll have a better idea later on this year."

"You aren't telling me something, Floyd. You two aren't either. Come and talk to me when you're ready?"

"I will, Gwen."

"Now it's time to go. Will you be here on Sunday, Floyd?"

"I'm not sure, Gwen. Some things have... have come up."

"I'm burning to know what, Floyd. You'll tell me in your own time I'm sure. It was a pleasure to meet you, Janie and Alvin."

They sat in silence for a few minutes as they watched Gwen walk away. Then Janie spoke.

"Well that told you, Floyd. Gwen's very forceful. But she's right as well."

"She sure is, baby. I wouldn't want to get on the wrong side of that lady. But she's definitely right about you, kid."

"I suppose so..." said Floyd.

"Suppose nothing, kid. But let's get one major problem out the way first."

"I can't really think of anything else, guys."

"We understand, Floyd. It's a shadow over you and us too."

"I've had a great afternoon with you guys, though."

"Us too kid. We should do this more often. It's diner, diner, diner, all the time."

"Let's do something regularly, Alvin?"

"We will, baby. If we can afford it. But I'm tired now. Let's go home?"

The next day they met with Ron Gershwin again. "The D.A likes your account, Floyd, but she's concerned you being an outsider in Medusa will go against you. We haven't been able to get anyone in the town who will back you up or take your side."

Floyd nodded his agreement. "I ain't surprised."

"We may have to think of different strategies against Sanchez's defence team, then."

"Yeah. I know. But it's true that many of the folks in Medusa admire Sanchez. Some are too stupid to know what he is. The rest would be too frightened to ask too many questions anyways."

"So we have the people Floyd grew up with who will say he's a troublemaker and the people who've known Floyd for three months in Woosterville who say he's a decent young man. Who will the jury believe?"

"Then we get lots of people who will testify that the kid is decent. The regulars at the diner. Sean Lynch. Gwen. Floyd's harem. Who else...?"

"Don't forget me, Alvin?"

"I could never forget you, baby."

"What about yourself, Alvin?"

Alvin paused in thought. "I'm not sure I can."

"What do you me you can't? This is Floyd we're talking about."

"Janie, it's not that I don't want to, it's whether I'm allowed to."

The prosecution lawyer spoke up. "It's true that Alvin's past may be 'colourful'. Could you do it if it was a closed session? Testify in Floyd's favour?"

"That might work. I have to ask permission. Let me make a call." Alvin left the room.

"So we have Alvin, who has some clout and all the Woosterville regulars. Who are your 'harem', Floyd?"

Floyd scowled. "It's Alvin's nickname for my friends. There's nothin' goin' on."

"Janie smiled. "They're all female, very attractive and they all seem to love him. He loves them back too, but he hasn't figured out which way or how yet..."

Floyd blushed. "I keep tellin' you ain't that sorta guy!"

"No, you aren't, my little monster. But perhaps you should be now and then?"

A little cough from Gershwin interrupted them. "So, they will provide written testimony of Floyd's character?"

Janie gave a little throaty chuckle. "And his other assets, I'm sure".

Floyd screwed his face up. "Can we keep it clean?"

"I can do that, Floyd," said the lawyer. "But a clean cut young man who is decent and has female friends without trying to take advantage of them in any way would work in your favour too."

Alvin came back into the room. "Yeah, they'll go for it. I provide written evidence as Alvin the diner owner and Floyd's employer. I can be there in court again but it has to be a closed session. On pain of death, I'm told. Behind a screen would be better."

"You can't have that much to hide, Alvin?"

"I wouldn't bet on that, baby. You can't be there. Or Floyd."

"But why not?" asked Janie.

"Because you don't need to know. Neither does the kid, here."

"But..."

"No but's, baby. If you get to know, I have to move on."

"You'd do that to me?"

"To protect you? I'd do anything, Janie."

"But you'd leave me?"

"Like a shot. You know things, you're in danger. I won't allow that. I...like both of you too much."

"You big goof! You can say that word, you know."

"Only in private, Janie. And we're not."

"We're probably going to trial in three weeks. The Governor is leaning on us to get this moving quickly. It would be a coup for him to nail Sanchez, especially as he's up for re-election next year."

"Anti-corruption, my ass!" said Alvin.

Gershwin smiled back. "You may very well think that..."

Then the lawyer paused in thought. "Floyd, can you talk to your friends, this Gwen and this Lynch guy?"

"Yeah, I can do that," said Floyd, "if I know what the hell to say."

Alvin interrupted. "I'll talk to Sean Lynch, Floyd."

Floyd looked at the older man suspiciously, but let it go. "If you say so, Alvin."

Gershwin made some notes on his pad. "I'll write you down some ideas, Floyd. They will have to have the permission of their parents, which may cause a problem. Do your best?"

Chapter 25 – Trials and Tribulations

Floyd met Gwen in the park as usual on the following Sunday. He was nervous because he would have to tell her and the girls about his past. "What am I gonna do if they hate me for it?" he thought.

"Floyd. How are you? I was delighted to meet Janie and Alvin."

"Thanks, Gwen. They enjoyed meetin' you too. Look, I have somethin' to say and the girls need to hear it to. Do you mind if we join them?"

"Of course not, Floyd."

When the girls spotted him, they mobbed him with hugs as usual. Mary kissed him and the others crowed with delight.

"Guys! Guys! This is Gwen, a friend. She's been helpin' me with learning. But you all need to know some things about me. Can we sit?"

"What is it Floyd?"

"It sounds serious...?"

"What can we do...?"

"Can you let me get a word in edgeways?" interrupted Floyd, more tersely than he liked. He was sure that they would all turn their backs on him once he'd told them the truth.

The all sat, looking curious.

"I use to live in Medusa. I'm illegitimate and the townsfolk called me 'Marlene's Bastard'."

The replies from the girls were sympathetic.

"Oh Floyd that's terrible..."

"Why would they be so awful to you...?"

"They should know better..."

Floyd waved his hands around to get them to quieten. "Guys! Guys! Let. Me. Finish."

Then Floyd spoke again.

"Medusa is run by a guy called Theodore Sanchez. He and his cronies run the place. People disappear, like my friend Zeke. They ain't seen again. You can guess what happened to Zeke and others."

He saw their responses: the girls with wide eyes, shocked at what he was telling them, Gwen with attention like a hawk.

"I'm a witness and Sanchez and his guys are on trial. I wanted to ask you if you would say that you know me and that I'm a decent guy..."

He paused, embarrassed by his tears. "I'd understand if you didn't want to..."

His confession as met with astonished silence as they all stared in amazement. Floyd looked at them and began to stand up.

"Where are you going, Floyd?" asked Gwen.

"I have to go. If none of you can help me, I shouldn't bother you anymore."

"Floyd, don't be an idiot," Gwen said. "I would be happy to provide a personal and professional reference to you."

"I'll do it, Floyd," said Marla, "like a shot."

"So will I!" replied Julie. Floyd was surprised at her enthusiasm.

Mary took his hand and looked straight into his eyes. "How could you think I wouldn't?" smiled Mary.

The rest of the group quickly followed.

Gwen took charge. "You do realise you're all minors. Under age. Your parents will decide whether they think you're able to do this?"

Floyd nodded at them. "Yes, that's right. The legal guys will write to you, but it's your Mom and Dad who say whether you can."

"There will be a riot if they don't!" grumbled Marla.

"I don't know what to say to all of you. Apart from 'Thanks'. You know I can't see any of you while this is going on? I'll make it up to you later."

"I can think of some ways, cutie," purred Marla.

"Is that all you think of, Marla?" said Julie.

"Well at least I do think about it, Julie."

"24/7? You're obsessed?"

"And you aren't…?"

Everyone else laughed at Marla and Julie's usual antics.

When he had to leave, Floyd was mobbed by them again with hugs and kisses. Floyd knew they would try to support him. That felt comforting as he worried about what would happen the next few weeks. He was still nervous at the idea of being a witness at Sanchez's trial.

The three weeks flew by. The diner opened but on reduced hours. Janie's 'sick aunt' continued to ail. The worst thing for Floyd was cancelling his regular dates with Mary and meeting with his regular Sunday friends. He wondered if any of them would speak to him again, or be allowed to by their parents, especially after the local cops had got in touch. He missed talking to Gwen as well.

Floyd was grilled and questioned over and over to get his statements right. Alvin and Ron Gershwin worked with him daily until Floyd was tired and surly. Janie acted as referee and the voice of sanity when things got too tense. But Floyd was cheered by the support of the people he knew in Woosterville. They all consistently wrote in his favour about his good nature and behaviour. Sean and Gwen's testimonies as academics also boosted his credentials. He felt ready and able to take on Sanchez and the court.

Floyd was unhappy that two of the girls' parents would not allow their daughters to write a testimony in Floyd's favour. He knew that it wasn't their fault, but Mary's mother and father's decision hurt him most of all. It slightly soured his feelings towards her. Worst of all, he could not speak to her to try and patch things up.

Floyd was petrified as he stood there, in the hallway of the court, Janie and Alvin with him.

"Are you ready, kid?"

"Yeah. I ain't frightened, Alvin."

"You're not nervous, Floyd?"

The boy laughed. "Hell, yes! But I won't let It stop me."

Alvin patted his shoulder. "Great. I'm proud of you kid."

Janie hugged him. "I am too, Floyd."

"Thanks, Janie. I couldn't have done it without you guys."

"We'll be sitting behind Ron Gershwin, rooting for you, kid."

They were interrupted suddenly: "The court summons Floyd Jensen to the witness stand."

Floyd froze.

"Time to go, kid."

375

Alvin and Janie could see Floyd pull himself together. "Let's go," he said, his voice neutral, as he been encouraged to do by Gershwin.

The swearing in process was a blur, but Floyd was soon seated in the witness box. Floyd looked around the room until he spotted Sanchez, sitting in the dock. He drew comfort from the man's anger. It was an older, fatter and greyer Sanchez than Floyd remembered, but still big, still powerful and still dangerous.

The one thing that still got to Floyd was Sanchez's eyes: those grey eyes, just like his own. Exactly like his own.

Gershwin, acting as defence lawyer was the first to question Floyd.

"Floyd, tell me about yourself?"

"I'm Floyd. Just an ordinary guy. But in Medusa I was known as 'Marlene's Bastard'. The locals treated me and my Mom badly. I never knew why, but nobody ever let up on us."

"Did you have any friends?"

"Only Zeke. At school and around the town."

"For the record, Floyd's friend was called Ezekiel Jefferson. And how did the townsfolk of Medusa behave towards Zeke?"

"They thought he was trouble. Called him a…a… you know, the 'n' word. Said he was trouble like they told me."

"For the record, your Honour, Ezekiel Jefferson was an African-American."

Gershwin turned back to Floyd. "Were you trouble, young man?"

"No. Me and Zeke minded our own business and my Mom and Zeke's folks warned us to take care while dealing with anyone in Medusa."

"What were Zeke's parents like?"

"They was quiet. Like they were frightened of everybody and anybody. Always nervous. They warned us all the time to steer clear of any dealings with Medusa people."

"So did you? Steer clear of trouble, I mean?"

"Yeah, we tried. But it seemed that every move we made we were scolded or insulted. When we got to our teens it got harder."

"How did it get harder, Floyd?"

"Sanchez. The mayor. His guys. They started to pick on us, but especially Zeke. It got worse when he got tall. He never got a moments peace from them."

"Did you fight back, Floyd?"

Floyd paused, not sure what to say. "Yeah, I did… I had to. I made it as hard as I could for them. It went on for years. They picked on Zeke more cuz he wouldn't fight back at them."

"So Floyd. Can you identify the gang who bullied you and Zeke?"

The defence lawyer, Kowalski, rose out his seat. "Objection. The prosecution use of the word 'gang' implies criminality and that has not been proved."

The judge replied. "Sustained. Would the prosecution limit itself to the facts?"

"Yes, your Honour. Floyd. Can you identify the individuals who bullied you and Zeke?"

"Yes sir. It was those three guys on the left. There was another guy but I don't see him here?"

Gershwin interrupted. "For the record, Floyd has identified Anthony Moscarra, Samuel Dempsey and George Lindberg. Do you know the name of the other gang member?"

"Yes, his name's Jake Kalb."

"For the record, Floyd has named Jacob Kalb as one of the individuals who repeatedly bullied Floyd and his friend Zeke."

"What happened to Zeke, Floyd?"

"We... we got to seventeen and we could hardly go into Medusa. The gang... I mean the 'individuals' over there gave Zeke hell. He tried not to answer back but it got him so angry. So he told them what he thought of them."

"Did they leave Zeke and you alone after that?"

"I never saw Zeke ever again after that, sir."

"Do you know where he went?"

"No. My Mom said he was probably dead. 'Like all the others', she said."

Kowalski got to his feet. "Objection, your Honour! This is all assumption! The witness is merely reporting gossip and slander."

The Judge scowled. "Mr Gershwin. Care to explain?"

"I'm getting to that, your Honour. Just one or two more questions."

"Very well. But I caution you not to test the court's patience..."

"What do you think your Mom meant, Floyd?"

"Well sir, she said that Sanchez... that guy over there in the dock on the right and the others had done it to others before. That they were all buried out there."

"Could your Mom say where, Floyd?"

"No sir..."

The defence lawyer stood again. "Objection, your Honour. There is no evidence here, just more slander!"

Gershwin looked at the Judge. "Your Honour, I'm getting to this. With your permission?"

The Judge nodded.

"What happened to Zeke's parents, Floyd?"

"I never saw them again with, after that day. Mom said they were probably dead too."

"Is there anyone else you can tell us about Floyd? People who simply disappeared?"

"Mom mentioned some guy she said she was sweet on. Before I was born. She said that S... that guy over there was up to it."

"That 'guy' being Theodore Sanchez?"

Floyd couldn't help his animosity as he pointed. "Yeah, that son-of-a-bitch, there! Him!"

The Judge hit the gavel against his bench and glared at Floyd. "May I caution the young man to keep a civil tongue in his head when he is in my court?"

Floyd looked chastened. "Sorry, your Honour."

"Be careful, young man. Report your evidence. Nothing more, nothing less. Do you understand me?"

"Yes, sir."

"Mr Gershwin. Carry on..."

"So. Theodore Sanchez. Do you think he was involved in any of these alleged disappearances?"

"Yeah, all of them. He runs Medusa and anyone who crossed him is usually sorry."

"Who else?"

"There was Gunter. Gunter Roland. He joined the army. Came back on leave and told Sanchez and his gang what they could go and do. I never saw him again either."

"So an enlisted man is possibly murdered alongside many others. Why do you think no-one in the town objected?"

"Well… I think it was because they thought they'd end up dead or disappeared too. Everyone in Medusa was scared of Sanchez or his gang."

The defence lawyer angrily protested. "Objection, your Honour! This defamation without a shred of verification has gone on long enough!"

The Judge looked back at Gershwin. "Mr Gershwin. This is clearly not evidence. What can you say to prove what this young man says?"

"We have the testimony of the missing gang… I apologise… the missing fourth member. He has told special investigators what they did and where the bodies are. Forensic teams have found at least fifteen bodies in the last few days."

Floyd sat there stunned. The court erupted around him.

The Judge angrily used his gavel until the court was silent. "Silence in court! Silence in court!"

Kowalski was quick to comment. "Objection! Your Honour, the defence has received no information about this so-called forensic team."

"Could you explain yourself, Mr Gershwin?"

"Your Honour. My learned colleague. I apologise to both of you and the court. This information was only received this morning. I would have naturally prefer to share this beforehand, but it is pertinent to Floyd's statements."

The Judge looked furious. "It is relevant, Mr Gershwin, but I would appreciate you following legal procedures in this court. This is not a circus!"

"I will ensure that all pertinent information is sent to the defence counsel in due course, your Honour."

"See that you do. Have you many more questions for this witness?"

"Yes, your Honour, I'm afraid I do."

"Then proceed."

"Floyd. What is your relationship to Theodore Sanchez?"

"There ain't one."

"Come now Floyd, tell us the truth. What do you know about you and your Mom and Mayor Theodore Sanchez?"

Floyd sighed. "He's... he's my father."

The court erupted again.

"Silence in court! Silence in court!" shouted the Judge. "If this behaviour continues I will clear the gallery!"

"So. Floyd. Theodore Sanchez is your father. How do feel about that?"

"Feel...? Dirty. It's like being related to snakes. He's a monster!"

"But you've always known he was your father haven't you?"

"No. Not until the DNA test a few weeks ago. I had no idea. I just knew I hated and feared him."

"Why fear? Surely he took an interest in you? Even if you didn't know, he must have?"

"Mom was scared of him. Everyone else was. She warned me to stay out his way. So I did."

"So you had no contact with him?"

"No. I use to see him starin' at me sometimes when he came to visit school. I didn't know why. I glared back. He didn't like that much. Mom made me take sick days if she knew he was visiting the school."

"Did you ever have any other contact?"

Floyd's face went red. "He... he used to visit my Mom regularly."

Gershwin looked intrigued. "Oh? For what purposes?"

"He... you know..."

"What, Floyd?" asked the lawyer.

"He came to have sex with her."

"Was this consensual, Floyd?"

Floyd Paused. He couldn't get the words out.

"Floyd?" repeated Gershwin.

"No. I remember... I was just a kid when it started. Maybe it was going on before, I dunno. He used to drag her into the bedroom. It happened a lot. She was always covered in bruises. Later on those... those men over there made me leave. I think... I think they joined in."

Gershwin spoke again. "How long was this going on for, Floyd?"

"Ever since I can remember. Sometimes weekly, sometimes monthly, sometimes less. They just showed as they pleased. It always scared the shit out of me. And terrified Mom."

"This was not a normal upbringing then?"

"No. Mom lived in fear. Frightened for me too."

"Did you ever speak to the defendant again?"

"Once."

"What was the circumstances?"

"He yelled at me at the grocery store, last Christmas."

"Why, Floyd?" asked Gershwin.

"I... I pasted a picture of his face on the baby Jesus in the crib."

Laughter ran around the court.

"Why did you do that, Floyd?"

"I was tired of him being everything. His face on everythin'. Everyone wettin' their pants because of him. I just did it. I hate him for what he did to Mom."

"Was this the act of a rebellious son getting back at his father?"

"No. I had no idea about that. I had no idea he was my father. I just hated and feared him."

"What did he do?"

"He yelled at me for ten minutes. I thought he was gonna kill me. His gang were there. They looked like they might kill me too. They were enjoyin' it."

"Did anyone strike you?"

"No."

"So what happened?"

"I got fired."

"Was this the first time you had been fired?"

"No. Once before."

"Tell us about that?"

"I worked for another local store. I had some trouble because of who I was. But I kept quiet and eventually people let me be."

"Because you were 'Marlene's Bastard?'"

"Yeah."

"So you were quiet and minded your own business and got on with your job?"

"Yeah."

"So why were you fired?"

"I didn't know but then I found out a few days later that Sanchez had bought the store. And then I got fired."

"So you don't have any proof?"

"No. But it seems too much of a coincidence to me."

Kawalski looked pleased. "Objection, your Honour! Even the prosecution can't prove that there was any malice on behalf of my client."

"Sustained. Don't waste the court time, Mr Gershwin."

"I understand, your Honour."

Gershwin continued. "Floyd. If the defendant is your father, that implies she had a relationship with your Mom. How do you feel about that?"

"Mom loathed him. She was scared of him. I don't think a relationship came into it."

"So how do you account for your existence?"

"I... I can't see that Mom would ever want him. As I said, she hated him. She panicked when his name came up. She never loved him, that's for sure."

"Did the defendant ever speak to your Mom, apart from his 'visits'?"

"No, as far as I'm aware. I never saw it. When Mom was ill, I told his gang she needed help. They still beat me up. When I got home with the Doctor she was dead. She might've lived if I'd got help."

"So the individuals over there in the dock stopped you getting badly needed assistance for your Mom, who was seriously ill and which may have contributed towards her death?"

"Yeah. They just laughed at me. And then they beat the living daylights outta me."

"Thank you, Floyd. Now, the local GP, Doctor Greg Masters, wrote that you hit your Mom. Is that true?"

"No. I could never do that. The Doctor said he been told to say that by the Sheriff."

"Can you prove that?"

"No. I couldn't then, neither. That's why I ran away."

"So how can you prove anything?"

"Doctor Masters can tell you."

"Your Honour. I have a statement by Doctor Gregory Masters stating he was forced to implicate Floyd in his Mom's death.

That none of it was true. She died of natural causes associated with stage three bowel cancer."

"Why is Doctor Masters not able to attend the court and submit evidence?" asked the Judge.

"Your Honour, I have a separate statement from Doctor Greg Masters stating that he was held virtual prisoner within the town of Medusa and repeatedly beaten by Theodore Sanchez and his 'individuals'. It includes his testimony about the repeated assaults on his wife and two daughters. The entire family are recovering with the help of trauma counsellors. None of them are currently able to face the stress of a court appearance."

The Judge nodded. "Very well. I accept the testimony of Doctor Masters which appears to exonerate the witness of allegations that he struck his mother which resulted in her death."

"A few more question, your Honour."

"Very well, Mr Gershwin. A few more. But only 'a few' more."

"Thank you, your Honour. Floyd. You were arrested by Medusa police on the outskirts of Woosterville. Can you explain that?"

"Well... I was on the run because they framed me for Mom dying. Doctor Master said 'run' so I did. I was inside Woosterville limits when they tried to grab me."

"Did you resist?"

"Yeah. But I knew they were Sanchez's men. The Sheriff is owned by Sanchez. They're just another gang in Medusa for Sanchez to use. Everything they do is controlled by him."

"Where did they try to arrest you?"

"I was hidin' in a garden on the outskirts of Woosterville."

"So, these Medusa cops were outside their jurisdiction, in plain clothes and they beat you up?"

"Yes, sir."

"What happened next?"

"I dunno. I was unconscious. Next thing I was in hospital. I was told the local cops arrested two of the Medusa cops, but one got away."

"For the record, your Honour, Floyd was severely beaten by these rogue policemen from Medusa, clearly outside of their normal area of jurisdiction. They were not wearing their uniforms. Another of them fled the scene in an unmarked car. The two so-called policemen are still in custody. The Medusa police department is part of a separate investigation by the FBI with legal proceedings to follow.

"Floyd Jensen alleges that the whole department is controlled by Theodore Sanchez. That is yet to be proved, but it does follow a pattern of corruption and intimidation within Medusa headed by Mr Sanchez."

Kawalsi leapt to his feet. "Objection! Your Honour, my client's guilt is not proven by any of these statements."

The Judge paused for thought. "I would regard a police force acting outside their normal powers as 'unusual'. Their beating of the witness in plain clothes is proven, but it does not imply that your client is involved, Mr Kawalski. However, it does point to unusual practices in Medusa, particularly their desire to arrest the witness seemingly at any cost. The actions of these two policemen from Medusa is clearly disturbing and pertinent to these proceedings. Please proceed, Mr Gershwin?"

"Thank you, your Honour. Floyd, describe your life in Woosterville to the court."

"I'm just an ordinary kid. I ain't nothin' special. People in Medusa treated me like shit. Sorry, everyone. Sorry your Honour... I always tried but no-one ever gave me a chance. But everyone in Woosterville I've met did give me a chance and I've been happy here. I don't want no trouble. I've seen enough."

"Thank you, Floyd. What Floyd is not saying is that he is a well-respected young man, with friends, a girlfriend, a steady job, a place to live and the friendship and affection of many in the diner where he works. He is also commended by two distinguished academics, Professor Sean Lynch of Woosterville University and Gwen Perloff, a retired Professor of Woosterville

University. They will testify to his intelligence and potential and they are collaborating to find funding to get Floyd into a local college as a student."

"Have you any more questions, Mr Gershwin?"

"No. Thank you, your Honour."

"Mr Kawalski? You have the opportunity to cross-examine the witness?"

"Thank you, your Honour."

"Floyd. You have a reputation for trouble-making in Medusa, don't you?"

"Some might say so, but I..."

"Answer the question, Floyd. Yes or no?"

"Like I said, I don't..."

"Yes or No."

"I don't have to answer a question like that."

The Judge intervened. "Young man, you do. Answer the question."

"But your Honour, he's tryin' to..."

"'Yes' or 'No', young man. That's how it works here."

Floyd scowled, but responded: "Yes."

"You had a reputation for trouble at school?"

"Yes."

"And in the town, too?"

"Yes."

"You continued to cause trouble in Medusa until you fled the town after the death of your mother. Isn't that true?"

"No. No, it ain't true."

"Many will testify to your poor behaviour, Floyd."

"That may be, but it ain't true."

"So a town of eight thousand souls testifies that you have been a long-term nuisance for seventeen years. And we are supposed to believe that a young criminal like you has suddenly 'reformed' and is a pillar of the Woosterville community and a would-be university student on top? Surely that's farcical?"

"Ask the guys I know in Woosterville. Ask them in Medusa. See who looks you in the eye."

"So you can terrorise them further, Floyd?"

"No!"

"So you can intimidate the good people of Medusa?"

"No, that's not true."

"But they all say so. And you agree. Don't you?"

Gershwin stood. "Objection! Your Honour, it has already been established that Floyd is of good character and that has been confirmed by many people in Woosterville. That includes a letter signed by one hundred and twenty four customers who regularly eat at 'Alvin's Diner'. I also have the testimony of several of his friends about his good character. Could the prosecution produce the same sort of evidence of Floyd's alleged criminality? Or is it purely slander?"

The Judge intervened. "Sustained. Mr Kawalski. Can you prove with specific evidence, by individuals or by group testimony that the witness is a troublemaker and intimidating towards the population of Medusa?"

"No, your Honour, but I'm sure we could..."

The Judge looked puzzled. "You don't have it available now?"

"No, your Honour, but I could..."

The Judge frowned. "So you don't have it now? How can we make a judgement if you don't have evidence? Not one witness?"

The Defence lawyer looked uncomfortable. "No, your Honour."

"Then there is no evidence that this witness terrorised anyone, do we?"

"Not at the moment..."

The Judge interrupted Kawalksi. "Then you don't have it. Let's move on, shall we?"

The defence lawyer looked confused for a moment. "Yes... yes, of course, your Honour."

Kawalski turned back to Floyd. "Tell me what you think of Theodore Sanchez, Floyd?"

"What do you mean?" said Floyd.

"Don't play dumb with me or the court, Floyd. What is your honest opinion of Theodore Sanchez?"

Floyd looked over the courtroom at Sanchez.

"The truth? He's a son of a bitch and I wish him dead!"

"So you'd kill him if you could, Floyd?"

"I didn't say that!"

"But you implied it didn't you?"

"No, I never meant..."

"You're a troubled young man who would attack or even attempt to kill your own father to satisfy your aggression and confusion? Isn't that true?"

"No! I hate him and I wish nothing but bad things for him. But kill? I couldn't."

"You'd do bad things to him if you had the chance, wouldn't you?"

Floyd didn't know what to say. He wanted Sanchez dead for all he'd done to his Mom, Zeke and so many others. But he'd always fought on his own. Everyone else had died or abandoned him. It was always just him. He looked across the room, this time at Janie and Alvin, for support.

It was Janie who reacted first. She gave him a smile and a 'thumbs up'. Alvin saw what Janie had done and responded in the same way, a smile and another 'thumbs up'.

It was all that Floyd needed. Janie and Alvin and so many people were still supporting him. He wasn't alone. He'd heard about Sean and Gwen and the girls and the regulars at the diner and everyone who had offered him friendship and welcome. He was no longer alone.

"Come along Floyd, answer the question."

"No. I wouldn't."

"Are we expected to believe a person like yourself, with a history of aggression and disruption, is neutral about my client, Mr Sanchez? A pillar of the community, mayor and servant of the town of Medusa?"

"Pillar of the community my ass!" said Floyd. There was a bubble of laughter around the court which was rapidly silenced by the Judge.

"Young man, can I suggest you stick to answering the question and not continue to make colourful comments?"

Floyd looked embarrassed. "I'm sorry, your Honour."

"Very well. Continue, Floyd. Answer the question."

"I wouldn't hurt him. I'd like to. But I won't. I'd like to see him suffer in the worst way. But that ain't up to me."

"So who do you think will give you retribution with your disturbed agenda against my respected client?"

"It ain't an agenda. I want justice for what he's done. But I can't decide it. Those guys over there, the jury. They'll hear me and so many others and they'll decide what should happen to Sanchez."

The Defence attorney hesitated. He'd tried to rile Floyd and get him angry. But the boy had resisted.

"Mr Kawalski, have you any more questions?"

"One moment, your Honour. I have one more question."

"Then processed with haste."

"Floyd. Your Mom. She clearly had many men in her life. Any one of them could have been your father. What did she do to you to make you hate your own father so venomously?"

Floyd paused again. The slur on his Mom was too much! But he knew that he was being goaded.

"My Mom had a quiet life. She went to work and she stayed out of trouble. She feared Sanchez and she had good reason. I know you're trying to make out she was some sorta whore. I know she wasn't. He did bad things to her and I was the result of it. That didn't mean she loved me the less. She never said he was my father and she wanted to make me free of any obligation to any man who could sire a child and then ignore it to live as 'Marlene's Bastard.' I'm proud to be 'Marlene's Bastard', but I'm ashamed to be known as Theodore Sanchez's son."

Floyd looked over at Sanchez, completely dispassionate, but he couldn't quite stop the smirk that appeared when he saw the rage in Sanchez's face. Floyd know that if they were in Medusa he'd be dead. But he was free of Medusa and Sanchez. Now and forever.

Floyd turned his gaze back to Janie and Sanchez and grinned back at them.

"You are alleging that my respected client assaulted your mother? A woman of dubious reputation within Medusa? You can't prove that at all."

"Maybe I can't. But when I see a woman so scared of any man and terrified of her son having any contact with the same man and I later find he's my father, what am I supposed to think? That it was all wine and roses? I saw what he did to her over and over. She was terrified for herself and for me!"

"Have you any further questions, Mr Kawalski?"asked the Judge.

"No... no, your Honour."

"Then you may step down, Floyd. I thank you for your restraint in such circumstances, young man."

"You're welcome, sir. Your Honour, I mean."

And then Floyd was gone from the court room.

Chapter 26 – A Night on the Town

Floyd sat in the side room on his own for an hour. He went over and over what he'd said, worrying that he'd not been good enough. It wasn't until a note arrived that he started to relax. It was from the Ron Gershwin, Janie and Alvin:

'Well done Floyd, my little monster! Janie'

'You did good, kid. Alvin.'

'Well done, Floyd. You did very well under such pressure. You have been such an asset to us all. Ron Gershwin. We'll speak later.'

Floyd began to calm down and was soon dozing. He stirred only when Janie, Alvin and Gershwin came into the room.

"Hey, Floyd, have we woken you up?" smiled Janie.

"Time to get moving, kid," said Alvin. "You need to eat."

Floyd's stomach gurgled in response which made the three adults laugh.

The four of them made their way down to a nearby restaurant. Floyd looked alarmed. This was expensive!

They were met at the door by a waiter who took them to their table.

The lawyer looked at Floyd. "No need to be alarmed. This is on me to celebrate this afternoon."

"I ain't ever been in anywhere like this before!"

"Don't get too used to it, Floyd?" joked Alvin.

"Oh I don't know Alvin, I think I could?" said Janie.

"Baby, anything for you. But do you want me to go bankrupt?"

"Well..."

"You do?"

"If I can get a better offer later, I might consider it?"

Alvin looked wary.

"Of course I wouldn't, you big goof! Let's enjoy the moment."

"Yeah, baby, there will be other moments later..."

"Is that a promise...?"

"They need to get a room. They never stop, Mr Gershwin."

The lawyer laughed. "After today, you all deserve it. But let's not forget Janie's support. We couldn't have done it without you..."

Janie looked embarrassed. "I only supported my two guys, like any decent woman would do."

"I couldn't have done it without you, Janie" said Floyd.

"Don't be silly."

"No, I mean it. I got stuck, but you and Alvin were there with the 'thumbs up'. You don't know how that helped. That guy would have made mincemeat of me without you there."

Alvin nodded. "Me too, baby. We wouldn't be here without you."

Alvin picked up his glass of wine. "A toast to Janie, who supports us all."

"Janie!" said Floyd, raising his glass of juice.

"To Janie!" said Ron.

"To me!" Janie smiled again as they all laughed.

"So what happens next?" asked Alvin.

"We have witnesses in Medusa. Still working on them. We don't really need them, but it would be the nail in the coffin of Theodore Sanchez if we could. Kalb, from Sanchez's gang, will testify on Friday. And then there's you, Alvin."

Alvin face grew hard. "OK. I'm all set."

"But didn't you already testify, Alvin?" asked Floyd.

"Yes, why again?" said Janie.

"Janie. Floyd. I have to testify. No-one will ever know it's me. You don't need to know any more. Let's say that I confirm Floyd's good character and I will present what I know about Sanchez."

Floyd couldn't let it go. "But how will..."

"No more questions, kid."

Janie interrupted. "But Alvin..."

"No more questions, baby. That's all there is to know."

The table went quiet. Luckily, the waiter approached bringing menus. Floyd didn't know what to do, so, the other three helped him select something suitable.

"I ain't sure what all these knives and forks are for?"

"Start from the outside and work your way in, Floyd," said Ron.

"Oh. Is that what I'm supposed to do?"

"It's what I do. Just do it confidently and no-one will ever notice."

"OK, I ain't got a clue but I'll do that confidently."

"No wine for you, Floyd," said Janie.

"Ah c'mon Janie, just a little drop?"

"No. You're still only seventeen. You can't officially drink in Woosterville until you're twenty-one."

"Ah c'mom. Alvin, just a small glass?"

"Kid, I wouldn't go against Janie's wishes. No wine for you. I'll get you a glass in about four year's time?"

Floyd sulked until the food arrived, which distracted him. The others talked about the trial, but he was too busy inhaling the meal.

"Floyd! For God's sake! It's great food! You can't just gobble it down like you're a pig!"

"Sorry Janie, but I'm starving."

"Don't choke yet, kid. We might want you back as a witness."

"Gee, thanks for your concern, Alvin."

Floyd reluctantly slowed down, but he loved the dish he was eating. "Chicken Marengo..." he mumbled while still eating.

"Don't speak with your mouth full, Floyd!"

"Sorry, Alvin. But it's so good! Better than what we make at the diner."

"It's about ten times the price too, kid. Do you want to subsidise me?"

Janie patted Alvin's arm. "It is good food, though, Alvin."

"Yeah, I know, baby. But we couldn't afford to sell food this glitzy."

"Couldn't we?" said Janie. "Let me have a think about that…"

The rest of the meal passed quietly with chat and banter.

Floyd, Janie and Alvin got back to the diner at 9pm. Janie was tired so she excused herself and went early to bed.

The two men sat in the den.

"You did good today, kid."

"You too, Alvin. And you'll do whatever it is you do on Friday. But will it be enough?"

"I'm not sure, kid. Everything points to Sanchez, but he's been smart enough to not be too directly involved. We've got his gang and the local cops. We've proved that everyone is terrified of him in Medusa. We've got fifteen dead bodies on the outskirts of Medusa. We've got twenty missing people in total, over twenty years. But pinning it directly on Sanchez? I don't know, kid."

"So I might not be free of him at all?"

"Kid. Don't worry about that. Even if he walks, Sanchez will be made understand that it would be a mistake to involve himself with Medusa, or you ever again."

"Is that as a diner owner or…?"

"What do you think, kid?"

Floyd let out a jaw-cracking yawn. "I think I gotta get to bed."

Alvin smiled at the boy. "Wise, Floyd."

"Night, Alvin."

"Goodnight, Floyd. This will soon be behind you, kid."

"I hope so."

Alvin remained seated in his chair for some time, brooding.

Over the next two days, the diner remained closed 'For Repairs'. Alvin and Floyd worked on cleaning the kitchen while Janie worked in the office.

"I have some ideas from last night," but she refused to say more.

They were all quiet, thinking about the result of the trial.

On the Friday morning, Alvin disappeared early without saying a word. Janie and Floyd knew where he was, but they continued to work in silence. In the evening, Alvin returned home. He looked exhausted.

"Alvin? How did it go?"

"It was OK, baby. I told everyone what a decent kid Floyd is and I damned Sanchez as much as I could."

"So what do you think will happen?"

Alvin sighed. "To be honest, I think he's gonna get away with it."

"How can that bastard get away with it?" growled Floyd.

"Kid. Sit down."

"We were told he'd..."

"I said sit down!"

Alvin waited until they were all sitting, then continued.

"This is how it goes, kid. Sanchez's gang are up to their necks in it. They'll probably be in jail for the rest of their lives. But with the exception of Kalb, no-one has been able to pin anything on Sanchez. He might get a few years for corruption, but no-one can pin any murders on him."

"So I'm under threat still?"

"No, Floyd. There are ways of persuading Sanchez it's best to start a new life somewhere else and leave you be."

"How are you gonna do that?"

"Ask no questions, tell no lies, kid."

"So what happens next, Alvin?"

"The prosecution will sum up on Monday and then the jury will retire to decide, baby."

"How long will that take?"

"Who knows, Janie? There's lots to consider."

"A few days?"

"Could be. They'll let us know when the jury is ready. I want us to be with Floyd when it happens."

"I don't need no..."

The older man cut in. "Yes you do, Floyd. That's the way it will happen. We were there for you in the court when you were a witness, we'll be there when the jury decides. OK?"

"Yeah. I guess so. Sorry for being a pain in the ass."

"Pain in the ass or not, we'll support you, kid."

"You know we will, Floyd" said Janie.

In the meantime, we've got some renovation to do, kid. While Janie sits and thinks in the office!"

Floyd groaned at the amount of work to come, while Janie laughed at the looks on their faces.

The whole weekend was spent painting and cleaning. It was back breaking work, but the diner looked fantastic afterwards: the walls and were spotless and the floor shone from polishing.

"I'm so proud of you two," said Janie. "The whole place looks great! Those guys will come to refurb the seating next week. But what about outside?"

Alvin and Floyd began complaining again.

"Baby, I'm beat. So is Floyd. We can't do it all. Can't it wait until next year?"

"I don't think it can, Alvin. Inside looks great, but the exterior of this place looks tired. But..."

"But what?" said Floyd.

"I think you two need a few days off. I'll cook. You just relax. OK?"

"You sure, Janie?"

"After all you've been through these past few weeks? It will be my pleasure..."

"I'm always interested in your pleasure, baby."

Floyd looked revolted. "Ah God, here we go again. Maybe I'll go and get a room for a change."

The couple laughed at Floyd as he fled up the stairs.

Two days later, Alvin got the call. "Janie! Floyd! The jury will be back in court first thing tomorrow!"

Floyd's heart sank. "He's gonna get away with it."

"Floyd! We don't know that!" said Janie.

"It's true, kid. We'll have to wait and see. Now, I think we should go out to eat."

"Where, Alvin?"

"Somewhere swanky, baby. Put your best dress on."

"What about me?"

"I'll have to get you a nice dress, Floyd."

"Har-har. I've got no decent clothes."

"Then we go shopping for a suit. Time to learn to look smart, kid."

They all met downstairs at seven pm, Floyd and Alvin dressed in charcoal grey suits, the younger man with a jazzy blue tie and Alvin wearing a conservative dark green.

"You look decent, kid."

"Thanks. I think I look like an idiot."

The Janie came through the door in a summer dress. The two men looked astonished.

"Janie! You look beautiful!"

"Baby, you look like a movie star!"

She smiled back. "You two don't look too bad. Come here, little monster. I need to fix that tie."

Janie came closer and Floyd was enveloped in her perfume.

"That'll do," she said and gave him a kiss on the cheek. "Don't get too carried away, Floyd" she whispered in his ear. "But when a guy with those eyes looks at a woman, she'd be a fool not to interested back. Remember that for the future?"

The boy reddened with embarrassment.

"Hey, what's going on here?"

"Nothing, Alvin."

"It doesn't look like nothing."

"Are you jealous, you big goof?"

"Sure I'm jealous. Have I got a rival for my affections?"

"You might have. It's your own fault for putting him in a sexy suit."

"I'll have to remember that." Alvin glared at Floyd. "Kid, after tonight, no more sexy suit-wearing near Janie. You get me?"

"Yeah! Sure! I don't want no trouble, Alvin." Floyd didn't realise they were making fun of him as usual.

Janie giggled. "Come on, let's go. Where are we going, Alvin?"

"That's the surprise, baby."

A taxi cab pulled in outside the diner and took them away into the city. When they arrived, Janie and Floyd were astonished.

"We can't afford this, Alvin!"

"Sure we can, Janie. It's my treat. For you. And a little bit for you, Floyd." Alvin grinned. "But mainly for Janie."

"But we can't eat here, it's too…"

"Baby, it isn't 'too anything' for you. There isn't anything in the whole wide world that isn't 'too anything'."

Janie hugged him and they both shared a passionate kiss.

"Is this where I have to tell you both to get a room again?" interrupted Floyd.

Janie and Alvin stopped, looked at him disinterestedly for a moment, and then resumed kissing.

Floyd grimaced. "It's me. I should get a room. Yeah, that's it..."

When they'd finished, Janie took Alvin's arm and they walked into 'Le Bistro Laurent', Floyd trailing behind. They were met by a fussy looking waiter.

"Good evening, Madame, Sir and young Sir. You have a reservation?"

"Good evening. Yes, I have a reservation under the name of McCall," replied Alvin.

"Mais oui! One of our better suites. If you would follow me?"

The waiter took them out into the back of the restaurant and into a large private room. The large windows looked out over Woosterville Bay.

Janie stared, open-mouthed. "Alvin, this is beautiful. It's like a fairy tale!"

"It sure is, Janie. Let's enjoy the evening."

And so they did. The waiters patiently helped Janie and Floyd with their menu selection. Alvin was surprisingly knowledgeable about French cuisine and he read the menu in French. The wine was perfect, although Floyd sourly drank his water. As the sun went down, the lights of the city pierced the darkness. They were content with each other's company, the food, and the view.

It was one of the happiest nights of Floyd's life. He was with his two closest friends. His family. There was no danger to him or to them. He didn't know what the future held, but was unworried. The present was pleasant enough. Tomorrow could take care of itself.

"You're very quiet, kid."

"Just thinking how lucky I am, Alvin."

"This isn't luck, it's just a decent night out."

"No, it's luck" said Floyd. "I've never had much of until I met you two. Now I'm the luckiest man alive."

"That's a beautiful thing to say, Floyd." said Janie.

"Poetic, baby. I do believe our foundling is a poet as well as being intelligent, a half decent cook and not bad with a paint brush. Will your talents ever end, Floyd?"

Floyd scowled. "Now you're just teasin' me again."

"Not really, kid. Janie and I just gave you an opportunity. And a kick up the ass when you needed it. When you put your mind to it, you seem to be able to do anything you want, Floyd Jensen."

"He's a real renaissance man, Alvin."

"He certainly is, baby."

Floyd became defensive. "I ain't that clever."

"That's debatable, kid. Once all this bullshit is over, I... Janie and I want you to go and study."

"I couldn't leave you guys to the diner on your own. And expect you to keep me for nothin'!"

"You'll still work for us, kid. You're welcome to stay as long as you like. But study is your future."

"We want you to get more chances in your life, Floyd," said Janie.

"What if I like being where I am?"

"Then we're mistaken about you, Floyd: Alvin, me, that guy Sean Lynch, Gwen and all the other people who have met you here. We all want you to try. If you don't like it, then don't do it."

"But we do expect you to try, kid," added Alvin.

Floyd hesitated. "I know you mean well, guys, but..."

"But what, kid?"

"What is it, Floyd?"

"I ain't got education. I ain't got finesse or class. Gwen says I'm 'primitive'. What can I do that thousands couldn't do better?"

"It's true, kid. You have no education. You're rough around the edges. Gwen thinks you have potential, but you need to study in order to bring out your talent. I had to, so you can too."

"Have you got education, Alvin?" asked Janie.

"More than I ever need, baby."

"Like what?"

"Oh, my folks made me study a degree. Then a masters. I hated it. But I finished it. Always was a dreamer and I loved the arts more than the sciences. But it did me no harm to learn how to think clearly and logically, you know?"

"So what's your top qualification?"

"It was another Master's in Forensic Science. Hard work, but it got to see and learn some interesting things. Not pleasant, but it wasn't dull. It started to be less fun about five years ago, so I retired. Lucky for me I met Janie when she applied to work at the diner. The best luck I ever had, baby."

"But it's poetry I like most of all. Expressive. Instant." He continued in a soft and refined voice as he looked directly into Janie's face. Gone was the everyday ordinary Alvin. She sat there entranced as he began to speak:

'But when the melancholy fit shall fall

Sudden from heaven like a weeping cloud,

That fosters the droop-headed flowers all,

And hides the green hill in an April shroud;

Then glut thy sorrow on a morning rose,

Or on the rainbow of the salt sand-wave,

Or on the wealth of globed peonies;

Or if thy mistress some rich anger shows,

Emprison her soft hand, and let her rave,

And feed deep, deep upon her peerless eyes.'

Janie's eyes shone and she looked away, embarrassed. Alvin smiled gently and he touched her cheek and made her look back at him. He too had shining eyes.

Floyd was too impressed with Alvin to object to their obvious affection. "That's so cool, Alvin! I never knew you could recite poetry?"

"Neither did I," agreed Janie, her voice thick with emotion."Will you ever stop surprising me, big goof?"

"I hope not, Janie..." murmured Alvin. And then he grinned at her and the spell was broken. "You can't beat Keats. Now, who wants dessert?"

Janie was still shocked. "But... you... you're so clever? You were making out you didn't know anything?"

"No, baby. What use is what I learnt working in a diner? Apart from a good understanding of human nature. The dark side of it, anyhow."

"But you could do so much more, Alvin!"

"I have already done what I wanted to do. I had a decent career. Then I didn't want to do it anymore. Then I retired and opened a diner. Then I met you and I felt complete. Then Floyd came along and it's what I always wanted. Never had any kids of my own, but I've got one in this kid here. What more do I want?"

"Oh Alvin, I didn't know you felt like that?"

"You didn't? I'm a big goof for real if I didn't make that clear enough, Janie."

"You are a big goof, Alvin. But you're my big goof."

"You know it, Janie! And as for Floyd here, he's off to college if he likes it or not!"

"Gee, thanks, Dad!" said Floyd, laughter interrupting the moment.

"So no more arguments, kid. You try it. If you genuinely don't like it, then don't do it. But it can't be just because you got out of bed wrong that day. You'll have to prove to me and Janie it's because you genuinely don't want to or aren't up to doing it. Deal?"

Alvin held out his hand. Floyd hesitated.

"Deal. Or no deal, kid."

"What the hell..." said Floyd and shook Alvin's hand.

"I'm a witness that you agreed to this, Floyd!" said Janie, smiling again.

"So, are we having extra dessert to celebrate?" asked Floyd.

Chapter 27 - Trial and Error

The court was packed with people as the Judge entered the court. Alvin, Janie and Floyd had just managed to get a seat at the back courtesy of Ron Gershwin. They all stood up as the Judge walked in, sat, looked around the court and spoke: "Please be seated."

He looked over at the jury. "Have you made a decision?"

One of the jury stood. "We have, your Honour."

"Please proceed,"

"Your Honour, we find Anthony Moscarra guilty of murder. We find George Lindberg guilty of murder. We find Samuel Dempsey guilty of murder. We find Theodore Sanchez not guilty of murder."

The court erupted. Floyd stared at Sanchez's look of triumph. His men looked beaten, but it was Sanchez's smile that did it for Floyd. He began to stand, but was quickly yanked back down in his seat by Alvin.

"Keep your head, kid," Alvin hissed. "Let him have his moment. It'll be all the sweeter after the sentences. OK?"

"But what can anyone do...?"

"Just wait and see, Floyd. Whatever you do, stay calm, don't let that son of a bitch goad you."

The Judge turned to the accused. "Because of the severity of your crimes, multiple homicide, rape, assault, intimidation and racketeering, I sentence Anthony Moscarra, George Lindberg and Samuel Dempsey to life imprisonment, with no possibility of parole. No town or city in this great country should be subject to your criminality without there being a harsh punishment. Freedom from criminals and thugs is part of the freedom we all enjoy. Without that freedom, we have no life and no liberty.

The judge looked at Sanchez. "Theodore Sanchez, the jury have found you not guilty and I respect their decision. I do find it difficult to believe that your close associates could terrorise Medusa without your explicit knowledge and involvement. Be sure that your sins will find you out eventually, Mr Sanchez.

"Court is dismissed."

Sanchez stood, shaking hands with his defence lawyer and his friends. He didn't bother to look at his gang members as they were meekly led away. He spotted Floyd at the back of the court and smiled again, making a 'gun' sign with his hand.

Floyd again made to stand up but Alvin stopped him. "Wait for it, kid. Look at his delight. Let him have his fun. He won't be smiling in about..." Alvin looked at his watch. "Ten minutes."

"What's going to happen?"

"That'll be a surprise for you, too, kid. Now look worried... yeah that's it! I'll look angry. Let him think he's in charge."

As the crowds began to leave Sanchez walked towards Floyd.

"Hey Floyd. Look forward to getting to know you, son. I hope you'll enjoy it too. My lawyer here is making an application for you to be taken into my custody. You're still a minor so I'll be looking after you in the near future. Just like I did your Mom."

Sanchez's eyes suddenly lit up. Any pretence of friendliness was gone. "We're going to have so much fun together, Floyd..."

"No... not a word" whispered Alvin, as he squeezed Floyd's arm. "Not just yet..."

"See you later, son, I have a party to attend to. We'll have our own party soon..." said Sanchez as he strode away, confident and in control, as he always had been in Medusa. As he made his way out the door, he was slowed down by the photographers and journalists asking questions.

The court was empty apart from Alvin, Janie and Floyd.

"I gonna kill him, Alvin," said Floyd. "I can't let him get away with this?"

"Not just yet, kid..." said Alvin.

"What are you up to, Alvin?"

"You'll see, Janie." Alvin looked at his watch again. "Five more minutes... just relax, both of you."

They fell into silence, Alvin seemingly at ease, but Janie and Floyd agitated and worried.

After what seemed an eternity, Alvin suddenly looked at his watch. "Let's move. Quickly! We need to be at the bottom of the court steps!"

They quickly got outside through a side door and were standing on the sidewalk, watching the crowds around Sanchez. He had walked down the court steps and was about to get into a large limousine. Before he could open the door, three dark blue cars appeared.

Several familiar looking men stepped out of the car and walked towards Sanchez, just stopping to grin at Alvin, Janie and Floyd.

"Theodore Sanchez, you are under arrest for money laundering and tax evasion under section 3 of the 'Illegal Source Financial Crimes Program'. You have the right to remain silent. Anything you say can and will be used against you in a court of law..."

Sanchez turned to the sound of Floyd's surprised laughter. "You fucking little prick, I'll kill you!"

Sanchez broke through the surrounding FBI Officers, running at Floyd, but the boy was ready. He dodged the punch and put one of his own squarely on Sanchez's nose. The older man was stunned enough to allow the FBI agents to drag him away, handcuffed, as he raged about what he would do to the boy.

Alvin patted Floyd on the shoulder with a big grin. "Nice punch, Floyd. That was sweet! Don't worry about the threats, kid. It will be explained to Sanchez that's such ideas won't be tolerated."

Alvin looked at his watch again. "I'll be doing that in about one hour."

Saul Hanser walked up to them. "Good job, guys. You got him so riled he threatened you, Floyd, in front of witnesses and the press. Nice punch, by the way. You were clearly defending yourself so there's no need to worry about any further trouble.

Hanser gave Floyd a nod. "It's been recorded on film too. We'll be encouraging everyone in the media to show it around the country. Janie and Floyd, I'll give you ride home. Alvin has some business to attend to."

The older man nodded sombrely. "I do. Not that it's anybody else's business. Yours or Janie or Floyd. Or anyone. Got it?"

"You're still the boss, Alvin."

"Good. Catch you later, baby. Catch you later, Floyd."

430

Janie and Floyd were escorted to a car and were soon home.

"What are we going to do after all that, Janie?"

"We need to relax. How about I make us some tea and something to eat and we sit in the den?"

"Yeah, sure, Janie. Want any help?"

"No, that's OK. Sit down and chill out."

They sat in silence the rest of the afternoon, just occasionally speaking, relieved it was over.

Alvin entered the precinct again. The local cops quickly jumped to attention and led him to Sanchez in the interview room.

Sanchez was in a chair, his hands handcuffed to the armrests, his nose taped up and bloody.

"Hey! Nice to see you again!" Said Alvin with a happy smile.

"What do you want?" growled Sanchez.

"Just to let you know that being convicted of murder would have been better for you. By the time the IRS and Feds are finished with you, you'll be looking at a few hundred years in jail, Mr Sanchez."

"All because of that little bastard! I'll..."

"No. You won't," interrupted Alvin.

"Are you going to try to stop me? A diner owner? I have guys who will..."

"No. You won't."

Without warning, Alvin punched Sanchez on the nose. Sanchez shrieked with pain. "You son of a bitch, I'll kill..."

Alvin casually reached across to Sanchez's hand. Found a finger, then twisted it violently to make it come out of its socket.

Sanchez yelled again.

Alvin grabbed Sanchez by the chin. "Look at me. You have nine more fingers. Then ten more toes. Then ankles, kneecaps, elbows and more."

Sanchez gasped with the pain. "You can't do this to me..."

Alvin reached again for another finger. The complaining stopped.

"Do you get the picture, Mr Sanchez?"

Sanchez whined. "What do you want?"

"You threatened Floyd. You threatened me. That will not be tolerated."

"I'll tell the cops you did this to me..."

Alvin violently twisted another finger on Sanchez's right hand.

As Sanchez sobbed in pain, Alvin spoke again.

"If you ever mention me, or Floyd or anything to anyone, what will happen to you will be extremely unpleasant. Do. You. Understand?"

He twisted Sanchez's broken fingers and as Sanchez squealed he said. "Do you understand me?"

"Yes! Yes! Please..."

"Good. Now, Mr Sanchez. Put any thoughts of harming anyone ever again out of your head. You'll notice that you've yelled and shouted and complained and no-one has come in to investigate. I can do whatever I like to you and no-one will ever come in."

Alvin paused and looked intently at Sanchez.

433

"So what will you do?"

"I'll… I'll never say anything about you or that little prick…"

Alvin grabbed Sanchez's broken fingers and he squealed again in response.

"His name is 'Floyd'," said Alvin. "Best remember that, don't you think?"

"Yeah… yeah… sure… please don't hurt me again."

"So what will you do?"

"I'll… I'll never say anything about you or… or Floyd. It's like you don't exist."

"Thank you, Mr Sanchez. I hope you haven't thought about hiring anyone for your dirty work?"

"No. I… I was gonna wait."

"Good. Then don't do it. I think we're done here. Please make sure we don't have to meet again."

"Yeah! Yeah! Whatever you say!" Sanchez sobbed again.

"You definitely don't want to meet me again, Mr Sanchez."

Alvin banged on the door. "Guys! Mr Sanchez has had a fall. Can someone patch him up?"

As the local cops came in, Alvin quietly slipped out.

When he got home he found Janie and Floyd sitting quietly in the den.

"Hey guys!"

"Alvin! Come and sit down. What have you been doing?"

"You know better than to ask. But it's all done. Never again. You're free as a bird, kid. I'm free too. Time we got on with our lives."

Alvin sat down and hugged Janie.

"Before I have to get a room, do you want something to eat, Alvin?"

"Thanks, Floyd. How about a ham sandwich, lots of salad?"

"Yeah, sure. I'll be sure to knock when I'm back."

But Alvin and Janie were too busy with their kissing to reply.

Chapter 28 – Moving On

The morning newspapers and news shows were full of Sanchez's trial, his smug smile at the acquittal and his subsequent re-arrest by the FBI. The threats to Floyd were repeated over and over so that no-one, anywhere, could be in any doubt at what Sanchez really was.

Saul Hanser had emailed a recording of Floyd punching Sanchez on the nose. Floyd watched it repeatedly on his laptop and enjoyed it more each time. He took satisfaction from seeing pictures of Sanchez looking battered and defeated. He found himself whistling a happy little tune as he watched himself punching Sanchez on the nose again and again.

"What the hell happened to him, Alvin?"

"Probably had a fall, kid?"

"Down the stairs? How many times? Know anything about that, Alvin?"

Alvin tried to look innocent. "Me? Perish the thought, Floyd. What would a humble diner owner have to do with criminal scum like Theodore Sanchez?"

"Nothin' at all. Or to do with a kitchen worker at the same diner?"

"You got it, kid. You'll not have to worry about that. He probably knows that well."

"OK. I don't know what will happen to him and I don't rightly care anymore. As long as they throw away the key?"

"It's likely. No-one could prove it in court, but he'll have no friends now. And when the IRS are done with him, he'll be in a cage for a hundred years. What they did to Al Capone, they could easily do with Theodore Sanchez."

"So that's it, Alvin?" asked Floyd.

"That's it, kid."

Floyd let out a huge sigh. "Good."

"Revenge enough for you, Floyd?"

"Yeah. As long as he can't hurt anyone else."

"He won't, Floyd."

"Cool."

"So what will you do now, kid?"

"Can we get back to normal? Diner, Mary, Sundays, Gwen, hanging out with my friends?"

"And study, Floyd?"

"I can't do everything, Alvin!"

"We'll manage that. I want you to call Sean Lynch tomorrow morning. OK?"

Floyd looked wary. "Do I really have to?"

The older man smiled back. "I think you do, Floyd, but I can't force you to do it. "

Floyd scowled as he thought about his options. Always working in the diner? The girls would be moving on to university and other things. Sanchez was in prison. Things were changing around him. What did he want from life? To stay the same or change himself too?

"Yeah, OK. I'll do it. Why not?"

It was a very nervous Floyd who dialled the number for Sean's office the next day.

"Hi. Is that Sean Lynch? Hi, it's Floyd Jensen. No, I'm good. Thanks for the reference you wrote for me. No, it's all done now. No, I promise not to punch anyone ever again on national tv!"

Floyd listened while the Professor spoke and then replied. "Yeah, funny you should say that. It's been suggested that I talk to you about me studying. No, I want to do it, I just don't know where to start. This afternoon? Have you got time? Cool, I'll be there. Bye."

They met in Sean's office at 2pm.

Lynch grinned in welcome. "Come in Floyd. It's so good to see you again! I am assuming your life as a court witness and clouter of criminals is now over?"

"I sure hope so, Sean!"

Lynch smiled again. "Good. We have some things to discuss, I think?"

"Yeah. I... I have to apologise for what I said in the gallery. I wasn't sure..."

"Floyd. Forget that. It isn't relevant to me as a Professor or you as a potential student."

"Oh! OK. So what's your interest in me?"

"Do you remember how we talked about the picture? The Venus?"

"Yeah. I do."

"Do you remember what you said?"

"Yeah." Floyd flushed with embarrassment. It all seemed such a long time ago. He'd changed and experienced so much.

"What did you say?"

"'It made me horny...' I was such a fool."

"No, Floyd, it was an honest answer. You're seventeen? What else would it make you do?"

"It was stupid."

"Not at all. But you talked about how the Venus contrasted with the women you'd met."

"Yeah. She... the Venus ain't like any real woman. Sorta like an ideal. Sexy but not really. The whores in Woosterville, they aren't like her. The Venus, I mean. Mary isn't like that, but she's real and more to me than any picture. But with the Venus there's so much. I remember sayin' to you. The sky and the trees and the servants and that big trunk and the flowers. And the little dog? It ain't just about her is it?"

"No, Floyd. It isn't. I've asked you lots of questions and tried to make you think. I do that with all my students. But you, Floyd Jensen, really do think about things and you give an honest and sometimes insightful answers."

"Just dumb luck, Sean."

"I think not. There's something there inside you and I want to set it free. To help you develop your talents and use them productively."

"Gwen says I'm primitive."

Sean laughed. "Ah, yes! The ever insightful Professor Gwen Perloff, who also thinks very highly of you."

"She's kind. And I enjoy talking to her. I've learnt so much off her to too."

"What has Professor Perloff taught you, Floyd?"

"I... it's hard to describe. She's made me think about how I look at things. How I really 'see' things. To see the things that ain't there. I sound dumb..."

"Not at all, Floyd. What else have you learnt from her?"

"I've learnt about me. Sort of. I know I don't think I can do anything, but I know I've got something... and I know I need help to understand 'it'. But I don't know what 'it' is. Does this make any sense at all?"

"It's my own experience too, Floyd. Professor Perloff will agree. Which leads to my next question, Floyd. Why aren't you learning, young man?"

"I'm too stupid, sir. Or that's what they told me at school. I gave up trying as everything I did was wrong or they told me it was. Until I didn't care either way."

Sean looked aghast. "Floyd, your teachers were the 'stupid', your school was 'stupid' and most the people you ever knew in Medusa were 'stupid', but you, Floyd Jensen are the least stupid student I've ever met."

"I ain't no student."

"But you could be, Floyd. The question is, do you want to be?"

"I like to know and I always wanted to know more. But who'd take a dumb-ass like me? And I seen lotsa pretty boys around here and I ain't gonna be another one of them!"

Sean laughed. "Come and have a look at this picture. This is Gabriel, my partner. You really aren't my type!"

"So what do you see in me?"

"I see something in your mind that I like. The way you think. Your thinking is primitive, as you've said, but that's to be expected."

Floyd grinned. "It makes me sound like some sorta caveman?"

"Absolutely! Academically, you're a caveman, Floyd, but I think you're bright enough to learn. And it's within my purview to offer certain students a grant to help them with studies."

"You'd do that for me?"

"Why not, Floyd?"

"How would I do it?"

"I'll set you some reading..."

"Holy shit, not more reading!"

"No reading, no grant, no studying, Floyd."

The boy paused in thought and then sighed. "When you put it like that, how can I refuse? OK. I'll do it. "

"Excellent! Now, what do you like doing most of all, Floyd?"

The boy hesitated. "I sorta like writing. Observing and writing. But that ain't learning."

"Of course it is, Floyd." Sean looked over at his overloaded bookcase, while muttering to himself.

"Right. A book on observation is first on your list. Another on structured writing. Ever written an essay?"

"Yeah but it was all a bore."

"Then I want you to read this." Sean picked a book from the bookshelf and handed it to Floyd.

"'Essay Writing for Dummies?' Gee, thanks!"

"It's what you need, Floyd."

"OK. Then what?"

"You read the 'Dummies' book. Then the book on observation. Then you write about how you observe. Contrast it with what you read in the book."

"I could never do that."

"You can't until you do, Floyd. I suggest you try."

"OK. I'll try. It's gonna be hard."

Sean nodded. "It's meant to be hard. You'll learn more about yourself. You'll stretch your mind. And I'll get to understand you better. Then read the next book. Look at how you write, all primitive and energetic. Then tell me what you think the book says about writing."

"But what if I like the way I do writin'?"

"Then explain and argue why you like it and why you want to keep writing like you do."

"OK. When do you want it done by?"

"First one in ten days. Second one in three weeks."

"Ten days! I'll never..."

Sean interrupted. "Ten days, Floyd. You have to learn to write to a schedule. I'll find out what you're good at and where you need some extra help. Now go off and start reading, young man!"

"I... is that it?"

"For now, Floyd. We'll look at your artistic skills later. First you need to know how to communicate."

"Yeah. I getcha."

"Off you go. Email me your first essay in ten days. Starting now..."

Floyd jumped from his seat. "I'll give it my best shot, Sean."

Sean smiled. "Of course you will. I expect no less. Get reading!"

When Floyd had gone, Sean made a phone call.

"Alvin? Hi it's Sean Lynch. Yes, good thanks. I've just met our young scholar. He's got ten days to write an essay. Yes he can. Just encourage him. Yes, that would be great. Then he has another one in three weeks. Yes I am pushing him. He can do it. If he can't, we know where to start. Yes, Of course I will. By the way, the new coffee is great! Thanks for that. Yes, if I can put more customers your way I will. A revamp? Just give me a date. Gabriel and I will be there. I'll be happy to help. And you, Alvin. Bye."

"That's Floyd sorted. Now what else?" Sean groaned. "All this marking to do...

He picked up the phone again. "Gabe? It's me, love. Yes. Marking... I know that! Phone me at eight? Love you!"

He smiled and got to work.

Janie and Alvin hardly saw Floyd in the next week outside working hours. He missed meals and was silent when they saw him.

"You OK, kid?" asked Alvin.

"Yeah. I'm just... hell, I don't know what I'm doing!"

"Can we help you, Floyd?" said Janie.

"I dunno, Janie. I've read the book and made notes. I've written stuff down, but I think it's garbage."

"How do you know it's garbage, kid?"

"I... I don't. I just think it is."

"Want me to read it?"

"I don't want to take up your time, Alvin."

"You won't be, kid. Just print me a copy and I'll let you know what I think. OK?"

"Thanks, Alvin."

The next day Alvin came back with the essay.

"What do you think, Alvin?"

"It's not bad, kid. You need a bit more structure, though."

"In what way?"

"The introduction is good. It told me what you want to say. Then you write OK about observation. But your conclusion starts adding new ideas."

"Oh! OK, I getcha. Anything else?"

"It isn't you writing this, kid."

"What do you mean? I ain't no cheat!"

"No, you aren't. You're too honest by far. But when you write this, you're doing it to please. What you think Sean will like. You aren't writing what you really think. I can tell."

"If I'm too in his face, he might not like it."

"Floyd. Being 'in someone's face' is what you're good at. It's a strength, if you do it right. You're blunt, but to the point. What you notice is usually important. What you've done here is avoid being blunt in case of not being liked. Against your nature. "

"So I should tell it as it is?"

Alvin laughed. "Within reason, kid! Say it as you see it, but explain yourself. Can you do that?"

"I think so."

"I'll leave you to it, then."

Alvin headed to the kitchen.

"How is he Alvin?"

"He's OK, baby. He just needed a gentle kick up the ass."

"He's not that bad, is he?"

"No. He just needed a few pointers. Floyd is a bright kid. He gets it. He just needs our help now and then."

"I don't think I'll be able to help him at all, Alvin."

"Janie, you have no idea what a help you are to him. And me too. Forget about Floyd for a while. He'll manage fine. What were you thinking about for our relaunch?"

It was a grumpy and tired Floyd who emailed his essay to Sean a few days later. He expected to fail.

"Sean will just laugh at it," he thought.

The following Thursday he arrived at Sean's office once more.

"Hi Floyd, have a seat. So, how do you think you did?"

"I don't know. I ain't got no way to know."

"Fair enough. Do you want to hear what I think?"

"Yeah. Sure. "

"It's naive. Primitive. No surprises there. You have strong opinions and you sometimes back them in your arguments and evidence. But not enough. There's no quotes at all. You have some problems with structure and your sentences are too long and tend to wander off. You confuse observation with just looking at people or things."

Seeing Floyd's face, Sean carried on. "Before you get too upset, you should understand that most my new students do it, too."

"Does that mean I've failed?"

"Of course not. I know a lot more now about what you think about and how you think about it. It's not bad for a first attempt. I've written some notes. Now start reading and writing for the next essay. You've got twelve days."

"Is that it?"

"It is. What more do you want?"

"I dunno. I put my heart and soul into this and we're done in five minutes?"

"That's the way it works. You did well, now do better. Off you go."

"But..."

"Anything more to add, Floyd?"

"Not really, but..."

"Then off you go, write me the next essay."

Floyd angrily got out of his seat, but before he could storm off, Sean spoke again.

"Between you and me: well done, Floyd. I'm pleased so far. Now shoo! I have too much marking to do."

The next few days were a nightmare. Everything he felt he should do when he wanted to write was wrong. According to the book, anyhow. He grumbled at Janie and Alvin endlessly.

"Structure this. Plan that. There's no fun or spontaneity in what I'm supposed to do. Where's the fun in planning everything to the smallest detail?"

"Have you put that in your essay?" asked Alvin.

"No. It sounds silly."

"If you think it's silly, why are you saying it to us, kid?"

"Because I write how I write. Silly or not."

"Then argue it in your essay, Floyd."

"It's true, Floyd," said Janie. "If you want to enjoy what you do, then do it the way you want. If doing it their way makes you unhappy, then why do it?"

"It's how to succeed, Janie. If I want to succeed I have to do it this way. No-one will read my stuff if I can't structure better."

"Then what are you bitching about, then, Floyd?"

"I dunno. I think I have to think some more."

Alvin sniffed the air. "Is that the smell of burning, Janie?"

"I think so, Alvin. Or is it Floyd's brain starting to work more?"

"If you two are just gonna make fun..."

"Of course we are, kid. We'll never stop until you start to think. You can do, it, though."

"Yeah. I suppose I can. I have to get back to it."

It was a drag. Reading. Note-taking. Thinking of ideas. Discarding them. Thinking again. Sometimes Floyd wondered if he could sleep, his head was full of so many contradictory ideas.

"I have to have a day off," he said to Janie in the morning. "My head is full of cotton wool. I can't think straight."

"Go and meet Mary. If she's not available, try Marla. She'll take your mind off everything, Floyd..."

Floyd grinned. "She would. But I want time with someone I like, not get eaten alive by Marla. I ain't sure she's good for me."

"I'm glad you realise that, at least, Floyd."

"I'll see you later, Janie."

"Sure. Have a good day. Can you be back for eight? I want to talk to you and Alvin about the revamp."

"Yeah. I'll be there."

Mary was free, so they spent the day wandering around the park. Floyd didn't enjoy Mary's fascination with window shopping, going into the stores and 'sometimes' buying something, but he put up with it in good grace. Floyd noticed that she seemed distracted and down.

"Are you OK, Mary?" he asked.

Mary suddenly looked sad. "Can I talk to you, Floyd?"

"Sure you can. What's wrong?"

"I got an offer from a university, Floyd."

"That's great! Where from?"

"Boston."

"Boston? But that's way over in Massachusetts. Which one?"

"Boston College. If you don't want me to go..."

"No. Mary. It's a great place. Even I've heard of it. You can't turn it down."

"But what about us?"

Floyd paused. "We'll always be friends, won't we?"

"But I love you, Floyd. But it doesn't sound like you love me?"

"I do love you, Mary. But you know what I've been through the last year. I'm only seventeen years old. So are you. I want us to always be friends. But you've got a life in Boston to look forward to. New friends. You might meet another guy. How could I stop you? Why would I want to if it made you happy?"

Mary hugged and kissed him. "Are you sure?"

"What else can we do? When do you go to Boston?"

"Eight months."

"So let's have eight months of time together. No regrets, Mary."

Floyd and Mary met all of the girls in the park as usual, but the weather was turning cooler into October. They tried some other diners nearby, but the food was nothing like Alvin's. One by one they told him of their university offers. They were all going away. He tried not to hide his disappointment that all of them were leaving him behind.

Marla was heading for Central City's university. "You can come and visit me any time, Floyd. Day or night."

Julie was taking a year out to travel. "I'm going around the world!" she said excitedly.

The other girls were scattering to universities, jobs and to travel. No-one was staying in Woosterville.

"You'll be all alone, Floyd. What will you do?"

"If I can write the second essay I might get a scholarship. But I ain't sure I've got what it takes. It's so hard to do!"

The girls scolded him.

"We know you've got a brain, Floyd..."

"Cute and clever, Floyd..."

"We know you can do it..."

"I guess you all have more confidence than I have?" Floyd groused.

"We want you to do your best..."

"Can we help...?"

"We'd do anything to help, Floyd..."

He looked at them all. These girls who were his closest friends, apart from Janie and Alvin. His 'harem'. The thought of 'anything' piqued his interest, but he quickly put those sort of thoughts aside.

"No. I'll be OK, guys. But thank you. I want you to all focus on your own studies. I want everyone to know how clever my friends are."

"And you too, Floyd!" Mary replied.

"We'll see..." said Floyd, but he felt a little more confident because of their support. And he was flattered by their attention.

"When's the diner opening up again, Floyd...?"

"Yeah, we want good food again, not like this garbage..."

"We like Janie and Alvin, we'll tell everyone…"

"I dunno. Janie wants to speak to me and Alvin tonight. I've gotta go soon, it's nearly seven."

It took Floyd ten minutes to get out of the diner with all the hugs and kisses and more hugs. Despite the fuss, he enjoyed the looks he got from all the other guys sitting around. They were jealous. That made Floyd even happier.

Floyd met Janie and Floyd in the diner office at eight. They both looked deadly serious.

"Is it bad news, guys?"

"No, kid. At least not yet."

"What's gonna happen?"

"Floyd, we've started to lose money. There's enough reserves to last a year, but we can't go on like this for much longer."

"So will you close down?"

"Not yet, kid. I have money to prop us up, but I don't want to do that if we can't get more customers."

"We can't waste Alvin's money, Floyd."

"So what can I do to help?"

"You can't, kid. Not directly. But Janie has a plan to go upmarket."

"Upmarket? Where do the customers come from?"

"The university. Sean Lynch said he'd help. Your girlfriends. The regulars."

"Most of the girls are off to university in about eight months. Mary is going to Boston University."

"Oh, Floyd. What will you both do?" asked Janie.

"We'll be friends and then she goes away."

Alvin scowled. "That's tough, kid. We really like Mary."

"I don't want to think about it. How can I help with the revamp?"

"We're hoping that when you go to regular classes and mention the diner. Give out vouchers to get people here. Take to the student association. Could you do that?"

"Sure. If they'll listen. And if I get into Woosterville College."

"You will. And try some charm, kid?"

Floyd smirked. "Me? Charm?"

"You've got charm, Floyd Jensen. You just need to use it," said Janie.

Floyd grinned. "I might have to get another harem first?"

Janie laughed. "Whatever works for you, Floyd?"

"Just be careful, kid. Study comes ahead of romance."

Floyd grinned again. "If you say so, Alvin."

"Janie and I will talk to our contacts. Do your best. That's all you can do, Floyd."

The next week went quickly. Janie finalised the menu and Alvin ordered in supplies. Floyd found some of the new meals tricky, but soon got the hang of most of the recipes.

"Yeah, I got it, Alvin. It's stew."

"No. Floyd, it's called 'Beef Borginion'."

"Yeah. Beef stew."

"No, Floyd. 'Beef Borginion'. The name is important. If people think it's just 'stew' they won't pay. If they think it's French and fancy, they'll pay more."

"I can't even say it. Beef Bor-gin-on?"

"Beef Bor-geen-yon."

"Beef Bor-geeng-gon?"

"Beef Bor. Geen. Yon."

"I got it! Beef Bor. Ging. Yong."

"No, Floyd. Beef Bor. Geen. Yon."

"Shit! Beef Bor. Geen. Yong."

"Nearly, kid. Keep practising."

"I can cook 'em all, but I'll never remember all the names."

"You will, Floyd. Give it time, kid!"

"How is it you know all these dishes, Alvin?"

"My folks ate out a lot. Fancy restaurants, you'd call them. Helps to have learnt a bit of French and Italian too."

"You can speak French and Italian?"

"Mais oui! A bit rusty, kid. I like Italian better, the language of love."

Janie walked into the kitchen. "What's this about love?"

"We're talking about the language of love, mio cuore…"

"Who can resist when you talk to me like that, Alvin? You should learn a language, Floyd. Girls will love it."

"Maybe. I might have to for my studies. French or Italian?"

"That's up to you, kid. Depends what you go on to study?"

"Another thing to think about. Jesus! When does it stop?"

Alvin grinned. "It doesn't. That's life, Floyd."

The night of the grand re-opening of Alvin's Diner had arrived. The place was spotless, painted inside and out and well furnished. They were all nervous, especially Floyd.

Sean Lynch had volunteered to give an opening speech. "If it help and gets more of my colleagues here and their students, why not?"

"Do I have to wear that uniform?" whined Floyd.

"Yes. You look smart. Our female customers will want to see you. They will come back. And they'll tell their friends."

"I hate it."

"Hate it all you like, Floyd. But that's what you'll be wearing. For the photos too."

"Photos? Awww, Janie. I don't want a camera pointed at me lookin' like this. I feel like a clown."

"You don't look like a clown. Tell him, Alvin."

"You look decent, kid. Very smart. Attractive, even. When you stop scowling. Stop complaining. It's only tonight. We'll see how it goes."

The doors opened at 8pm and the guests came in. Floyd's friends immediately came over and made a fuss.

"Floyd. You look cool."

"I love a man in uniform," said Marla, kissing him on the cheek, as she pinched his behind.

"Hey!"

"Just having fun while I can."

"Leave him alone, Marla. He doesn't want you all over him," said Julie.

"He'd never want you all over him in a million years, Julie."

"Take that back, Marla, you..."

"Guys! Guys! Let's have a nice evening, shall we? There's lots of university guys here. Why don't you go and talk to them?"

Marla's eyes lit up as she saw the male students. "Catch you later, guys."

"Me too. I'll talk to you later, Floyd." Julie hurried after Marla.

"Mary. What do you want to do?" asked Floyd.

"I could stay with you?"

"I'm gonna be busy cooking and serving. Why don't you go and talk to the university guys?"

"Are you sure, Floyd?"

"Of course. Have a great evening, Mary."

Floyd felt a pang of sadness as she went over to the older university students and was soon talking to them animatedly. She'd blossomed in the few months he'd known her and she'd become much more confident. "Even if she'd stayed, she'd find someone better," he thought bitterly.

Janie appeared from behind him. "That was kind of you, Floyd."

The boy scowled. "She'd better off with some clever guys, Janie."

"Don't talk so foolish, little monster. She loves you. I can see it."

"Maybe. But there ain't no future in it, is there?"

Janie shrugged. "No. Maybe not, but you've got a friend for life. I can see that."

"I know. I'll always care for her, but she's going away."

"Time to get cooking, guys," said Alvin.

The guests were seated and it got quieter as they looked through the new menu.

"Janie, you start on the left, Floyd at the far end. Time to take some orders, guys."

The evening was a whirl of activity. Taking the orders, advising the meals, choosing wine and buttering up the customers. Most were kind and appreciative, some were just plain ignorant. Floyd smiled until his face hurt.

Then it was into the kitchen working with Alvin to cook the starters and main course. The food went out as they made it. Sometimes Floyd, but more often Janie served the food.

They were delighted with the comments. Everyone loved the food, even the less friendly diners.

Janie tapped him on the shoulder. "This is going well, Floyd. Good job keeping smiling with that jerk on table eight."

"Yeah. He's just looking for a free meal. He'll soon be gone. As long as he doesn't say bad thing about us."

"He won't. It takes too much effort. Hold the fort while I talk to Alvin."

"Sure, Janie."

It was quiet while the diners ate their starter and then the main course. Floyd wandered around to each table making sure everyone was happy. Sean Lynch waved Floyd over.

"Floyd, this is great food. Did you cook this?"

"Not just me. Alvin too."

"Congratulations. Another talent you have. By the way, this is my partner, Gabriel."

Gabriel was a slim Hispanic man, good looking almost to the point of being pretty. He looked Floyd up and down as if checking out a rival.

"Hi. Pleased to meet you Gabriel."

"You too, Floyd. Sean has told me a lot about you."

"Hope it wasn't all bad?" joked Floyd.

"No, he really likes you. I almost started to feel jealous."

"Now, don't start that again, Gabriel," interrupted Sean. "Floyd here is a capable and intelligent young man and student at the College next September. That's as far as it goes."

Floyd looked incredulous. "I'm a student?"

"Yes." replied Sean, looking puzzled. "Didn't I tell you?"

Gabriel laughed at Floyd's astonishment. "Floyd. Meet Sean. The most wonderful, kind man in the whole world. But sometimes I wonder if he has a memory at all..."

"I didn't tell you? Oh. Well let me tell you now. I liked your second essay. It was much better. You've got a long way to go, but I've secured you funding to start at Woosterville College in September. Question is, do you want to do it?"

There was no hesitation. "Yeah. I do! Of course I do! When do I start?"

Sean laughed. "We'll talk next week, Floyd. Now, have you got a dessert menu?"

"You're on a diet, Sean," interrupted Gabriel.

"Oh Gabe. It's just one night."

"But your doctor said..."

"Stuff and nonsense to my doctor. I'm having a lovely evening out with you and friends and Floyd, Alvin and Janie have excelled themselves. I want my pudding!"

Gabriel looked heavenward. "I give up. But tomorrow you're back on the diet."

"Tomorrow and tomorrow creeps in this petty pace..."

"You think I'm petty?"

"Of course not! I just think we should enjoy the night, Gabe. Let tomorrow take care of itself."

Gabriel stopped in thought, then smiled. "I can do that. Sean, let's have fun!"

A delighted Floyd left them to their bickering. Gwen Perloff rolled her eyes at the couple. "The food is wonderful, Floyd, darling. Well done to the three of you for putting on such a fine night."

Floyd smiled. "Thanks, Gwen. And me a student too!"

She looked up at him, smiling. "About time, darling! Do me proud, won't you, Floyd?"

He reached down and hugged her. "Always. I could never have got to this point without you, y'know?"

She gave him a squeeze. "All that life to live! I feel a little jealous!" Then she pushed him away. "Enough of this sentiment. I want my dessert too, darling!"

"I'll get you guys some menus. Give me a second?"

He walked over to Janie. "I got in."

"College?"

"Yeah."

"Oh Floyd, I'm so proud of you." and she kissed him on the cheek. "Go and give Alvin the good news."

"As long as he doesn't try to kiss me too."

"Now, Floyd. Before I embarrass you in front of everyone?"

It was at that point that Floyd saw everyone staring.

"Anyone for dessert?" he said, trying to look like he wasn't mortified.

Seeing the nods, he grabbed the menus. The girls were particularly curious about Janie's kiss.

"Have I got a rival?" smirked Marla.

"Have I got a rival too?" said Mary too, coolly.

All the girls around the table teased him, but Floyd took it in good grace.

"Just excited about some good news."

"What news?" they all asked.

"I got offered a place at Woosterville College."

The table erupted with cheers and claps. They were so pleased for him! He was shocked at their enthusiasm.

He spotted Mary looking at him, her eyes shining. "Not so stupid as you think, Floyd?" she said.

He grinned self-consciously. "Guess not, Mary."

Floyd noticed a couple of the male students glaring at him. They didn't seem too pleased for him and they didn't like the attention the girls paid him.

"Buncha assholes," he thought.

"Anyhow. Guys, can I take your dessert order?"

That pacified the surly students, but Floyd could see that a few of them looked like future trouble? He sighed. Another set of problems to overcome, but not tonight.

"All part of life. Decent folks and assholes. Screw them anyway," he thought. He kept a polite smile fixed to his mouth and made his way into the kitchen with their orders.

"How's it going, kid?"

"Good, I think. No complaints. A coupla jerks from the university trying to show off to the girls. Nothin' we can't handle."

"Great. What's the dessert orders?"

"Oh. Here. I got some news as well."

"Good or bad?"

"Good, I think."

"Well spit it out, Floyd."

"I got accepted into the College. Sean just said."

Alvin smiled and grabbed Floyd in an intense bear hug.

"Oof! You'll crush me, Alvin. Get off!"

Alvin laughed and let him go. "I promise not to hug you too often, kid. Only when I'm proud of you."

"I can never get a straight answer from you."

"No. And you never will. Now, let's get the desserts started."

Janie came in with the rest of the orders.

"How's it going, baby?"

"It's been so positive, Alvin. Why don't you go out there and see? Floyd and I can finish up here."

"OK. Shout if you want anything."

When he was gone, Janie tuned to Floyd. "Did you tell him?"

"Yeah. He was pleased."

"How pleased?"

"He almost crushed me to death!"

"Same old Alvin. You know how much he cares about you, really."

"Yeah, I know. I really do know now, Janie."

"We'd better get to it, Floyd. I'll do the cold desserts, you do the hot?"

"Sure, Janie."

An hour later, they were done. Deserts had been eaten, coffee drunk and everyone sat around chatting. A man with a camera came up to Janie.

"Could I take a picture? I'm with the Woosterville Gazette. That was a great meal and I'd like to feature you next week?"

"Sure. But not without my two guys."

"No offence to them, but I'd rather just you in the picture, lady."

"No. The two guys are part of this. Alvin owns the diner and we couldn't do this without Floyd, neither."

"OK. If you insist! Let's do it. But you in the centre."

"Floyd! Alvin! Get over here for some pictures."

Alvin looked like he didn't have a care in the world, but Floyd was incredibly nervous. The journalist took dozens of shots with the three standing in different positions, but Janie always in the centre.

The photographer tried to put them at ease. "Kid, try to relax. Smile a bit more. No, that's a grimace. How do the guys here get you to smile?"

"I'd know how to make him smile!" Marla called out.

Floyd's resulting grin was picture perfect.

They were exhausted as the last of the guests left the diner.

Janie gave Alvin and Floyd a hug. "I'm so proud of both of you! I'd call that a success!"

"It went better than I thought, baby."

"I didn't screw up, either," said Floyd.

"I'm beat!" said Alvin.

"Me too," agreed Janie. "Let's lock up and head up to the den. I'll catch you guys up."

Alvin and Floyd were sitting quietly when Janie came in with a tray holding a bottle of red wine and glasses.

"Here you, go. A small glass for you, Floyd. Don't tell anyone!"

"As if I would, Janie!"

"Cheers! To my big goof and my little monster. My helpers!"

Floyd pulled a face at the wine. It was his first glass.

"Not to your liking, kid?" asked Alvin.

"Not really."

"It's an acquired taste, Floyd, "agreed Janie. "One that you won't be acquiring yet."

"I can live with that."

"So do you guys think tonight would work on a regular basis?"

"Sure, baby. A diner the rest of the week upmarket on Saturday nights? Why not?"

"Everyone liked the food. Really liked it. You looked great in your uniform, Floyd. Handsome and in control."

Floyd blushed. "It was all an act, Janie."

"It was a good act, kid. Remember that most of us are just doing the same."

"You act, Alvin? You seem so sure of yourself."

"I am sure of myself. Or that's what it looks like. Who can tell? Only me..."

"I can learn that."

"Sure you can, Floyd. Here and at College."

Janie yawned. "I think I need to sleep. Goodnight, Floyd. Coming, Alvin?"

"I'll just be a minute, Janie."

"You did well tonight, Floyd. I am proud of you. The way you were tonight is a long way from that frightened kid I met eight months ago."

"It seems like years ago, Alvin."

"Maybe it should feel like that kid. That chapter of your life is over, now. I'm tired, kid. Goodnight."

"Night, Alvin."

Floyd sat for a while taking small sips out of his wine glass. He still made a face, but it didn't taste as awful as it did at the start. He chuckled to himself. "Wine drinking, Woosterville College student, Floyd Jensen. Up yours, Sanchez! Up yours, Medusa!"

He finished the wine, got up, stretched and yawned, then headed for bed.

Chapter 29 – Burying the Past?

A few weeks later Floyd was summoned once more to the precinct, with Janie and Alvin. Saul Hanser greeted them.

"I just wanted to keep you guys up to date about the trial of the Medusa cops. We've got Floyd's statement, so he won't have to testify. Everyone agrees he's gone through enough. At the very least the entire sheriff's office are facing custodial sentences. Corruption, racketeering, intimidation, the list goes on. You can forget about them bothering you again, Floyd."

"Do I have to have another conversation with them, Saul?" asked Alvin.

Saul looked amused. "No, that won't be necessary, Alvin. For some reason none of Sanchez's associates want any more to do with Floyd. We don't know exactly what happened but we think Sanchez put the word out."

Alvin smiled too, a wolfish grin. "I wonder what got into him? Perhaps he's decided to reform and turn his life around...?"

Saul grinned back. "Sure looks like it, Alvin!"

Floyd looked at both of the men suspicious. They were up to something, but he had learnt that it was best to keep his nose out of it. He was safe, that was the main thing to focus on.

Saul's smile faded and looked grim. "We won't bother you any more Floyd. But I thought you should know we found the body of a young black man out in the digs around Medusa. About seventeen. DNA confirms it. I'm sorry, son."

Floyd was speechless. He had put Zeke out of his mind with this new life, but it all came back with a vengeance. The laughter, the silliness, their camaraderie.

Zeke was dead. His only friend in Medusa. The only friend he'd ever had in the entire world before he'd come to Woosterville. There would be no more horseplay and fun and dreams about the future. Ever again. Floyd could not have stopped his tears, even if he tried.

Janie soothed him like a child as he wept. "Oh Floyd..."

Alvin stayed quiet, but the fury radiated from him.

"We couldn't find any remains of Zeke's parents, so we have no reason to believe they aren't alive somewhere out there. We simply don't know."

Floyd wiped his eyes. "Thanks, Saul," croaked. "Thanks for letting me know. Will there be a funeral?"

"Sure. We'll let you know. It won't be in Medusa. You have my word on that."

Floyd was quiet and stayed that way for several days.

"I'm worried about him, Alvin," said Janie.

"Just let him be, Janie. Keep him busy in the kitchen. It will pass."

"How do you know that, Alvin?"

Alvin looked saddened. "From too much experience, baby. Far, far too much."

Janie, Alvin and Floyd attended Zeke's funeral and were there at the graveside. Floyd threw a baseball mitt into the grave. "That will keep you outta trouble, buddy," he murmured.

Saul motioned him over. "We did some investigation and found where your Mom was buried. We thought she should be free of Medusa, too."

In the next section of the cemetery was a plain white marble headstone:

Marlene Jensen

Much Beloved Mother of Floyd

Rest in Peace

"Thanks, Saul. Can I have a minute on my own?"

The usually stern-looking cop looked sad. "Of course you can, Floyd. It's the least we could do for her and for you."

Floyd stood at the graveside and he talked. About all he'd done and seen and experienced.

"We got that bastard Sanchez, Mom. He'll never hurt anyone ever again. I ain't stupid and I have a future, better than either of us would ever have imagined. I won't let you down.

"I'm not a scared kid walking alone home in the rain any more. I'm still 'Marlene's Bastard' but I ain't ashamed of that either. I've got friends and a girlfriend and I know now how to learn and I'm going to Woosterville College! How about that for a nobody kid from that backwater shithole?"

Janie and Alvin noticed how quiet he was again for a few days, but Floyd felt a sense of relief too. He smiled grimly: "It's my life now and I'm going to succeed or screw it up my way..."

All the loose ends had been tied up and there was nothing left of Medusa to hold him back.

Or that's what he thought...

Afterward

Thanks go to Lucy Kong Creative for the fantastic cover and to Victoria McDonagh for reading my first draft and criticising it in a positive way. It's the better for it!

Thanks also to Dee Miller, proprietor of Minor Oak Coworking in Nottingham for creating a great supportive and friendly creative space. Much of the first draft of 'Life and Liberty' was written there.

I dedicate this book to my lovely Mum, Una Parr, who is a poet in her own right. I am appreciative and grateful to have inherited some of her talent.

She was ninety years old in August 2019, so a major Happy Birthday and lots of love from me!

Aidan Parr

September 2019

Other books by Aidan Parr:

Of the Sea: an anthology of Prose and Poetry

Life, Nature and the Spirit: poems by Mary Winifred Parr
(Editor)

Printed in Poland
by Amazon Fulfillment
Poland Sp. z o.o., Wrocław